EDEN UNDONE

What if Eve had said, 'No'?

Anna Lindsay

First published in Great Britain in 2015

Instant Apostle
The Hub
3-5 Rickmansworth Road
Watford
Herts
WD18 OGX

British Library Cataloguing-in-Publication Data

A catalogue record for this book is available from the British Library

This book and all other Instant Apostle books are available from Instant Apostle:

Website: www.instantapostle.com
E-mail: info@instantapostle.com

ISBN 978-1-909728-23-3

Printed in Great Britain

*Dedicated to Him. And to those
whose love and friendship have proved true...
as well as to the memory of those beloved ones
who have already returned Home.
With love, and gratitude, always.*

contents

a note about naming

Throughout this book, names for God are used interchangeably, depending on which facet of His character is to the fore.

Glory, Majesty, Love... all these are wholly Him yet none by themselves encompass Him.

part one

chapter one

And God said, 'Let the land produce living creatures according to their kinds: livestock, creatures that move along the ground, and wild animals, each according to its kind.' And it was so. God made the wild animals according to their kinds, the livestock according to their kinds, and all the creatures that move along the ground according to their kinds. And God saw that it was good.
Then God said, 'Let us make man in our image, in our likeness, and let them rule over the fish of the sea and the birds of the air, over the livestock, over all the earth, and over all the creatures that move along the ground.'
So God created man in his own image,
in the image of God he created him.
(The Book of the Beginning 1:24-27)

Memories of memories, without shape or form. He was floating up, rising, surfacing through inchoate shadows. Fragments of impressions, feelings. Light and dark. Palms to rough bark. Knuckles on soft soil. Dust. Wordless sounds. And then – explosion of lucidity, consciousness. Opened eyes meeting the face of Love, radiating joy.

'Your name is Adam,' He said. 'Welcome, my beloved!'

And, 'Come. Come with me.'

Now the LORD God had planted a garden in the east, in Eden; and there he put the man he had formed. The LORD God made all kinds of trees grow out of the

ground —trees that were pleasing to the eye and good for food. In the middle of the garden were the tree of life and the tree of the knowledge of good and evil. … The LORD God took the man and put him in the Garden of Eden to work it and take care of it.
(The Book of the Beginning 2:8-9, 15)

'I've got something to show you. Close your eyes,' He said.
The world moved.
'Look,' He said.

It was a garden. The man knew it was a garden, knew the word, knew the name. Garden. Eden.

There were trees. Trees of every kind, shape and size, as far as the eye could see. And flowers. Riots of colour, exuberant cascades, shy petals in tiny nooks. A gentle breeze filled Adam's lungs with the subtle afternoon perfume: nothing cloying, nothing clashing. A bird chirruped. Curious eyes turned to them, drew towards them. In the distance, some animal let out an ecstatic bugle of welcome.

And a moment of stillness, breathless, expectant.

'I planted it,' He said. 'For you. Do you like it?'
There were no words. Words aren't sufficient for the first glimpse of beauty, first breath of awe. Only the heart that fills until it feels as if it could explode from joy.
Only a nod, and the heart that leapt.

God rejoiced.

And a thundering of hooves, pounding of paws, as noses nuzzled and soft fur touched. *'Welcome,'* they said. *'Welcome. We have been waiting for you. Come and see! Come and see! Come and stay!'*

'Will you?' He asked.
'Yes,' said Adam. 'Oh, yes!'

chapter two

Every precious stone adorned you:
carnelian, chrysolite and emerald ...
You were anointed as a guardian cherub,
for so I ordained you.
You were on the holy mount of God;
you walked among the fiery stones.
You were blameless in your ways
from the day you were created
till wickedness was found in you.
Through your widespread trade
you were filled with violence,
and you sinned.
So I drove you in disgrace from the mount of God,
and I expelled you, guardian cherub,
from among the fiery stones.
Your heart became proud
on account of your beauty,
and you corrupted your wisdom
because of your splendour.
So I threw you to the earth.
(Fragment: The Lord's Lament 28:13-17)

He had kept most of the gems. Smuggled them out with him when he was cast out from Heaven. Idiot ...*One*..., not to have realised that the gems were being sneaked out. Or worse, to have realised and not cared. He couldn't quite bring himself — not even now, when he was entitled to his fury! — to curse God. Not that it would be blasphemy, of course. How could it be, when that ...*One*... had shown Himself to be so weak? It was simply that, well... and so what of it? It could not, would not, *could* not be interpreted as weakness on his own account. If anything, Lucifer thought, it was, well, proof that he had been maligned. And it certainly could *not* be taken as proof that deep inside he was aware of who (a pause. Even in his own thoughts he could scarcely bring himself to think of ...*that Being*...) ...the *One*... was. He was no mere throne-bearer, worship leader, guardian of the holy places, cherub, he! He, Lucifer,

9

who by rights should be *on* the throne, not merely bearing it. He, Lucifer, the most beautiful in all the hosts of heaven: he who had been adulated by all, and had been called the bright morning star, son of the dawn. Even without the living jewels whose fire had reflected his beauty before and still showered him with their lustre now.

And power. For the umpteenth time, Lucifer nursed his bile against his Creator. What did that ...*One*... know about power?! Power was for using. Power was for creating more power, bartering for what you could get, and simply grabbing what wasn't up for exchange. Power was created by those strong enough to lust for it, strong enough to foment dissension. Power was there to weaken everyone else and to make oneself look bigger. Power went to the strongest. The strongest *deserved* power.

He himself could *not* have been created. Could not. Particularly not by that... that ...*One*... who had failed to surrender His throne to him. Granted, he had no specific recollection of what he'd been doing when light was separated from dark, and dark from light, but... but that did not mean he had been created. Or, even if he *had* been created, then certainly not by that... that *weakling* who occupied the throne and wielded the power he craved, the throne and power which should by rights be his...

Take the Earth. The Earth was supposed to be *his*. To use as he saw fit. To take the things he wanted. Such as more gems. He was certain that with gold and jewels one could accomplish all sorts of things. Precious stones reflected his beauty, dazzled and awed those around him. Especially the living jewels, the stones of fire, which adorned Heaven and in which he had clothed himself too. Granted, those he had smuggled out were losing their life and becoming... hard... but they were still precious. And still reflected his beauty. And still instilled awe. And where you could instil awe, you had power. And power... power was everything.

What use was power if you didn't use it to exploit those around you, if you didn't use it for yourself, if you chose instead to use it for others? Sign of a weakling, that was, and by the end he'd even managed to convince others of the angelic host of the same thing. Managed to convince them that *he* would run a far tighter ship if *he* were in power rather than the present incumbent. With, of course, the right incentives to those loyal to him...

Didn't that count for something, that he'd succeeded in convincing some of the lesser angels that the power should be his?

And where were those beings now? Scattered. Weaklings.

He was surrounded by weaklings, that was the problem. Above and below... Why, even the fact that he'd been exiled from Heaven was proof of that impotent ...*One's*... weakness and stupidity. Now if *he*'d been on the throne, he'd have known the right way to treat a menace as powerful, beautiful and... and... and *powerful* as himself. If the roles had been reversed — hah! — *then* Heaven would have seen what Power truly meant. And *he* wouldn't have been so idiotic as to leave his enemy running loose...

There, he'd said it. The ...*One*... was... the *enemy*. All that faff that the ...*One*... had said about grieving for Lucifer, all that mourning his so-called corruption, all that pleading with him to throw away his pride and come back to be forgiven. Forgiven?! How *dare* He? How *dare* He suggest that Lucifer was wrong? Or patronise him by mourning for him? Just signs of weakness, hypocritical cant to cover up a Lord too weak to do what needed to be done. Lucifer wasn't going to fall for it. Would not be taken in by that pretence of love. Love? Even the word now tasted disgusting to him. Slimy. Lucifer spat. The horrid taste remained, and the churning of his insides. Love? Pah!

Well, He'd regret it, Lucifer vowed. Power was his by rights, and since the ...*One*... had been stupid enough to let him loose...

Nursing the dimming gems and his enkindling grievance, Lucifer beat his great wings and continued to roam the world of his exile.

chapter three

Now the LORD God had formed out of the ground all the wild animals and all the birds in the sky. He brought them to the man to see what he would name them; and whatever the man called each living creature, that was its name. So the man gave names to all the livestock, the birds in the sky and all the wild animals.
(The Book of the Beginning 2:19-20)

They danced there with him, leading the way, showing him, welcoming him. *'Welcome,'* they cried, the merriest confusion of sizes and shapes and colours, till he could scarcely begin to take it all in.

The colours alone – just glancing around him – why, if he'd been the one to create green, and if it had occurred to him, then, well, perhaps a single shade? But here – just the greens alone, in too many shades to even begin counting. And that was just the greens. Every colour was a celebration of variety on its own; put them together and the infinite colours sang of their Maker's joy and unbounded exuberance. And then there were the textures. And the shapes! And the interplay of them all! And then the animals! Fur and feathers and scales, rough and smooth, big and small!

He hardly even knew where to start. There was so much to do, so much to learn! It was so gloriously new, so endlessly challenging, so full of awesome wonder.

He put up his hand toward one of the leaves caressing his face. It was delicate, a fresh green, unfurled from a branch with smooth silvery bark. *Birch.*

But even as he was touching it, he became aware of a chorus of voices, getting louder by the instant. *'We're coming! We're coming! Wait for us! Here, let us through! We're here! We're here!'*

With a rush and a rustle of undergrowth, a parting of surrounding hooves and paws, whiskered faces and feathered wings, two new somethings careened out of one of the bushes, through the throng and hurtled against his legs in a flurry of silky fur, wet noses, wagging tails and furred paws, bowling him over.

With a thump, Adam landed on the soft grass, laughing.

'Welcome! Welcome! Oh, welcome!'

It took a few seconds, but finally the two somethings succeeded in untangling themselves from Adam's legs and each other, and Adam found himself looking at two pairs of excited eyes. 'Hello,' he said. 'Er, I'm Adam. What about you?'

'We're… we're…'

They almost floundered for an instant, until He said gently to Adam, 'Actually, I thought *you* might like to Name them all. Who do *you* feel they are, Beloved?'

It was his first Naming. He could feel their Name shaping itself in his heart and mind. It was the right Name, he could feel it, the Name that belonged to them. 'Dog,' he said.

The two bounded up. *'We're dogs! Yes! Dog! We're dogs! Here, did you hear? Did you hear? He's named us, he has! We're dogs, we are!'*

They chased each other ecstatically round and round the clearing, weaving in and out of the surrounding forest of legs and hooves and paws, while Adam picked himself back up off the soft sward. One of them was so excited that he tumbled head over heels before continuing the romp, and then they both landed, panting, pink tongues lolling, back at Adam's feet.

'We're coming with you,' they said. *'We're here! We're here!'*

Adam laughed, rubbed their ears, and then looked up into the next pair of great brown eyes, set in a long face with a velvet nose and a black mane. A happy *whoosh* of warm sweet breath fanned his face. *'Lord Adam!'*

'Horse,' he said, and with a joyful nicker, Horse made way for the next somethings.

They were all there, big and small, welcoming him, receiving their Names, while God beamed with delight.

Lion. Swallow. Elephant. Sheep. Mouse. Bear. Bee. Cat. Eagle. Rabbit. Giraffe. Beaver. Owl.

Glorious Tiger with her stripey hide.

Tall Serpent with his proud carriage and jewelled colours.

Cow and Bull with their glorious horns.

The pair of Squirrels with their pitter-patter of tiny paws, scampering and skittering along the branches, leaping featherweights from twig to twig, bushy red tails held high.

'We're here too! We heard! We heard! Welcome, Lord Adam!'

Adam's heart danced a jig of pure joy, and the soaring paeans of praise rising unprompted to his lips harmonised with the hushed choirs of angels above.

chapter four

You were ... perfect in beauty.
You were in Eden,
the garden of God;
every precious stone adorned you.
(Fragment: The Lord's Lament 28:12-13)

And Eden. Eden should have been *his*. *Was* his by rights. He'd been there when the
...*One*... was creating it.

The ...*One*... had even asked whether he liked it! Of *course* Eden had been meant
for him — why else would the ...*One*... have shown it to him and to the other
angels, if not because He'd secretly been intending to give it to him all along? And
then... then to discover that it had actually been meant for that... that... *creature!*
That weak, fragile little two-legged monstrosity that He'd created out of dust, raised
from the mere fabric of the world itself, given life and consciousness by His breath! How
dare He pass Lucifer over in favour of that... that *mud*-man? *He* didn't have the power
that Lucifer had. Nor his perfect beauty. Nor his wings. Nor his position. *He* hadn't
been a throne-bearer to the Almighty. What *right* did that interloper have to... to
usurp his rightful prize?

And to add insult to injury, now that he'd been banished from Heaven, he wasn't
even allowed back into Eden either! When anyone else could have plainly seen that
Eden was his by rights, and that in mere deference to his former position he should at
the very least be given Eden to set up his residence. As... as an apology for the way
he'd been shamefully passed over *and* then banished. Banished! When by rights his
ambition should surely have led to his promotion! So Eden was, after all, his by rights
— he'd set foot in it long before the ...*One*... had created that thing. He'd been
there first. How *dare* He then snatch it away again to give to that creature!?

Well, if he couldn't have Eden, then it was up to him to see that that creature
wouldn't have it either. Or the ...*One*... Lucifer would show Him. He'd see. He'd pay.
No one was going to mess with him.

And then, who knows, once he'd evicted that... *squatter*, then he'd have shown
that idiot ...*One*... just who had more power — he or the squatter — and then the
...*One*... would see sense and give Eden back to him.

After all, Eden should have been his in the first place.
And if he couldn't have it, then no one could.

chapter five

The LORD God made all kinds of trees grow out of the ground – trees that were pleasing to the eye and good for food. In the middle of the garden were the tree of life and the tree of the knowledge of good and evil.
(The Book of the Beginning 2:9)

Joy upon joy, awe upon awe, wonder upon wonder. Each step they took together, each corner they turned, each dell he explored in God's company, it seemed to Adam that they came upon something new and more beautiful than the one before. Sometimes he'd almost have walked past it had Glory not drawn his attention to it and opened his eyes to see it properly and share God's passion for it.

It wasn't just the animals who had different names and personalities, likes and dislikes. The plants did too, and during his walks with Glory, Adam got to know each of them.

'This one,' He'd say, 'likes your help keeping it trimmed,' and the vine put its pretty blush into its grapes. Or, 'This is the Avocado. See how her fruit covers itself? Try it!' and so Adam peeled the glossy, knobbly black coat and tasted the perfect nutty richness within, buttery-soft and satisfying. They shared merry laughter when the fruit – so ripe that the coat came away in easy strips – skittered out of his hands and left a creamy green trail along his arms and down his leg.

Adam rinsed himself in the nearby brook, cool and sparkling as it burbled along its bed, and flicked some of the water towards Dog, who had been bounding along beside them. Dog responded by plunging in and spluttering with delight, and the two of them enjoyed a brief splash-fest before emerging again, dripping, onto the bank, water diamonds glistening before the warmth of the sunshine dried them again deliciously. Dog decided that shaking himself vigorously and making the water droplets fly up in great arcs was almost the best bit about getting wet.

Cherries – huge, rich, black, bursting with flavour – became an instant favourite. And the flowers on the tree (for all the trees in the

Garden had both flowers and fruit on them at the same time) also took his breath away with their beauty. Beauty down to the smallest detail.

'You are free to eat from any tree in the Garden,' He said, 'but you mustn't eat from the Tree of the Knowledge of Good and Evil, for when you eat of it you will surely die.'

'What does "die" mean, Lord?' he asked then.

A great sadness crossed His face. 'It's when someone is cut off from my presence, Adam.'

A chill ran down Adam's spine. Cut off from Love's true light? That... that would be like drawing breath and finding no air, opening his eyes and seeing nothing. Conceivable only in the dimmest fashion, but gut-wrenching even at that remoteness. No, dying was not something to which he felt drawn...

But then, 'Come, Dearheart!' and the moment of the shadow of fear melted in the light of His Love, tucked away from experience and stored only in knowledge.

They bent down to speak to Mole, who had swum his way up through the rich soil to greet them and had now emerged, sneezing and blinking in the sudden sunlight, with his great shovel paws resting atop his little mound. Crumbs of soil still covered his velvet fur, and his nose twitched. *'Welcome my Lords, welcome,'* he snuffled. *'My burrow is yours, if you'd like to visit? It's cool and restfully dark,'* he added, squinting in the unaccustomed light, and plainly convinced that any sensible being would be equally uncomfortable in so much blinding brightness. *'If you give me a few minutes, that is, to make the hallways a little wider?'*

Adam gravely thanked him, touched by the invitation, but reassured him that they were quite happy up here in the fresh air, and might find soil quite difficult to breathe in.

'But there's lots of air here!' defended Mole, *'in between the soil. And the roots. I like roots,'* he added. *'The roots here are lovely. Ask the Lord. **He** knows.'*

Glory smiled and assured him that indeed He knew; and Mole, finally convinced that the Lord Adam would not be joining him and Mrs Mole for tea, disappeared again in a flurry of earth as he burrowed down again into the welcoming blackness, full of the clean scents of soil and roots.

And the Lord showed Adam how the loam crumbled, and spoke of the different types of soil and how this one was loved by such a tree, and that one was loved by another. Adam ran his fingers through the soil, feeling its beautiful texture, and marvelled anew at the vastness of God's conception that knew and loved every atom of this world He had created, from the depths of the earth, and the crumbs of the soil, to the trees that fed on it and the Creatures that lived on – and in – it.

And Dog, in his enthusiasm, got his muzzle covered by the loose dirt where Mole had been, before deciding that perhaps he, too, was too large to breathe the air in between the soil and had perhaps better stay up top instead of taking up Mole's invitation.

chapter six

Then God said, 'Let us make man in our image, in our likeness, so that they may rule over the fish of the sea and the birds in the sky, over the livestock and all the wild animals, and over all the creatures that move along the ground.'
So God created mankind in his own image,
in the image of God he created them;
male and female he created them.
(The Book of the Beginning 1:26-27)

Worship. Joy. Marvel. The expectant hush filled and grew among the angelic hosts. The Godhead – three strands of a single cord, distinct and yet One – was about to complete His creation, precious mirror of Their heart. First male, and now female, in perfect complement. In Their own image. The wonder of such honour. Such awesome privilege, that this new relationship carried the very fabric of the universe in its existence. Such blessed beings, for whom I AM had crafted such a beautiful world and outpouring of His Love. And whom He had crowned with that ultimate gift, the ultimate freedom, the ultimate grace, the ultimate sigil of His image: free will.

Holy, holy, holy. Honour and glory to Your Name.

chapter seven

The LORD God said, 'It is not good for the man to be alone. I will make a
helper suitable for him.'
(The Book of the Beginning 2:18)

Adam, at Glory's suggestion, had asked Wild Boar and his mate to snout the soft soil into long straight furrows. Wild Sow teased her husband that she could see exactly where he'd found a truffle by the way one of his furrows suddenly made a small zigzag, and then they'd gambolled off together to hunt some more under a likely tree she'd spotted earlier.

And now Adam was walking with the Lord while He explained to Adam how to sow the seed in the newly tilled field. Adam's toes curled luxuriantly in the gentle earth, warm and soft under his sole, tickling as it trickled through his toes. He could see the trail where he had followed the furrows. Right foot, left foot. Heel to toe, softly pressed into the soil to mark his passage. Glory, Adam had noticed, never left footprints behind. His tread was so light that even on tender turf, not a single blade of grass was disturbed, yet His majesty was so glorious that one could always tell where He had walked by the new flowers that sprung up in His wake. Here in the field a similar phenomenon was happening: where He had passed, the grain was already waking into green shoots. Perhaps, Adam thought, the reason he could never spot Glory's footprints was because he should be looking wider: the whole earth was His footprint, His signature. Adam felt the deep joy he always knew in His presence, and marvelled anew at the awesomeness of this perfect, beautiful world. He skipped for a few steps, dancing with the sheer delight of life.

God gently interrupted his reverie. 'You haven't asked me.'

'Asked you, Lord?'

'About the animals. Male and female. And yourself.'

'Myself?'

Love waited.

Adam stuttered. 'But... but... but I've got *You*, Lord. I... I don't need anyone else.'

Love waited again.

Adam suddenly thought his toes looked very interesting. Especially the way the smoothness of his toenails contrasted with the crumbles of soil dusting them. Yes, toes, he decided, were definitely —

'Dearheart, look at Me.'

It appeared that his toes weren't going to be allowed to occupy his attention. Adam raised his eyes to meet Love's.

'But... but...!'

The Lord breathed on him.

Ohhhhhhhhh.

There. Tucked away in the deepest corner of his heart, that tiny shadow, camouflaged as zeal. Had it not been for God's spotlight on it, revealing it for what it was, it might have grown, unperceived, from shadow to substance. Not zeal for Him. Not that *he*, Adam, didn't need anyone else. Just... yes... Now he could see it for himself. A shadow of a fear. Fear that God might not love *him* as much if there were someone else besides him receiving a share of His love...

'Ah, Beloved. Don't you know? There will *always* be enough love for you. I will be here for you until the end of days. I will not grow tired or weary. Neither the present nor the future, nor any powers, neither height nor depth, nor anything else in all creation, will be able to separate you from My love. I have enough love for you *and* for her, for your children and for all creation. How else do you think I could create you, if not from the outpouring of Our love? Trust me, Beloved. My love *is* sufficient for you.'

The nascent insecurity of which Adam hadn't even been aware until that instant melted in the warmth and tenderness of His gaze.

'Though, of course, whether *you* choose to continue loving *Me* above all else, or whether you allow yourself to become distracted, is a totally different question, and one that only *you* can answer!'

Adam spluttered. 'Me, Lord, abandon *you*?!? Never! Never!'

Glory grinned, His radiance sparkling, and for a moment Adam whirled in an effusion of iridescent butterflies that He had called into joyful being.

'So, *will* you trust me in this, Dearheart?'

'Yes, Lord.'

'Then close your eyes and sleep, Beloved, and I will bring her to you, and you will understand.'

chapter eight

So the LORD God caused the man to fall into a deep sleep; and while he was
sleeping, he took one of the man's ribs and then closed up the place with flesh.
Then the LORD God made a woman from the rib he had taken out of the man,
and he brought her to the man.
(The Book of the Beginning 2:21-22)

Adam sat up and rubbed his eyes. His left side – the side of his heart –
felt... refreshed somehow. As though the fibres of his being had been
taken out, washed and put back all sparkly clean and stronger even
than before. And... lighter somehow, too. As though a burden he'd
never previously noticed that he carried had suddenly become shared,
and the load reduced, so that he could breathe in God's radiance even
more deeply than before.

He almost wondered at that, but then... then he saw her.

Had Adam stopped to think about what he would have expected *her*
to be like, he'd have guessed that she'd be, well, like him. Identical,
more or less, apart from the genitals, just as so many of the animals
he'd just Named were to their mates. Well, maybe a little smaller than
him. Or covered in plumage, perhaps; radically different in colouring
from him, like some of the birds. Then again, he wasn't a bird. So
perhaps she wouldn't be covered in feathers either, even pretty ones.
Horns? He'd noticed that some of the beasts only had horns on one
gender. Usually, come to think of it, on the males. And – he'd double-
checked by patting his own head – horns were something he didn't
have. Not even little tiny ones. Let alone the gloriously proud
headpieces sported by some of the Creatures. So, well, she'd probably
be pretty much like him, he'd have guessed.

But not... not like *this*.

Similar, yes, sort of. Two arms, two legs, one head, similar
arrangement of eyes and nose and mouth (oh! What a beautiful
mouth!) But... but where his own sides were lean, muscular, planed,
she had... curves. Glorious curves, beautiful curves, wonderful curves!

Curves he just knew would... fit. Where he was lean, she was lithe. Where he was tall, she was slender. Where his torso was smooth, rippled only with muscles, she had two perfectly shaped breasts. Where his hair was short, dark and densely curled, hers was long (so long!) and silken and oh, so beautiful! Where...

He suddenly realised that he was sitting there with his jaw hanging open, and scrambled up to meet her.

And in that instant their eyes met, and she laughed with delight.

It was the most beautiful, musical, lilting laughter he'd ever heard, silver notes pealing on golden air. His heart felt as though it had leapt into his throat while simultaneously playing percussion in his chest.

Oh!

Ohhhhhhhhh!

Not a replica of him. Not a rival. No.

This... this *she*... was... part of him, his perfect complement, as he was hers. Every fibre of his being *knew*, now, what Glory had meant: this *she* was... his partner. Bone of his bones, flesh of his flesh: perfect in her own right as he was in his, and yet together they... together they were greater than the sum of their parts.

Woman.

Ohhhhhhhh.

Yes.

Wow.

chapter nine

What is mankind that you make so much of them, that you give them so much attention?
(Torment of a Patient Man 7:17)

No! How could He? How dare He? Rubbing salt into his wound. It was bad enough that He had made a... a *pet* of that two-legged mud-man, that usurper. And given the creature *his* Eden, the Eden that should have been his, *was* his by rights. The mud-man, dirt-digger, dust-drudge, *Human*... could have been dealt with. Somehow.

But now — as if all that wasn't bad enough! — now the ...*One*... had done *that*! All Creation was abuzz with it. Celebrating, if you please! A *female*. Woman. So that to top everything, that ridiculous creature could now *breed!* Increasing, in *his* Eden.

Well, he'd see about that.

This time, it was personal.

And whatever he was going to do, he'd have to do it quickly. Soon. Now. Before that vermin multiplied.

chapter ten

Let the heavens rejoice, let the earth be glad;
let the sea resound, and all that is in it;
let the fields be jubilant, and everything in them.
Then all the trees of the forest will sing for joy;
They will sing before the LORD.
(Song 96:11-13)

It was Glory who led the impromptu dance – headlong, joy-filled, passionate, in perfect step. It seemed as though the whole of Creation was thrumming with the beat of that dance, whirling, spinning, laughing, coming together and yet allowing each dancer the space to rejoice with their own steps in the abundance of transcendent freedom. Godhead, Woman, Man and beast, weaving together ever-new yet always perfect patterns in the intricacy of melody, while the Fireflies' light seemed to syncopate with the glittering stars, and Glory's radiance reflected itself on all around, from the open Heavens above to the tiniest dewdrop below.

Adam, of course, had met all the animals before, when he had Named them, but this was the first opportunity the beasts had had to actually meet Eve (and vice versa), and so the Dance became a double delight as Creation met its Lady.
'Welcome!' 'Welcome!' 'Welcome!'

There was no formal structure to the Dance, no expectation or pressure on any participant. Some of the dancers seemed blissful merely swaying, others enthusiastically romped to and fro, still others swooped and soared, and yet somehow all were woven seamlessly into the Dance in equal measure. The two Dogs couldn't quite decide whether they should be attending on God or on the Man or the Woman, and so they found that their own steps warped and woofed from one to the other, while the Elephants added rhythm both with their great feet and with their bugling. Across the waters, the Dolphins leapt with great sprays of salt in a minuet with the Flying Fish, and on land even the trees seemed to join in, waving and bowing in time to Spirit's music, honouring the Great Musician. All were woven into the Dance. And in the centre of it all, Glory and Adam and Eve, their hearts thrilling, reeled and leapt, twirled and twisted, ducked and dived, pivoted and pirouetted between them all, in Joy's exuberance.

It was impossible to tell how long the Dance lasted. Time stretched, yawned, and happily settled itself back down to drink in the sight. And at some stage Adam and Eve flung themselves, flushed, happy and almost breathless, onto the soft grass. In blissfully contented companionable silence, they watched the others continue their celebration in the warmth of the evening air until, nestled in each other's arms and Glory's glow, they drifted off to gentle sleep.

It had been a long day, a wonder-full day, a glorious day.

Their first.

'Sleep fully, Beloveds.'

* * *

It was the sound of a low, hopeful moo that first woke Eve the following morning. Silken warmth against her skin told her that Adam was still slumbering, but as she stirred and stretched, he too awoke. They exchanged excited grins. So much to explore! So many new things to discover!

They looked over to where Cow was standing, patiently waiting for her Lord and Lady to wake, while all around the chorus of birdsong heralded the new day.

Cow's udder was full. *'Will you help me, my Lords? I can't reach!'*

They scrambled up, honoured by the trust, delighted to help, but not entirely certain what to do.

'Glory?'

'Yes, Dearhearts.'

'Er... How do we tend Cow?'

Glory's Presence took form in the clearing and pointed out a large gourd nearby. Overnight, it had ripened and been hollowed out by some of the Mice, and dried by God's warmth, and now it stood ready for use.

'Here. Just put it on the ground, and stroke her udder just to get the flow started, and then she can do the rest. Here, let me serve you first, so you can see!'

The creamy milk frothed into the gourd, while Cow breathed a sigh of contentment and gratitude.

'Here. Taste it and see!'

They shared great draughts of the rich drink between them. Lion, drawn by the wonderful smell of the fresh milk, came to bid them good morning and to receive his own portion, while his smaller relative, Cat, came too, and tried to outdo her tawny cousin in purrs of appreciation.

Cow basked in the compliments, enjoyed a few lush mouthfuls of grass, and suggested that she come back at the same time the next morning. The purrs redoubled, and agreement was unanimous. The breakfast partnership was established.

It seemed that Glory had read their hearts when He suggested that they spend the rest of the day exploring the Garden and beyond. 'I thought it might be lovely if we all had a day of rest after yesterday!'

There was a chorus of delight, and some excited debate. Lion had heard from Eagle that there were some beautiful prairies to the south of the Garden, which he wanted to explore. Cow preferred to stay here where the grazing was so perfect. Cat was happy anywhere so long as she could curl up and snooze in the sun, and the two Dogs, who had enthusiastically joined the little breakfast group by this stage, were happy anywhere their Humans chose. Eventually, the two Humans (and Dogs) decided that they would first have a quick dip in the azure sea before heading north-east to explore the beautiful mountain range whose snow-capped peaks they could see gleaming in the morning sun.

The water was warm, and so clear that they could see each rainbow-coloured fish dart through the flowering corals thirty feet below. Adam spotted a conch shell lying empty on the white sand, and dived down to bring it up for Eve to exclaim over. They marvelled together at the glorious lustre of its mother-of-pearl. Sea Turtle joined them and offered them a quick ride on her broad carapace, while the Dogs contented themselves with challenging the waves to a race to the beach, and Spirit blew bubbles into the gently lapping wavelets kissing the shore.

And then, bare skins still glistening with the water prisms from their swims, they set off for the mountains, running and leaping with easy strides to celebrate the sheer joy of the morning. Dogs succeeding in keeping up with them, though they occasionally raced off on their own before rejoining them, tails wagging wildly. Gazelle joined them for the first part of their run too, though she elected to stop before they reached the first ascents, and others accompanied them for different stretches. It was, reflected Eve as she leapt over a mossy brook, burbling to itself in the sunlight, just a continuation of last night's great Dance, and she felt Spirit laugh and hug her in agreement.

The Garden gave way to the foothills, where fruit trees were blossoming and hummingbirds were hovering, and those in turn gave way to beech trees and then great pine forests which reached up almost to the snowline in the golden sunshine. The sun-warmed zephyr gently ruffled Eve's silken hair, now dry again after her swim, and carried the flowers' fragrances to the little group as they finally halted on a great granite outcrop. Down below, spread out in all its glory, they could see the Garden. The beauty of the sparkling gulf waters at its southernmost edge was equalled by the lushness of the Garden's trees and flowers. Even from this distance, they found they could focus on any point they chose and see each orchid's petal, each flick of a browsing ear, as clearly as if they were next to it themselves.

There, in the centre, they could see the Tree of Life and the Tree of the Knowledge of Good and Evil (Adam passed on Love's warning to Eve); there, just by that boulder with the dappled shade, Eve could make out Hare, combing his ears; there, by the river, Adam pointed out Hippo taking a mud-wallow. There, the Dogs excitedly recalled a particularly fascinating smell they intended to explore further; there, Chamois (who had bounded up with them on this last ascent) marvelled at the way Serpent's beautiful colours gleamed even when the elegant creature was swimming in the river; there, Glory delightedly showed them Caterpillar undergoing her secret transformation in her silken cocoon. High above, the two Eagles shrilled with rapture as they surfed a perfect updraught.

The little group drank in the scene with all their senses. Hand in hand in Hand, they looked and looked and listened and showed and shared.

Eve grasped for a word to encompass the sheer beauty around them, and failed. No word could quite capture the awe, the wonder, the magnitude of what surrounded them. No description could do it justice; only adoration. Perhaps this was why the angelic hosts cried, '*Holy*': no other word was big enough.

'Thank you,' she whispered.

'My pleasure, Beloved,' He murmured back.

And then, teasingly, 'Race you all back!' and they laughed and leapt and loped in light-footed elation back down the slopes and across the vast land to Eden, in time to celebrate dusk bringing out the evening stars in the deep skies.

chapter eleven

You who practise deceit,
your tongue plots destruction;
it is like a sharpened razor.
(Song 52:2)

The question was... how? How to get rid of the usurpers, when the ...*One*... had handed them everything?

Distrust? But how? How to destroy that perfect bond they had been given? How could he inject the poison that was needed to show that insufferable ...*One*... how misguided He had been in honouring *them* instead of himself? How to sow a flaw which would make it impossible for the ...*One*... Almighty, Maker of Heaven and Earth, King of kings and Lord of lords, the Perfect One, to continue in perfect relationship with His *im*perfect Creation?

All he needed to do was...

Ah. Oh.

Ah. But if he could simply find a proxy...

So he couldn't set foot or wing inside Eden itself. But there was nothing stopping him having a quiet word or two or three with one of its inhabitants when they emerged from its boundaries.

The question was ... which one?

One of the Birds, perhaps. But no, the Birds flew too high to Heaven. He couldn't risk being spotted. Not that he was doing anything wrong, of course: why, anyone would agree that he had a right to speak to whomsoever he chose. It was just that the ...*One*..., the Enemy, might have, well, told the heavenly hosts to be on guard. As if they could guard against him, who had been the mightiest, the most beautiful of them all, the most deserving of praise! How dare they guard against him when they should be adulating him, worshipping him? How dare they guard Eden against him when it should have been *his* in the first place? Of course, *He*, the ...*One*..., would know irrespective of whom he approached, but He'd already proved His idiocy in allowing Lucifer loose, and could be counted upon not to intervene when the moment came, even if He was (futilely!) protecting them as much as possible by safeguarding Eden from Lucifer for the moment. Something about allowing His Creatures free choice. Or free will. Or something equally ridiculous and namby-pamby. Well, he, Lucifer, would soon teach Him proper respect... Him, the ...*One*..., Them... Deity, the Imperial We... Time to teach the ...*One*... some respect.

So. One of the other Creatures, then. One sufficiently close to the mud-men to be listened to. One of the Cats perhaps. No, too direct. One of the Cattle? No, too... simple. One of the Rodents? He shuddered. No, too small, too insignificant: whichever Creature he turned to his will should at the very least mirror his own former beauty. It was necessary, for his revenge to have its full impact and send tremors of suitable fear through the hearts of his Enemies. Cast him out, would They? Overlook him, would They, and give Eden to the usurpers? Underestimate him, would They, and allow him still to roam? Patronise him, would They, and invite him to repent and come back to Heaven for all to mock? (Not that They called it mocking. *They* said it was grace. Grace? *Grace?* Hah! How stupid did They think he was! As if he'd fall for that! Of *course* They intended to mock him. After all, that's what *he* would do in Their place. No siree. He wasn't going to be taken in!) He would show them. Whichever Creature he used, it had to be a fit envoy for his status...

Ah. Of course! What other Creature was so bejewelled, so elegant, with such sharp intelligence? What other Creature drew such universal gasps of awe at his beauty?
    Yes.
    Of course.
    And oh, so simple to find, when all knew for a fact that Serpent took his daily morning swim up and down the great river that ran through Eden and out beyond it!
    And Serpent... yes... he would be easy to... enlighten, made to see the wisdom of asking oh-such-an-innocuous question at the right moment in the ear of the right person... Lucifer grinned, and would have been astonished had he seen a reflection of himself at that moment. Since his exile from Heaven, his beauty had continued to dim. Like the living jewels he had smuggled out from Heaven, the further he got from the source of Life and Beauty, the less he reflected that glory and the duller he became. But now, when he grinned, there was not even a trace of that former beauty left. It had been replaced by a grotesque parody which distorted his features and for a moment revealed the ugliness of the corruption within.

33

chapter twelve

You ... fill me with joy in your presence,
with eternal pleasures at your right hand.
(Song 16:11)

After feasting again first thing with the breakfast bunch, they'd spent the rest of the morning fascinated as Weaver Bird had shown them how he sewed his nest together. Lion had taken himself off to go and explore a new corner of the savannah he'd seen yesterday, and Cow had gone to lie down in her favourite pasture, but Monkey had joined them soon after. Monkey had brought them a fine straight strong spike he'd found growing on one of the trees, for them to use instead of a beak. With Spirit's encouragement, Adam had realised that by making a little hole at the wider end and threading it with one of the fibres from a palm tree, they could stitch leaves together. Some of the leaves they tried simply tore, but others such as the vine leaf and the lotus leaf turned out to be quite sturdy, and soon the Man and Woman had created several little leaf pockets. Monkey had laughed and had tried too, imitating them, but had abandoned the exercise when he was distracted by the sight of a beautiful banana tree nearby.

He brought back some of the fruit for them.

'We could fill some of the pockets with berries for breakfast!' Eve had exclaimed, thrilled, and they'd shown their invention to Glory, who'd hugged them with proud delight at this first demonstration of the creativity they had inherited from Him.

'Not quite as elegantly as Weaver Bird!' grinned Adam, who was still entranced by the beauty of Weaver Bird's masterpiece.

'Ah, but our pouches aren't having to carry such a precious burden yet, are they?' reminded Eve cheerfully, and perched the one she had just completed on Cat's head, upside down. Cat blinked her great eyes and then shook her head till her impromptu hat fell down. She proceeded to bat her new toy around, up in the air, back and forth between Glory and the Humans and herself, and then over to Monkey and Dog. Dog took it and shook it with delight before racing back with it to Cat. The air rang with their merriment for a while, until Serpent and the two Otters joined them, and the leaf-hat decided it was time to end the game by hitching a ride with a passing puff of breeze.

The Otters had come to invite their Lord and Lady to join them for a swim in the river. *'We've found the most beautiful little pool where the river has swirled by the river bank! Come and see! Come and see!'*

Serpent concurred on its beauty, and together the little group had gone to delight in this new gift, where fronds of ferns leant over the bank, and River Vole had built a little nest. Glory had withdrawn fractionally – though His presence still filled every breath they took, of course! – to craft some stalactites and design some new snowflakes for the mountain peaks. ('Did you notice,' He'd asked them the day before, when they'd got back to Eden, 'that each snowflake is different? No two the same. Actually, it was Spirit's inspiration. Isn't She awesome!' And Adam and Eve had determined to look more closely the next time they went up there, awed anew by such abundance and passion for creativity and detail.)

And now they were all sprawled on the soft grass in the centre of the Garden, a little way from the pool, where the two Great Trees threw dappled light all around, and the Crickets sang a duet with the Honeybees. Monkey had scrambled up a tall tree to bring them all some dates, and now the group lay, blissfully sated, simply enjoying... *being.*

The Humans loved this spot. The leaves of the two Great Trees shone in tones of lambent gold and silver and copper, scattering a play of light where the leaves caught the sunshine and Heaven's radiance. Their leaves brushed together softly in musical arpeggios which harmonised with both the Crickets' duet and the heavenly hosts. The warm afternoon sun gently fanned them, and wove Creation's songs into the air.

The friends were sharing tales of some of the wonders they had already discovered.

Monkey was attempting to share the exuberance he felt with his effortless sailing from branch to branch. *'It's so... easy! It's such a wonderful moment, that weightless moment in between branches, when you've let go of the last one and the new one is flying towards your hand, and your tail just gives you that perfect balance and direction and...! You could try it, you know! Though He hasn't give you much of a tail, has He!'* He was disconcerted for a moment as he looked at the tailless and undoubtedly heavier Humans who were stretched out, wearing only their own beautiful skins. The two Dogs thumped their tails instead. Monkey scratched his head. The Dogs had tails, but they lacked his clever hands to catch each twig and branch as it swung up towards him. It seemed that Glory had given that particular gift to him alone in that group. *'Anyhow,'* he chattered enthusiastically, *'it's... wonderful! It's glorious! It's what I was made for. Yes, yes, yes!'* He jumped up and down, flipped a somersault in his enthusiasm, and caught a date that Eve smilingly tossed towards him.

'Did you see the grain we planted yesterday?!' Adam had exclaimed. 'Where Glory passed, it's already grown a foot! He's promised that we can harvest it together. And,' his eyes danced with eager anticipation, 'He said we could cook something together from it.'

Knowing how delicious everything was that Love served them, Eve's mouth watered at the mere thought. Not that she could imagine how it was possible to better what He'd already given them – but then again, every time she thought it was impossible to top what He'd already done, He'd go and do precisely that.

The Dogs had discovered that their noses could sort not merely different smells, but different times. *'It's as though He's let us... see... with our noses,'* they'd tried to explain. *'Like layers and layers, where each scent has come from and where it's gone to, and even **when** it went! Layers and layers! Like the Dance, but... but, with smells! Try it, try it!'* Eve and Adam had laughed and attempted to sort out the myriad fragrances, standing up with their eyes closed. They fell over each other instead, to the others' merriment, and now Adam lay with his head in Eve's lap, breathing in the clean perfume of her sun-warmed skin. He might not be able to untangle the skein of smells as the Dogs could, but as he lay close to her, her fragrance filled his nostrils and posted a thrill of joy straight to his heart. Eve ran her hand over his hair, marvelling anew at its texture.

It was the moment Serpent had been waiting for. The beautiful being he'd met that morning during his swim had been right. If the Man and Woman were so perfect, so deserving of God's honour, then *why* could they not do all that the beasts could do, and more? Such as using their noses to sort the smells like the Dogs did?

The dazzling stranger had taught Serpent to question his assumptions. In just that single meeting, he had taught Serpent to look at things differently, had seeded questions. Why was it, the resplendent stranger had asked, that Man and Woman were Lord and Lady of Creation? What precisely *was* it that made them so special?

The stranger had been most insistent, however. 'You can't challenge them directly,' he'd advised Serpent. 'They're not as beautiful or as tall or as graceful as you, or... or as intelligent as you, but you'll still need to be careful. Catch them when they're unawares... I hear... I hear that there's a particular Tree in the centre of the Garden, isn't there?'

And then the stranger had enlarged his idea.

So now Serpent turned to the Woman and feigned confusion. '*Did God really say, "You must not eat from any tree in the garden"?*'

And Creation trembled, and held its breath.

chapter thirteen

A sly tongue brings angry looks.
(An Anthology of Sayings 25:23)

And Eve laughed, a merry peal, crystal chimes on the afternoon air. 'Why, Serpent!' she hooted with mirth. 'Not eat from any tree in the garden?! Why on earth would Love say such a thing?! You know as well as I do that He's given us *all*, each and every one of us, every seed-bearing plant on the face of the whole Earth, and every tree that has fruit with seed in it! It's only from the Great Tree of the Knowledge of Good and Evil that we mustn't eat!'

'*But why?*' Serpent persisted. '*Surely you should be allowed to eat from that one too!*'

And Eve laughed again. 'Oh, Serpent. What on earth has got into you? You know as well as I do that it's not that we're not *allowed* to eat from it, but that Glory loves us enough to warn us not to!'

'*But why? You will not surely die, for God knows that when you eat of it your eyes will be opened, and you will be like God, knowing good and evil. And besides,*' he continued urgently, '*I can't see why it isn't good for food like all the other trees.*'

Eve chuckled. 'Goodness, Serpent, you really are in a mess today, aren't you?! Why do I need to be like Glory, when He's already who He is, and has created us to be who *we* are, whole and perfect already in His love?! He's given us… *everything*. His love. His trust. Each other. All this…' – and she swept her arm around to indicate the vastness of His gift. 'Don't you know that? Have you forgotten it already?' She giggled and shared a look of bemusement with Adam.

'Just wait till I share that with Glory. You are a funny one, Serpent. Why on earth would you want me to do something that would cause Him sadness?'

'*Adam?*' Serpent began, but the moment was lost, and the conversation on which he'd allowed himself to pin excited hopes was ended.

And Creation breathed again, and remained whole.

* * *

The friends ran up to the Lord to chatter excitedly as soon as they saw His presence brightening in the glade. Majesty heard them all out, as always effortlessly untangling each voice from the gloriously chaotic jumble. But gradually they became aware that His countenance was darker, sadder, sterner than they had ever witnessed before, and one by one they fell silent.

'Serpent,' He called.

And again. 'Serpent.'

The Earth trembled at His voice.

Serpent's tall form strode elegantly and unrepentantly before Him.

'What is this you have done?'

Serpent shrugged nonchalantly. *'Nothing. I simply asked...'*

Majesty stopped him. 'Do not fool yourself, Serpent. Did you think I would not know? Be thankful, be grateful that you did not succeed in introducing disobedience, did not succeed in destroying our Relationship. The whole universe would have groaned had you succeeded. And you, too, are part of that universe.'

Serpent shrugged.

Majesty sighed. 'Ah, Serpent. Do not let yourself go down that road. Think, and come back to Me.'

Serpent decided to brazen it out. *'I didn't do anything. I simply asked...'*

Majesty looked at Serpent sadly.

'What? I didn't do anything! I just asked...'

'Serpent. Serpent. Think! Come back!'

Serpent shrugged.

'Ah, Serpent. Since that is your Choice... then you may stay here, but to remind you, and all Creation, how terrible the consequences would have been had you succeeded, I Speak this: You will crawl on your belly from this moment forth, that all may see and remember what you did. For everything we do, and everything we Choose, has its Consequence, and the consequences are ours to bear. For that is the nature of freedom. This is your Consequence, Snake.'

And before their shocked and grieving eyes, Serpent's limbs shortened, shrivelled, changed, and were absorbed into his body. And now, instead of towering over them all with his graceful form, he lay his full length on his belly.

'Come, Children,' He said sadly, and led them away to allow Snake the privacy he needed to adjust to his new form. And name.

chapter fourteen

The LORD loves righteousness and justice;
the earth is full of his unfailing love …
Let all the earth fear the LORD;
let all the people of the world revere him.
For he spoke, and it came to be.
(Song 33:5, 8-9)

It was a subdued little group that left Snake to his privacy.

And yet, in its own way, the episode had increased Creation's reverence for its Creator, to whom Relationship mattered so much that the consequence even simply for its *attempted* destruction was so unequivocal.

'Will Snake be alright, Glory?' asked Eve

'Ah, Beloved. That's up to him to choose. We cannot force another's heart choices. We can only love him.'

'And his legs? Will they grow back?' questioned Adam, still shocked by what his friend had brought about on himself.

Glory shook His head sadly. 'No. Consequences are rarely drops of water to disappear with the first ray of sunshine. Consequences are… real. But,' He consoled the little group, 'Snake will soon discover there are joys to his new form, if he allows himself to do so. There will be things that he can do without limbs that he could never have done before. Wait and see!'

'Will we still be able to play together?' asked Monkey, who had developed a fondness for the way his towering, elegant friend could play hide-and-seek with him by reaching up into the branches and tickling him wherever he was crouched.

Love smiled affectionately. 'Yes, little one. If he chooses to. Just differently now that his form has changed.'

'Yippee!' Monkey yodelled, and swung himself round a passing branch in relieved jubilation, playfully pelting Dogs and Man with a couple of nuts he found close at hand.

Man pelted him back, and then Monkey, deciding that a rough-and-tumble was no rough-and-tumble if your playmates couldn't join you in the trees, came back down to grass level, where a thoroughly satisfying romp and chase and tickle ensued till all lay gasping and laughing together at Glory's feet.

They lay there for a moment, delighting in the contrast between the coolness of the tender grass under them and the warmth of the sun on top, and then Adam turned himself over to look up at Glory again with serious eyes. 'Father, what did you mean when you said that the whole universe would have groaned if Snake had succeeded in dislocating our Relationship?'

Love hugged him. 'Exactly what I said, Dearheart.'

Adam was baffled, and Eve asked his question for him. 'How?'

Glory looked at them both with a gentle smile. 'Imagine if you were to lose Snake. How would you feel?'

They meditated on this for a moment, before Dog spoke for them all. '*Emptier. As though a piece of me were missing.*'

'Exactly. And how would your friends feel if they saw that you were feeling emptier, even if they'd never met Snake themselves?'

Another pause while they thought about this chain of effect. '*Sad because they'd see me feeling unhappy.*'

'Yes. And those who were *their* friends?'

Eve's eyes widened. 'It'd be like the Great Dance, except in reverse! Everyone would be emptier in the end, on and on and on!'

'Yes, Beloved. Because what affects one affects you all. And now imagine that the Relationship you had lost was not simply Snake's friendship, but Creation's Relationship with its Creator…'

Adam was still groping to understand the full enormity of the tragedy they had just averted.

Love turned to him. 'Adam. What happens if your head decides to go swimming and dives into the pool? Can your body cut itself off from your head and stay dry high up on the bank, or does it follow where your head leads, into the water?'

Adam grinned at the image of the rest of his body sitting up on the bank while his head took itself for a swim. 'It follows, of course!'

'Just so. And I created the two of you, and your children, and all who are born to your line, to be the Head of My Creation, to care for this world and to nurture it, to lead it and above all – above all! – to serve it. To rule it, in other words, in Our image. Creation relies on you. And therefore on the Relationship that we share, the love and life and freedom I have given you to choose our partnership, for which I created you. And so if that Relationship were to be broken, it... it would cascade through Creation, and Creation too would suffer. So, you see, if you had chosen to put your trust in Snake, or in yourselves, above Me, and eaten from the Tree, that breach of trust would have breached the universe in turn, and all... would have borne the consequences of your Choice.'

'Oh,' said Adam humbly. 'That seems ever such a big responsibility!'

Majesty laughed, and hugged them again. 'Of course it is, Beloveds! The biggest there can possibly be. But that's why you're not on your own: together, we can fulfil it. And now,' He said, 'there is a time for sombreness and a time for joy. And you have used your freedom today to keep Creation whole, in perfect step with Me. And *that*, I believe, calls for a celebration!'

chapter fifteen

Their tongue is a deadly arrow;
it speaks deceitfully.
With their mouths they all speak cordially to their neighbours,
but in their hearts they set traps for them.
(The Prophet's Oracle 9:8)

The Earth was too bright. The Earth was *still* too bright. It was starting to hurt his eyes just to look at its perfection. It was nothing to do with his former glory dimming and him consequently finding it increasingly difficult to look into the Light he had once served. This, *this*, he convinced himself, was a deliberate ploy on the part of the …*One*…, the Enemy, to rub salt into his wound.

By rights, by now the Earth should have dimmed, should have shown up with darker veins where that damned Relationship had been disrupted and poisoned. But instead, yet again, he was surrounded by incompetents, while the Earth continued to blind him with its reflected glory. Fool reptile, failing him!

He'd heard that Snake had merely had his form and name changed. By rights, Snake should have been destroyed, wiped out, obliterated. Punished. If not by that idiotically soft-hearted …*One*…, then by him. He *needed* to hurt something, to destroy something, to take out his righteous fury on something — anything — and Snake deserved it for failing him, failing in such a simple task as gulling those impostors. The mere thought of lashing out at something and making it suffer warmed him, brought temporary relief to his injured pride. Power. Power to inflict suffering. Slowwwly. Painfully. To teach that incompetent a lesson. Yes.

But even *that* had been denied him. The Earth was *still* bright. Still perfect. Still in Relationship with *Him*, that …*One*…, that Enemy. The Earth… still gave him no foothold, when he had banked on today bringing him triumph, evicting that vermin from his Eden. How *dare* that selfish, sanctimonious …*One*… deny him the right to hurt others?

Well, he could wait. If he could not lash out at Snake, then at least he could groom him. Carefully, slowly. So that next time there would be no mistake, no failure, and Eden would be his.

Perhaps, thought the being who had once been Lucifer, he would start by offering Snake a sympathetic ear. Feed his sense of injury, blind him to the justice.

Yes.

That should work.

chapter sixteen

The beams of our house are cedars;
our rafters are firs.
(Love Song 1:17)

Eve unfurled luxuriantly on her bed of warm, soft moss. She could hear Adam singing joyfully to himself and his Creator as he bathed in the pool nearby. It was fed by a hot spring and had the most soothing jets of bubbles which rose up to massage whichever part of you was closest to them. Eve remembered some plants she'd noticed the day before, with the most delightful fragrances. If she experimented, she thought, she was sure she could create some combination of them which would be blissful when rubbed on her skin in the pool. Perhaps Adam might be interested in it too. And they could see if Spirit would join them and all create it together. Yes, that sounded as though it would make a perfect day: a walk to find the plants, and then time to experiment until they found a satisfying combination. And then using that combination on each other in the pool. Oh yes! She hugged herself and laughed with delighted anticipation.

This Man she had been given, and for whom she in turn had been created, this perfect partner! Everything about him delighted her. His adoration of Glory, and Glory's delight in him. His joyful friendships with the Animals. The depth of her friendship with *him*. His strength. His passion. His intelligence. His insatiable curiosity about the world they had been given, his unabashed fascination and awe at every new thing that Glory revealed. The unreserved abandonment of his laughter, his joy, his love. The way they each *knew* what the other was thinking, the way they shared everything. The way the sunlight glossed his gorgeous ebony skin – so different from her own fairness! – with bluish highlights. The countless tender little gestures of love that he showered on her and on all around him. Like this orchid which he had left by her head for her to see when she woke up, or the way he always checked that others had food in front of them before he himself would eat. The way he had of unconsciously running his hand through his hair when he was thinking. The silken touch of his skin on hers, his warmth when they nestled together at night. The way she could feel his muscles ripple under his skin when he moved, the reverberation of his heartbeat when she lay her head on his chest...

And now he was in the hot pool, bathing. By himself. Before even the breakfast bunch turned up. No one else. By himself. By *himself*...!

Eve scrambled out of bed and headed across to the hot tub to join her husband under the great camellia.

* * *

In the end, they had time for that and more that day.

The Birds had got together to weave a coverlet of feathers for their Lord and Lady, with down on the underside. *'We each chose our most beautiful feather to contribute,'* they explained, proudly showing off the gaps where a tail feather had been plucked here, or a wing feather there, or an indentation where the down had been. *'And Weaver Birds wove them together. Do you like it?'*

Adam and Eve were speechless, touching the precious gift with humble awe and marvelling at the way the feathers refracted the light in shimmering tones of iridescence. 'It's stunning,' they assured the Birds. 'Beyond anything we could have imagined. Thank you, thank you! But... are *you* going to be alright, each missing a feather?'

The birds chittered with laughter. Robin reassured them. *'Oh yes, don't worry. Glory saw what we were doing and has promised us that the feathers will grow back, even more beautiful than before! Not that we knew that when we started,'* she admitted, *'but we wanted to do it anyway. Just to say we love you.'*

Eve was still stroking the treasured gift, entranced by the beauty of its making and the enormity of its giving. 'And its patterns! Its symmetry! How did you think of it?'

Hawk tilted his head to look at her with his piercing gaze. *'Male and female, remember? And we each gave a feather. 'Course, some of us are plumed differently from our mates, but we used those for the centre of the pattern.'*

Eve held the soft, supple quilt to her cheek, and then to Adam's. 'Thank you,' she repeated. 'It's perfect.' And Glory, when they showed it to Him, agreed.

And later still in the day, when they'd successfully developed not one but three different plant concoctions which smelled heavenly when rubbed on their skin (and one or two utter failures, which *should* have smelled wonderful but didn't!), and resolved to spend other days, too, when the whim took them, experimenting on combining plants, and after they'd then *used* one of the fragrant creams on each other in the pool, they snuggled up under the precious coverlet. Overhead, the stars sparkled above the sweet-smelling cedar tree's sweep of branches, while the cicadas' zithers serenaded Creation in the evening air.

'We could stay here, couldn't we, Dearheart? Just like the Birds have their nests, and the Moles have their burrow. I mean, we could always sleep somewhere else if we chose, but somehow we seem to end up here in the evenings, on this moss bed under this cedar, with the pool nearby and the stars overhead, and the glade where we all meet for breakfast. And now we've been given this coverlet... Do you think that maybe this is our nest?'

Adam laughed and held her to him. 'I'm sure it is, Beloved. We can ask Glory, too.'

And Glory smiled and reassured them that the Earth was theirs, and everything in it, and that that moss bed was the absolutely perfect spot for their home if that's where they chose.

chapter seventeen

'In repentance and rest is your salvation …
but you would have none of it …'
Yet the LORD longs to be gracious to you;
therefore he will rise up to show you compassion.
(The Book of the Far-Seer 30:15, 18)

Just as Grace had assured them, Snake discovered that his new shape allowed him to do things he'd never done before.

'Now you can join me *in* the trees to play! And we can both play catch!' was Monkey's ecstatic reaction when Snake effortlessly slid up a tree. Swimming, too, turned out to be easily graceful: he could enter the water with scarcely a ripple now, and propel himself as lightly, it seemed, as the Birds did in the air with their wings and tails. Holes and crevices, which before would have been far too tight to accommodate his limbs, now presented no problem, and allowed him to explore places where his friends could not go.

Or former friends.

For although it was true that his new shape permitted new things, and although his friends behaved towards him with as much joy and love as before, and although, if anything, they were even more solicitous for him than they had ever previously needed to be, the words of his other friend, his *new* friend, had dripped in his ear and been allowed to seep into his heart.

His new friend had been flatteringly outraged on his behalf at the injustice of the Consequence which had been laid on him. Except that his new friend didn't call it Consequence. He called it *punishment* and *unfair*. The fact that Snake could do things with his new shape that he'd never been able to do before was irrelevant, it seemed. What mattered was that his first shape had been his by rights, and it had been taken from him unfairly, pettily. 'When all you did was ask,' his new friend had pouted dazzlingly, and reminded Snake to dwell on what he had lost rather than on what he had been given. The fact that his new shape was a consequence not merely of his attempted destruction but also of his refusal afterwards to admit or take responsibility for it was also, it appeared, irrelevant. 'Unfair,' whispered his new friend. 'Unfair.'

His friends? 'Hah!' had snorted his new friend sceptically. 'Don't tell me you've let yourself be taken in by all that rubbish, have you? Do you really think they love you just the same? After all, you tried to betray them. You tried to destroy their precious Relationship. Do you honestly think they love you just the same, unconditionally? Looking like you do now? All long and stringy and without legs?' and Snake had allowed Doubt to creep in and begin its corrosion.

It would have been so easy to allow himself to slip back into the easy embrace of his friends, to respond to their devotion with his own, to glow with the warmth of their love and their admiration, to *believe* them.

'I thought you were elegant before,' Eve had said to him the other day as she gave him a hug, 'and I couldn't imagine how Grace could make you more so. But now... now you're not just elegant; you're... *streamlined*! Oh, Snake, isn't He wonderful? Who could have imagined that He'd turn even the Consequence you caused into something beautiful?'

And Snake had felt himself growing inside, melting, healing.

But: 'You haven't let yourself be taken in again, have you?'

'But why? Why would they pretend?' he'd asked.

'Ah. That's the cunning bit, you see. They're so devious that of *course* it wouldn't be obvious. But don't let yourself be taken in. They don't love you. They just *pity* you. They're... condescending. Look at you. Not even tall any more. Just long and stringy and without legs. Of course they're not telling you that 'cos they're not your true friends. *Real* friends tell you the truth. I'm your real friend. Don't let yourself be taken in by them.'

* * *

Eve was concerned about Snake. He seemed to be withdrawing from them inside. 'I thought perhaps he was just adjusting to his new form and simply needed a little time,' she confided worriedly to Adam, 'but he seems to be growing into his new form, just as Love promised. I watched him swarm up a tree yesterday. Beautiful! It's… inside… that something's wrong. But he won't talk to me about it.'

'I know, Beloved. I've noticed it, too. I tried to get him to come swimming with us yesterday. He did, but… it was almost as though he couldn't meet my eyes.'

They sought out Love.

'I know, Beloveds.'

'But can't You *do* something?' they cried. 'It's like his limbs when they shrivelled – except this is worse, watching it happen inside him, watching him go away from us, watching him imprison himself! Oh, Father, can't you, won't you, *do* something?'

Love shook His head and shared their anguish. 'It's the one thing We cannot do, Beloveds. We cannot force his heart. If We did, there would be no freedom; only slaves and mindless creatures. He is the only one who can choose to come back to us. We can only continue to love him unchangingly.'

'I miss him,' grieved Eve.

'So do I, Beloveds. So do I.'

chapter eighteen

Shout with joy to God, all the earth!
(Song 66:1)

In time, it seemed, Snake came back to them a little. He started joining in Monkey's games again, and swimming. Even, sometimes, laughing with them. They were glad. The knot they instinctively knew was still there would melt, they hoped, with time; and meanwhile, they delighted in him.

And in all the newnesses which continued to unfold with every day.

For Eden had welcomed glorious miracles to her realm. Miracles that squirmed and squealed, crawled and gambolled, scampered and raced, burped and hiccoughed adorably. The Nest, as Adam and Eve had called their dwelling, had expanded considerably. Cedar was lending his lowest branches as beams for the Nest. Lion had led Elephants to his expanse of savannah, and the three of them had come back with smug delight and a huge load of long, golden grass. Glory had helped them make it into a snug thatched roof around Cedar's branches. Elephants' clever trunks had helped put the finishing touches on the top.

'*And we didn't even eat the grass on the way here!*' they'd proudly told Eve and Adam.

'*We did eat some before we loaded the rest on our backs, though,*' Elephant Cow pointed out. '*But not once we'd loaded it. Because we wanted it to be for you.*'

Knowing just how much foliage Elephants were capable of eating before their tummies were full, the two Humans had been properly touched and impressed.

And now the latticed walls echoed with the joyful sounds of the new miracles. Dog had had seven, and Cat likewise, and both had decided to share the awesomeness of these new creations with their Humans. It was practically impossible to place foot or paw or hoof on the ground without narrowly missing one adorable bundle of fur or fluff or another. For, of course, even the other Creatures who had not officially set up Nest in the same home as Adam and Eve still spent much of their time visiting in a steady and jubilant and gloriously chaotic crowd.

Just at the moment, Eve had two purring kittens round her neck, an adoring squirming puppy in her arms, and a couple of chipmunk babies perched merrily on her head. The puppy was trying to wash her face for her.

Adam was similarly adorned with one of Lion's two cubs and a baby marmoset. The baby marmoset was deliberating whether to stay where he was or use Eve's passing braid to swing himself up to join his chipmunk friends.

Cheetah was leaning against Eve for Eve to absentmindedly scratch her beneath her ears, and Horse had popped in to tell them that he and Chimpanzee had been given some spare branches by the Trees to bring by for use as firewood in the new stone oven.

Adam grinned with delight at the news. 'Thank you,' he said. 'I'll go by the Trees later and thank them too for their kindness.'

Horse looked around optimistically, and Eve laughed. 'Yes, of course you may,' she said, correctly interpreting his timing as a hope for an invitation to supper. 'I'm guessing that Mare and Foal are outside?'

Horse nickered enthusiastically.

Eve grinned. 'I'll get the bran mash out, then!'

Of course, there was sufficient for them all. There always was when Glory was around in the abundance of His love, and He always was.

They'd built a table outside for those who chose to use it. Or at any rate, for placing the various dishes of bran mash or nuts or fruit or milk or honey or baked extravagances upon. Dinner was always a time of exuberant praise and thanks and delight, of celebration, of fellowship, with Glory at the centre. Just at the moment, conversation was inevitably filled with the latest doting anecdotes from all and sundry, leaving everyone in gales of infectious laughter.

One of Bear's cubs had found the new flour mill by the weir and had rolled in the flour. *'By the time I found him,'* Mama Bear apologised, *'I'm afraid he was so white that I thought for a moment that he was one of Polar Bear's cubs come to visit! I'm afraid he's managed to scatter that lovely new flour you all made!'*

Elephant trumpeted that there was no need for worry – he'd managed to blow all the flour back together into its proper pile. *'Spirit helped,'* he added, *'and kept any stray bits of chaff from getting back in.'* There was a unanimous chorus of thanks. Ever since the Humans had built the little flour mill under Glory's help and guidance, the scrumptious, crusty, fresh loaves which were now baked on a daily basis were eagerly shared between all.

Inevitably, conversation turned to Eve's own tummy, bulging with promise, and the topic of excited discussion throughout Creation for the past several months. *'When? When?'* they asked.

Eve laughed. 'Well, Spirit and Glory have told me that it'll be very soon now. Perhaps even tonight.'

Adam beamed ecstatically. A baby! *Their* baby! *Eve's* baby! *His* baby! He'd spent days creating a – what was it that Glory had called it? Not a pocket... a crib, that was it! Sort of like a pocket, but bigger. And sturdier. Baby-sized, according to Glory. He was rather hoping that the baby would look identical to Eve, with her long-lashed, huge blue eyes, and perfect alabaster skin, and long, silken, golden hair down almost to her knees. Glory had informed him that baby girls weren't born with the same curves as their mothers, but He had promised that if it was a baby daughter, she would eventually grow into curves. Adam secretly hoped that the baby would be a girl. As beautiful and intelligent and loving and compassionate and thoughtful and curious and adoring of Glory as her mother. A girl. Lots and lots and *lots* of baby Eves.

He'd been a fraction disappointed when Glory had told him that Humans would generally only have one baby at a time. Eve had laughed at his expression and had kissed the tip of his nose. 'I'm sure we can have more when we choose to, Dearheart,' and at that consoling thought, Adam had brightened up considerably.

And in the meantime they had a household full of little ones, so perhaps it was just as well that Eve was only bringing a single one into the world, or they might not be able to lavish him or her with enough attention. Though he suspected that with all creation around to adore the baby, lack of attention was probably not going to be too much of an issue.

And baby Adams... well, he conceded that baby Adams would be wonderful, too. Lots and lots of baby Adams, to grow up with the baby Eves and with the puppies and lambs, cubs and baby snakes, calves and kittens.

He'd spent the last few months adoringly following the contours of her changing shape with his hands, eyes and heart. So beautiful! So awesome! So wonderful! That the Creator had not limited Himself to merely creating them, but had allowed them, too, to create. In His image!

His attention was unceremoniously brought back to the moment, when Eve touched his hand and grinned excitedly. He looked at her, stunned. 'Now?' he asked incredulously. *'Now?'* And in awed amazement, a third time.

Eve's eyes sparkled. 'Yes. Now.'

'It's coming! Now! We're going to have a… *baby*! A *baby*. *Our* baby!'

Supper exploded into sheer joy as the Creatures each volunteered their help. Privacy, of course, was an unknown concept. Mama Bear took charge. *'I'm the biggest here with any experience. No offence, Elephant, but your Cow is still nattering with Giraffe on the other side of the Garden. So clear some space for our Lady, you lot. No, Dog, thank you, but I don't think she'd fit into the basket with your puppies. Thank you, Sweetheart, but no, I don't think she'd be better off flying to your eyrie. Yes, thank you, Glory, that's wonderful! Right, now, my Lord, if you'd just let her lean on you. One, two, three. It's a boy!!!'*

And Adam, awed, astonished, amazed, astounded, found himself holding his… *son*. Look! His *son*! Ten fingers! Ten toes! 'Oh, Father. He's so perfect. *Thank* you!!!!! Look! Look! We've got a *son*! Isn't he… *wonderful!'*

Eve laughed with pure delight.

And with a clamouring and rejoicing, a jubilation and felicitation, Creation delighted with them.

And Eve exclaimed in wonder: *'Look, Adam! He's got a belly button! That's where he was linked to **me**! A **belly** button!'*

And the two awed new parents looked at each other's smooth stomachs and then back in amazement at this tiny being with the new feature which marked this new generation and all future ones from themselves.

chapter nineteen

In the beginning was the Word, and the Word was with God, and the Word was God. He was with God in the beginning. Through him all things were made; without him nothing was made that has been made. In him was life, and that life was the light of all mankind.
(The Record of Grace 1:1-4)

The arrival of baby Cain did not, in fact, much increase the usual glorious chaos in the household. As Adam had half-guessed beforehand, Creation offered itself as a profusion of babysitters, all vying for the privilege of caring for the little Lord. Indeed, the problem was in *limiting* the help received, not in finding it.

Mama Bear had apparently appointed herself honorary secretary of the baby's social diary, and was as stringent about his care as she was for her own cubs. Rabbit, for example, was excluded from babysitting. *'It's not that Rabbit doesn't mean well,'* she explained to Cain's Human mama. *'It's the fact that Rabbit only feeds her own litter once a day. So she forgets that Cain wants to be brought to you to suckle more frequently.'*

And indeed, the quantity of milk that Cain chortlingly drank from Eve's breasts was avidly approved by the Creatures, who would have happily provided their own milk for him, too, if Eve had permitted it. She didn't, usually, though she was aware that occasionally one or other of the beasts would slip him 'an extra little drop' here or there. Cow, for instance, was always pointing out how much excess milk she had every day.

But the baby was clearly thriving, and they knew that Glory and all the heavenly Host were watching over him day and night as well, so whatever extra Cain was receiving was clearly not endangering him.

In the evenings, the household often quietened down slightly, as the daytime shift of non-resident animals returned with their younglings in tow to their own nests or burrows or quarters, and before the night-time shift started dropping in, *'just to check, m'Lady, that you're well.'* It was fortunate that Glory gave new strength to them to enable them to be as gracious to the later shift as they were to the daytime Creatures, but even so, Eve sometimes politely but firmly explained to them that Humans were not by nature as nocturnal as they were, and would be grateful for some rest.

But tonight was one of the rare evenings that they had time more or less alone with each other and with Glory. Cain was in his crib, gurgling happily to himself, and Eve and Adam were nestled down under their beautiful feather coverlet at Glory's feet. One of the kittens had sneaked in to join them and was now fast asleep with her tiny paws in the air and her tummy warm and tight as a drum from the milk she had drunk before bedtime. She'd spent the afternoon unstoppably chasing her own tail, and those of the other youngsters, and was now oblivious to the rest of the world. Man and Woman spent a few minutes watching the gentle rise and fall of her tummy before exchanging tender glances with each other and with Glory. So serenely peaceful, after such whirlwind energy during the day!

The birth of Cain and all the other Eden younglings had given them all a new and breathtaking insight into the depths of His love for them. That Glory – Creator, King of kings, Lord of lords, Maker of Heaven and Earth – should love them as His children, was almost beyond fathoming.

The time when Cain would be old enough for bedtime stories would come. For now, though, it was their turn. 'Please tell us again, Father,' begged Adam.

Glory laughed. 'Again?!?'

'Yes. Please!'

'Very well. In the beginning, We created the heavens and the Earth. Now the Earth was formless and empty, and darkness was over the surface of the deep. And My Spirit was hovering over the waters. And so We said, 'Let there be light.''

'And was there?' Eve asked sleepily. She knew the answer, of course, but it thrilled her every time she heard it, sent shivers of awe down her spine.

Father laughed gently. 'Yes, Beloved. There was light. With a big bang! And I saw that the light was good, and I separated the light from the darkness.'

'What did you call the light, Father?'

Father gentled their hair and smiled down at them. 'We Called it Light, Dearheart!'

Eve looked up at Him and grinned. This was all part of the Telling of the Story. 'I *meant*, what did you call the *time*?'

'I Named it... Time, Dearheart. Before that there was no Time. Only Me, with My Spirit and My Word.'

On this occasion, Adam was temporarily diverted from the Story. 'So, Father, how *did* You exist before Time?'

The Lord's radiance shone warmly. 'I AM, Beloved. You know that. I'm... outside Time. I'm the Beginning and the End, and every instant in between. I AM beyond the beginning and outside the end. A million years for you is as a day for Me: yet an instant of your time is as a thousand years for Me. I AM. I AM with the Sparrow as she builds her nest. I AM with the grass as his first shoot peers above the ground. I AM with the mote of pollen on the breeze, and I AM before the first mountain was created and until the same mountain becomes dust millions of years later. I AM...'

Adam mulled it over. 'Is a million years a long time, Father?'

Father laughed, and hugged them both. 'Not if you're I AM, Beloved.'

Eve murmured sleepily. 'Tell us the rest, Father?'

And as the Man and Woman drifted off to sleep, their heavenly Father took up the tale again. 'And We called the light "day", and the darkness We called "night". And there was evening, and there was morning – the first day. And then I said...'

He looked down at them.

By this telling of the Second Day, His beloved Humans had joined the kitten in a starfield of dreams. He kissed them tenderly on their foreheads and withdrew some of His radiance to let them sleep perfectly.

chapter twenty

Woe to those who call evil good
and good evil,
who put darkness for light
and light for darkness,
who put bitter for sweet
and sweet for bitter.
(The Book of the Far-Seer 5:20)

The knot, of course, was still there. It was simply hidden better. His new friend had insisted on that.

'You mustn't let them realise you're on to them. Don't give them that satisfaction. Pretend you believe their lies of friendship. Don't let yourself be taken in, but don't let *them* realise that you haven't. They're not your friends. How could they be? Look at you. Not even tall any more. Just long and stringy and without legs. Do you really think they love you? After all, you tried to *betray* them. You tried to destroy their precious Relationship. Do you honestly think that they love you just the same, unconditionally? Of course they're not telling you that. 'Cos they're not your true friends. *Real* friends tell you the truth. I'm your real friend. Now. We just have to wait till this young one is a little older. *Then* we can have revenge for what they did to you. Such pettiness! Such unfair punishment! When all you did was ask a question!'

And so he learned to hide the knot where it could grow undisturbed, and he pretended to join in.

Sometimes he pretended so well that for a moment he forgot the knot.

But whenever he did so, the next time he went to see his friend down by the river bank, outside Eden, his friend would remind him that those in Eden were merely toying with him, that what they called light was in fact darkness, and what they called sweet was in fact bitter, and the knot would harden again with the acrid thirst for vengeance.

So his friend would urge him to be patient, and to carry on pretending to be whole.

And all the time, Adam and Eve and the animals loved him, and yearned for him to allow himself to be set free from the dread cage he had chosen for himself.

chapter twenty-one

I praise you because I am fearfully and wonderfully made;
your works are wonderful.
(Song 139:14)

There was still so much to explore, so much to discover, so much to do. Every day brought new joys, new skills, new understanding. Usually they took the two boys and the two girls with them everywhere – Cain was now a strapping boy of about seven, and Abel a sturdy five-year-old, while the twins had just passed the toddling stage – though Eve generally put her foot down when it entailed activity she deemed particularly reckless. 'Yes, I know Glory is looking after us and is at our right hand and our left. But I still don't think that expecting one of the Archangels to be the children's bodyguard *again* is fair. Besides, Mama Bear has been fairly pining to look after them again.'

And so they'd leave them in the tender care of the children's delighted nursemaid, while they followed Glory to tend and joyfully learn more about the realm He had entrusted to them. With Him they soared on wings like eagles to the highest eyries, and visited Leviathan in the deep. With Him they roamed throughout Havilah, where there is gold, aromatic resin and onyx, and through the land of Nod, east of Eden. Sometimes they simply rested in Him, and other times He'd laugh joyously and urge them to trust Him before He introduced them to something 'just for fun'. Adam was particularly enchanted by the occasion He took them to a high snowy peak and got them to strap wooden boards to their feet to skim the powder-soft snow. Eve was more impressed by the time He suggested Calling the Dolphins to themselves in the sea and asking the Dolphins to take them on a gloriously wild ride round the bay, seated on their warm, soft backs.

Sometimes the Dogs came with them (*'Though we draw the line at being lifted up in the air by the Eagles, Glory or no Glory! We're Dogs, we are. We'll stay with our four paws on the ground, thank you!'*), though their pups invariably accompanied the children and were inseparable from them.

But even when they weren't roaming far and wide, Adam and Eve found each day filled with new marvels, new reasons to praise Him together with all the angelic host. Sometimes those marvels were the kinds that continued to unfold day by day before their eyes: the growth of the children, the way each child was so utterly unique, not merely in looks but in character and interests. Sometimes the marvels were developments of skills they learned from the Animals, or had invented themselves. Weaving, for example, or using clay to make pottery, which they discovered could be beautifully baked in their stone oven. Adam, they had realised with delight, was the more artistic of the two, and had a flair for colour and music – and cooking! – which brought joy to all around. Eve had a gift for practical things, for seeing a need and discerning how to fill it, with Spirit's inspiration. The little stone mill – which was still functioning perfectly to grind the grain into flour – had been her idea, for instance.

And both treasured the times when they would each walk alone with Glory, in different parts of the Garden, simply spending time with Him and letting Him show them what He would.

'I wonder how He does that,' Eve sometimes said, 'walking at the same time with each of us, wherever we are!'

Adam would invariably hug her at that, and reply, 'He's Glory, Beloved. He's I AM, every*where* and every*when*, remember! And I'm not, but I'm here *now*, and what do you reckon to...' – and hand in hand they would go to the hot spring, or to check that the boys weren't mischievously asking Caterpillar which foot he put down first, or to visit Tiger and take her some of the raw savoury fruit of the Bassar tree which she so loved and which was her main diet. The Humans preferred it cooked.

* * *

The children differed greatly in their characters. Cain, as the eldest and having enjoyed undivided attention from all of Creation for the first two years of his life, was constantly showing Abel and their sisters how to do everything, and was the undisputed leader of their little group of two- and four-legged friends.

62

'He'll make a great servant-king, if he only chooses to learn some humility,' observed Adam wryly, and took Cain with him to till the soft soil with the help of Wild Boar and his increasing tribe.

Abel was gentler and quieter than his brother, and loved nothing more than running out to meet Glory and sit at His feet in adoration, more often than not accompanied by one of his four-footed friends. Invariably, he'd bring that day's special treasure to show Him: a bright feather given to him by one of the Macaws; a perfect fruit he'd picked from his special tree; a leaf with a flawless drop of dew glistening at its heart. His most precious ones of all, he'd give to Glory, and Glory would gravely thank him and accept the gift. 'I've stored it in my heart,' he'd tell Abel, and Abel would glow with delight and run to tell his mother or father that Abba had treasured his offering.

The girls, though twins, were also disparate. Yan-î adored her eldest brother and would trail him wherever possible. M'burechet, on the other hand, was particularly musical, and would beg the angels to show her how to play their instruments, before spending hours alone in Spirit's company building one for herself, shaping the wood, tuning a gourd and harmonising notes while singing quietly to herself with melodies she'd picked up or devised on the spot.

Physically, all four were utterly unlike each other, too. Cain was a strapping lad with berry-brown skin, great grey eyes and his mother's dimples. Abel took after his father – sturdy, with ebony skin. His dazzling white smile seemed permanently set in his fine-boned face, and his startlingly long-lashed, green eyes seemed to look into the heart of everything he gazed at. The twins were still too young to truly show their adult traits, but Yan-î had beautiful, dark, almond-shaped eyes, golden skin and glossy black hair, while M'burechet had her mother's fairness, an adorable sprinkle of freckles over her nose, and rich, russet hair.

Adam and Eve had marvelled at this variety, until Spirit reminded them that Glory was Creator, fountain of variety, and that it was His nature to instil uniqueness into His children's line. 'Particularly when the children themselves grow old enough to have children, and their children have children in turn. How else do you think He could bring out the different facets of Our Being? You were created to be in Our image, remember, with the vastness and richness that entails? Or would you have preferred identical copies of yourselves?' She'd teased, and they'd grinned back at Her.

Sometimes Adam remembered his daydream of hundreds of baby Eves and baby Adams, but as ever, he now realised that Love's reality had vastly surpassed anything he could have remotely imagined. That his four children so far could be so... *perfect*, so... *unique*, awed and staggered him, and again and again he thanked Father for this privilege of being allowed to witness such a daily miracle.

chapter twenty-two

A violent [being] entices his neighbour
and leads them down a path that is not good.
Whoever winks with their eye is plotting perversity;
whoever purses their lips is bent on evil.
(An Anthology of Sayings 16:29-30)

The Earth was still too bright. But soon, soon, it would be his. He was no longer particularly interested in Eden itself — it was too bright, even by Earth's standards! — though he was still determined that since he couldn't have it, neither should the usurpers.

But Earth... ah, now that was promising. Soon, oh so soon, the wait would have been worth it. Soon, the disgusting waste of time pretending to be that incompetent reptile's friend would pay off. All he needed was that single drop of poison to act and Earth would no longer be perfect. And as he knew, imperfection and that vile ...*One*..., who was Perfection Itself, could not co-exist, could not mix.

He'd had time, these last years, to experiment. He'd taken some of the gems — not those he'd smuggled out of Heaven, but the ones which were already cold stone in the Earth's crust — and he'd played with them. Some — the ones with no inner flaw — withstood heat or pounding a lot longer than those which already had a weakness. But those with an inherent defect — he'd enjoyed smashing those, or subjecting them to heat and hearing the fatal crack, seeing the shattered smithereens fly apart, feeling them turn to dust under his destructive hand, and anticipating when the Earth itself would be his prey, no longer perfect, no longer able to survive the force of the ...*One's*... holiness, no longer in Relationship, and therefore abandoned. To him.

Ah! Soon. Oh so soon! The potentialities would become weaknesses, flaws, and then those same imperfections would... would explode in the presence of perfection, would become overloaded and would cause the whole of Creation to splinter apart. And that namby-pamby ...*One*..., he knew, would see the futility of allowing the imperfect Earth to blow itself to smithereens, and would therefore abandon it. And then it would be his. All his! All his, to ravage and devastate and play with as he chose. Ah, the triumph! Exile him, would they? But soon he would have the last laugh, when he caused it to be unfit, and discarded, and left to him to glean...

Soon, he promised himself. But first there were still things to do.

He'd have to endure that snivelling snake a little longer before he could laugh at its destruction. All he had to do was continue to prevent the idiot reptile from turning back to the ...*One*... whose perfect Love (Urgh. *That* word again. Vile, disgusting word! He spat.) would drive out all fear, would melt the festering knot he'd so carefully nurtured these past years. Yes. All he had to do was keep its attention away from the fact that it is our choices that shape and eventually form our character, not our circumstances.

There was just one more piece he had to sneak into place for him to be able to savour every instant of his triumph.

And then...

And then Creation would no longer be too bright.

chapter twenty-three

What a [being] desires is unfailing love.
(An Anthology of Sayings 19:22)

At long last – oh, so long! – it seemed that Snake was beginning to allow himself to… breathe… again. Of course, they could sense that the cage in which he had trapped himself was still there, that knot which he'd never released since he had brought the Consequence on himself. He had still not opened up to his friends, let alone to Glory, to allow it to dissolve. But if his unfurling, uncurling, continued as he spent more and more time with Cain, then, they hoped, he would finally allow himself to become whole again, and through that friendship with Cain, come back into full Relationship with them all.

They weren't quite sure what had been the precious catalyst that had allowed Snake to feel more at ease in Cain's company after so long holding himself back, but whatever it was, they were glad. As for Cain himself – grown now into a beautiful young man, and still accompanied everywhere by Yan-î – it was easy to see the delight he took in Snake's witty conversation, and in the supple elegance which allowed the two of them to swim and climb together.

The Creatures were overjoyed. As the boys had grown into maturity, it had become clear that Cain's giftings lay with the soil, with plants of field and trees of orchard, whereas Abel's joy manifested itself above all in walking with Glory to serve his four-legged friends. Where Cain loved nothing better than scattering the grain after asking Wild Boar to till the fields, and watching with delight as Majesty caused them to sprout and ripen fast, or getting the Birds to help prune a vine until each was perfect, Abel would spend hours roaming with Glory, in the Garden or out beyond it, spending time with each Creature, learning from it, helping where he could, serving where he might. But the amount of time Cain spent with any Creature – beyond those he needed to serve the land – had grown limited. Only some of Dog's pups occasionally accompanied Cain. So the Creatures were delighted that, with Snake, Cain was rediscovering the pure joy of friendship with one of them.

'And,' said Adam, 'perhaps the fact that it's Snake, of all Creatures, to become so close to Cain, is perfect. Perhaps Snake will remind Cain of Father's majesty and grace towards him, and will encourage Cain as well to grow in the depth of his friendship with Glory!'

Eve smiled up at her darling Man, dimpling, and Adam felt his heart bound and lurch with pure joy as he always did when he looked upon the beloved whom Glory had given to him. His skin tingled deliciously. 'Yes,' she agreed, 'that would be wonderful. Every time I see Snake, I marvel again at Glory's grace, how He turned a Consequence into something so beautiful. But I suppose Cain has only ever heard about the Consequence second-hand. So spending time with Snake should allow him to appreciate Glory's grace with fresh eyes.'

And, indeed, the times spent with Cain were among the most blissful that Snake knew. Everyone, it seemed, approved. Even his friend, usually so scathing about all the inhabitants of Eden, seemed to be in favour. In fact, come to think of it, he'd even been the one to suggest that Snake befriend Cain in the first place! It was the first time in a long, long time that Snake had been allowed to simply enjoy a friendship without having it marred by his friend's baleful warnings, and he basked in it.

chapter twenty-four

But you have turned justice into poison
and the fruit of righteousness into bitterness.
(The Book of the Peasant Prophet 6:12)

Snake had just sloughed his skin and was now gleaming in his handsome new coat. He loved this moment, when he had shucked off the old one and was resplendent in the new. In recent years, these were the only times when he had felt... clean. The problem was that the newness was only ever fleeting. Within minutes, Snake felt, that sense of lightness, of freedom, of cleanness, would vanish.

He had come to meet his friend at their habitual daily meeting place by the river just below Eden. The friend who always told him that he was Snake's only true friend. The friend who was always outspoken about the great injustice, the unfair punishment, done to Snake. The friend who never failed to remind him that Snake was no longer tall, just long and stringy and without legs. The friend who somehow never failed to remind him of his guilt. Strange how in Eden neither Glory nor anyone else ever seemed to view him that way. But then again, his friend had said that it was the very fact that they *didn't* mention it that proved that they weren't his real friends.

And now he was waiting for his friend at their usual trysting place, with his old skin curled empty beside him.

He didn't have to wait long. Within instants, his friend had arrived. His eyes gleamed with delight when he saw the empty skin.

'Ah. You remembered.'

'Yes. But I still don't quite understand why you need it.'

'Don't be silly. I don't need it. I just thought that you might like me to accompany you back into the Garden.'

'But... but why don't you just come as yourself?'

'I've already told you lots of times. I could if I wanted to. But then everyone would look at me and admire me, and I'm doing this for you, so that they can all look at you and see that you've finally made a real friend.'

'But...!'

'But? How do you mean, 'but'? Snake, I'm doing this for you. And this is how you thank me?'

Snake hastened to apologise, and helped his friend into the discarded skin. It was astonishing how cleverly his friend made himself look like Snake. If it weren't for the holes here and there in the skin, his friend might have been born into it.

His friend sounded satisfied for a moment, and Snake was relieved. He wasn't sure why his friend's company made him so keen to avoid displeasing him. After all, his friend had always been nice to him, had always declared his partisanship for Snake against those who had so unjustly punished him. Still, there was no denying that he was glad that his friend sounded satisfied.

'Now. Shall we go?'

'Go?'

'Yes, of course, dear Snake. You didn't think I was just doing this for fun, did you? Come on, let's see if this works.'

They headed towards the Garden. At the boundary, though, his friend unaccountably stopped dead. It was almost as though he'd come against an invisible stone wall.

'Actually, I've changed my mind, Snake. This would be boring, going like this in this old coat! Come on. I've got a better idea!'

He explained his idea. Snake was uncomfortable with the notion. *'But why?'*

'Oh, Snake, not again! I've just told you. Look, it'll be much more fun if they don't even know I'm there. That way I can see how they behave towards you for myself. And *then* I'll know how I can help you most when I put on the skin and come in as your friend!'

'But I thought you said ...'

His friend sighed long-sufferingly. 'Look, Snake, do you want me to help you or not? Here I am with this wonderful idea, and all you can do is dig your heels in. Metaphorically speaking, of course, since I know that ever since that unjust and unfair petty punishment you don't have your lovely tall legs any more. Or feet. Or heels.'

It took a little while, but Snake eventually allowed himself to be convinced.

And then it took a little while for them to experiment by trial and error. The first few times, when Snake allowed his friend to completely take over his body, or half take it over, they unaccountably stopped short at the boundary again. His friend explained each time that he'd simply changed his mind and had an even better idea.

But finally they found the balance. Snake was in control of his body, and only the most tiny tendril of his friend's mind insinuated itself into a corner of Snake's own mind. It felt... unpleasant. Cold and slimy. But his friend pointed out that if he was going to so much trouble on Snake's behalf and enduring at least as much discomfort, then the least Snake could do was thank him instead of complaining.

They didn't venture far into the Garden. Just a few yards (Snake could feel his friend looking through his eyes), and then his friend nudged Snake's mind and suggested that they'd worked hard enough that day and could do it again on another day. But his friend seemed satisfied about something.

This most recent time, it had only been the tiniest tendril of his friend's mind, the most ephemeral of filaments inserted into his own.

Even so, Snake just wished it were time to slough his skin again.

chapter twenty-five

'Seek first his kingdom and his righteousness, and all these things will be
given to you as well.'
(The Taxman's Testimony 6:33)

They'd walked the barley field together that morning. Wild Boar and Cain had tilled and sown it a few weeks back, and now the grain was almost ripe. So this morning Cain and Glory had gone together to view it. Cain wanted to see when it should be harvested. Two of Dog's pups, now fully grown and delighted at the opportunity to accompany the young Lord Cain today, bounded along beside them.

'Isn't it a glorious day? A glorious day! Yes, yes, yes! Oh, thank you, Glory, thank you!' and they'd be off, racing each other up and down the rows of nodding grain, or stopping to sniff Rabbit's news by a barley plant here, and a message left by Hare there.

'They're having a party down in the Glade this afternoon and left a message for us to join them. Shall we? Shall we? Shall we?'

Cain was thrilled to see that the grain should already be ripe for harvesting the following day, and Called the Elephants with his mind to ask for their help on the morrow. They were grazing down in the south of the Garden, but cheerfully assured Cain they'd be there.

He looked with delight back at the way they had come. As usual, when Glory had passed through the fields, the grain in His wake was even richer, fuller and more plentiful than it had been before.

'Oh, Glory, this is wonderful! Tomorrow's harvest will be another perfect one.'

'Cain, Beloved.'

'Yes?'

'Tell Me. Why do you love tending the fields?'

Cain was astonished. 'You know why, Glory! It's just so wonderful! Getting Wild Boar to till them, and then sowing the seed and seeing it sprout up so tall and perfect until it's ripe, and then getting the Elephants to help harvest it, and seeing it all collected and bound up and then threshed and ground…'

'Cain, Dearheart.'

'Yes?'

Love waited.

Cain looked baffled.

Love waited some more.

Cain fidgeted.

And then... 'Ohhhhhh. Oh Father! You're right. I'd... I'd got my eyes so stuck on getting it all done perfectly that... I almost forgot the Heart of why!'

He flung himself into Glory's arms, and Glory laughed and hugged him. 'I know, Beloved. I know.'

They walked on, hand in Hand, and Cain sang with the joy of the renewed lightness that came of having lifted his eyes up from the detail to focus back instead on the Giver of that detail. And the two pups vaulted over each other in ecstatic delight and cleared two rows of barley before careening off in a headlong circuit of the field.

chapter twenty-six

'Why are you troubled, and why do doubts rise in your minds?'
(The Doctor's Testimony 24:38)

They were basking on a sun-warmed rock above the pool after an energetic swim. Snake had won the underwater swimming stretch, whilst Cain had gleefully won the diving challenge, and now both were sprawled contentedly on the smooth stone in the glorious sunshine. One of Snake's smaller cousins, a sweet little grass snake, had come to join them, and was joyfully coiled around Cain's forearm, a bright green highlight on Cain's beautiful brown skin. Snake's other friend lay watchful and alert but quiescent in his mind, an almost imperceptible presence.

In the last few days, since their first experiment, Snake's friend had wanted to practise this piggyback exercise increasingly often, it seemed. *'But I thought you just wanted to look!'* Snake had exclaimed in dismay the first couple of times, to be reminded that it was, after all, for his sake that they were doing this. And in the meantime they had practised so often that by now it almost felt like second nature to Snake.

A hummingbird dipped and bobbed nearby in his stunning plumage, his slender beak finding the loveliest nectar in some scarlet trumpet flowers, and some young yellow canaries were earnestly trying to teach some butterflies to sing. *'Look! Listen! Just open your beaks and trill!'*

The butterflies were giggling (such dainty motes of happiness on the tapestry of air!) and pointed out that Glory had created them without beaks. *'But we can fly together!'* they pointed out, and fluttered merrily in a dance with their feathered friends above the sunbathers.

Cain sighed blissfully. Today was another perfect day. He told Snake about that morning's walk with Glory. 'And I hadn't even realised, you know, that I'd almost been starting to look down so much.' He laughed ruefully and added, 'That... that instant of realisation between the time you finally see it and the dross melting away is still uncomfortable, though, isn't it! But oh, isn't He wonderful!' He laughed, carefree and joyously, in the restored fullness of Relationship.

It was an area that Snake didn't feel up to exploring too fully. Oh, how he longed for that freedom himself! But it was out of reach. He'd carried his knot too long to want to let go of it. It had become part of his identity. His, all his. He couldn't, didn't want to let it melt away.

Especially not now. Not now that he was hosting that tendril of... of what his other friend called friendship, but which felt more like... darkness. Cold, slippery, slimy darkness.

Snake decided to deflect the subject. The guest in his mind sprung to complete and utter alertness. *'Glory doesn't have to remind Abel as often as He does you, does He?'*

Cain laughed uproariously and rolled over on to his belly to look at his friend. 'No, of course not! Abel spends so much time with Him that he's always got his eyes open and free. Abel never tangles himself up like I do! Wise lad!'

He chuckled at the unlikely image of his younger brother, who still brought every day's greatest treasures to Glory, becoming so focused on detail that he'd lose sight of the Author.

The guest in Snake's mind reared its head and nudged the knot and awoke old doubt. And Snake said, *'I guess that means Abel is His favourite then, doesn't it?'*

And Cain hesitated. 'I don't *think* so,' he replied.

And then they changed the subject by mutual unspoken consent. They dived back into the pool (Grass Snake hurriedly slipped off Cain's arm first) and splashed and frolicked and laughed and delighted in each other's witty banter.

And then they were joined by Yan-î, whose company Snake enjoyed almost as much as her brother Cain's, and they all trooped off, barefoot in the soft grass, to pick some of the luscious raspberries which everyone adored, and carry them home to the Nest for supper.

Favourite? Favourite? He didn't *think* so. But... favourite?

chapter twenty-seven

'Today if you hear his voice, do not harden your hearts.'
(Song 95:7-8)

Snake was coiled up in a fork of his favourite bough. It belonged to a great Copper Beech, with smooth bark and rich colours. Its leaves rustled gently, soothingly, in the breeze, and dappled sunlight filtered onto his back in warm patterns.

Glory settled down beside him. His other friend retreated to the deepest part of Snake's knot. His other friend was curiously shy about looking out of Snake's eyes when Glory was present, Snake had noticed. Strange, considering his increasing boldness at other times. But when Glory was present, he'd noticed, his friend generally found reasons to withdraw completely from his mind, or else, as now, when there'd been less warning of Glory's arrival, to crouch immobile and imperceptible in the deepest corner of Snake's knot.

Actually, Snake had to admit that he found Glory's presence a bit of relief. Of *course* he was appreciative of what his friend was doing for him. But… but still it was nice to not be sharing his mind for a moment. Even if, as always, the knot remained. Ever present.

Glory smiled at him, and a tiny twig budded and sprouted from the bough, just where Snake had fleetingly wished for a little more support for one of his coils. *'Thank you,'* he said.

Glory caressed his head tenderly and gently rubbed the furrow between Snake's eye ridges, where one of his scales had been itching. It felt lovely, and Snake sank his chin, eyes half-closed with contentment, onto Glory's lap for more cosseting.

'Oh, Snake. Beloved. You know how much I love you. Won't you let Me heal you?'

Snake stiffened. How often had Grace shared that yearning with him? How often had he been on the verge of saying yes; how often had he almost been taken in by that Love?!

Deep, deep, deep inside the knot, the wisp of the other shuddered, cringed. Almost as if it were afraid.

'I can't lift it from you if you won't let Me,' He said.

'I'm fine, Glory. Really. It... it doesn't bother me. Not any more. I've had it so long. It's part of me. I'm fine, really.'

'Oh, Snake. You don't have to go down that road. There's still time to turn back. Come back, Beloved. Come back.'

But Snake was sticking to the safety of the familiar knot. 'It's who I am, Glory. I've had it for so long. I can't let go. I don't want to let go. I'm fine. Really I am.'

And Glory, grieving, sat with him a while, and then withdrew again. Free will could not be free if it were forced. And Glory, King of kings and Lord of lords, was nothing if not God, the Giver of true freedom and Respecter of the free will which was His gift.

chapter twenty-eight

'Greetings, you who are highly favoured! The Lord is with you.'
(The Doctor's Testimony 1:28)

It nagged at him. Favourite? Favourite?

He sought out Father. 'Glory... Glory, is it true?'

'Is what true, Dearheart?'

'You know. What Snake said. That Abel is Your favourite?'

Love laughed. 'Why, of course it is, Beloved!'

Cain was momentarily stunned. He'd been hoping, expecting, vehement denial.

But, 'Of course it is, Beloved! How else could it be? Abel's My favourite Abel, just as you're My favourite Cain.'

Oh.

'I am?'

Glory laughed richly, joyously, merrily, lovingly.

'Of course you are, Dearheart! There is no one else like you. You are unique, precious in my sight. I love you as I love no one else. Just as I love Abel as I love no one else. And Snake. And your father and mother. And your sisters. And Dog. And Cat. And Lion. And all their children. Each one of you is my favourite *you*. I have known each one of you from before you were formed in your mothers' wombs, from before *I* created you: I love each one of you in each instant of time. I AM.'

Oh.

'But... but what about this morning? You don't have to constantly remind Abel to look up from the details!'

'Beloved. Just because you're different from Abel doesn't mean I love you any the less. Or any the more. You are simply different. I delight in your passion for completeness of the Harvest, your delight in the details. I simply grieve when a shadow threatens to come between us when you focus so much on them that you forget to look up and breathe in My Life: it hurts Me to see you when you stunt yourself like that. So every now and again I remind you to look up again! That's *because* of My love, Dearheart. It's not because I love you any the less! Remember, you are My favourite. Just as Abel is. And every one of My Creation.'

The warmth of His breath filled Cain's being and brought the balm of His peace.

Holy, holy, holy.

chapter twenty-nine

In his arrogance the wicked [one] hunts down the weak,
who are caught in the schemes he devises.
(Song 10:2)

Soon. Soon. Oh, so soon. Just a little while now, and the Earth... would be his. It was all coming together. And this time, the incompetent reptile would not be allowed to mess things up.

Soon. Soon his power would be revealed. Soon he would be free to use that power as he chose, unfettered. Soon the Earth would be at his... 'mercy' — and even that word would lose its vile taste of holiness. Soon those incompetent weaklings who'd abandoned him when he was so unjustly exiled, the lesser angels, would see his power and come crawling, snivelling back to him from wherever they'd been hiding all these years. Soon all would see him, and tremble.

Oh yes. Revenge would be so sweet.

Soon.

chapter thirty

They sharpen their tongues like swords
and aim cruel words like deadly arrows.
(Song 64:3)

They were sitting in the great glade in the centre of the Garden a couple of days later, where the two Great Trees – of Life, and of the Knowledge of Good and Evil – sang songs of root and branch, soil and sunshine, to all Creation, in tones of rustling leaves and glints of gold and silver and copper. The air was filled with the heady perfume of the Trees' praise, and the boughs of each lifted its precious fruit to the sunlight.

Cain was stretched out on the grass, wondering whether to tell the squirrels to harvest some of the apples tomorrow, or whether they should harvest the oranges first. Yan-î lay crosswise to him, her head on Cain's lap, contentedly humming a song of praise. Her stunning glossy black hair fanned out from them, and her limpid almond eyes were half closed. She'd spent the first part of the morning helping Adam bake some bread and roast a golden life-fruit from the great Tree beside her, for tonight's dinner, and then she'd gone out with Cain to tour the vineyards to the north-east of the Garden and prune them with the help of some of the Birds.

Above them – almost within lustrous reach of where she lay – were the rich red fruits of the Tree of Knowledge of Good and Evil, ever-present testament of the Great Relationship. The fruit perfumed the air like distilled bliss, the colours serenading her eyes, a visual reminder of the love knitting Creation to its Creator. She drank in deep lungfuls of the air, her heart filled with joy, and settled her head even more comfortably on Cain's lap.

Such times were the highlights of her days. Ever since she could remember, she'd adored her eldest brother and followed him around everywhere, as devoted as the rest of Creation to him. Everything he'd done, she'd mimicked; everything he'd said, she'd repeated, and he in turn had always doted on her, finding her the most succulent berries, giving her piggybacks, showing her the wonders that Glory brought forth in the fields.

And now the three of them – she, Cain and Snake – were resting here, simply enjoying each other's company in the late afternoon sunshine. They'd been inventing the punniest jokes they could think of and testing them on each other.

It was Snake's turn. *'Why don't ducks tell jokes when they're flying?'* he asked, and waited for the two Humans to guess or give up. They hazarded a few wild guesses and waited for the punchline.

Snake grinned. *'Because they'd quack up...'* he chortled, and slid away before they could pelt him with handfuls of the soft grass.

When they'd stopped chuckling, and Snake had returned to the cosy little dimple in the grass where he'd been lying before the punchline, Cain turned to Snake. 'Oh, I meant to tell you, Snake, I asked Glory about what you said. You know, about Abel being His favourite.'

Snake reopened his eyelids. In the depths of his mind, the Other lay coiled and tensed, every fibre alert. It reminded Snake of his games with Cain where they would bat a gourd between them and try to get it between two posts: that same contained explosiveness of action that preceded a strike. But all he said was, *'Oh? And? What did Glory say?'*

Cain gave a cheerful grin. 'He said that of course Abel was His favourite, and that I am too, and you Yan-î, and you Snake. He said that each one of us is His favourite us, all unique.'

The two Great Trees above them sang of sap and bark, life and leaf, as the gentle air caressed their foliage with its airy touch.

But now the Other gripped Snake, shook the knot, fanned it to an inferno, and set it loose to wreak its long-harboured destruction. And Snake asked, sounding puzzled, *'But how can that be? I mean, how can each one of us be His favourite?'*

Cain shrugged indifferently. 'Don't know. I mean, when He said it, it all made sense. I... I *think* He means that no two of us are alike. Even the leaves, if you look at them closely, differ in some tiny particular, don't they? Even the blades of grass! And us – well, we're us, aren't we, and we don't even *look* anything alike. I mean, look at Yan-î here. I mean, apart from her being a woman and all! But look at her lovely golden skin, and her long legs and lovely curves, and her breasts –

they're slightly smaller than M'burechet's, have you noticed, and a slightly different shape? And the beautiful plane of her cheekbones?'

Yan-î lay unconcerned by this scrutiny of her body, as they all were. Bodies were simply the beautiful containers that Glory used to contain His breath, as natural as every other facet of His craftsmanship.

'Whereas I,' continued Cain, gesturing down at himself, 'well, look at me. Completely different colour to Yan-î, for starters. And taller, and I'm more passionate about Harvest than she is. So I'm different, but just as wonderful as she is. So I think that's what Glory meant, that He loves us uniquely and so each uniqueness is His favourite uniqueness... It sounded better when *He* explained it, though,' he added cheerfully.

'But... but... wouldn't you say that Yan-î is your favourite sister?'

Cain paused. It was true. He adored M'burechet too, of course, but Yan-î... well, Yan-î was special. It was for Yan-î that he'd always brought the biggest pears, the juiciest cherries, the glossiest strawberries.

'Y... Yes,' he conceded, slightly reluctantly.

'So would you say that both of your sisters are your favourite, then?'

'Well, no,' he admitted.

Now Snake was on home turf, and he pressed his advantage. *'So, then, if you have a favourite favourite, doesn't it make sense that... that Glory does too?'*

And deep, deep inside Snake, a tiny part of himself was crying, pleading, begging himself not to do this. Not now, not to his friends, not again.

But the Snake of a quarter-century of pent-up thirst for revenge for perceived unjust punishment was not going to let go. At last. This, this was what the Other had groomed him for. This was what he had bided his time for. This was the payback for all those years he had pretended to believe their lies of love for him...

And Cain said slowly, 'Well, maybe. But...'

'But you'll never know, will you?'

'But...' began Cain.

*'But you never **will** know, will you, Cain? And you'll always wonder. Always unsure. Always uncertain. Precious Abel. Perfect Abel. Abel who follows Glory around like one of the Dogs, lapping up His radiance. Favourite*

Abel. You'll always wonder if Abel isn't Glory's favourite favourite. Just like Yan-î is for you. And you'll never know, unless...' and Snake trailed off.

Cain had sat bolt upright. 'Unless...?'

'Nah. You wouldn't do it anyhow. Not brave enough. Too much of Glory's boy.'

'Do *what*, Snake?'

'Ah, forget I said anything. You wouldn't do it anyhow. So you'll never know, will you?'

Cain was desperate now, reaching for the lure. 'I will. Do it, I mean. Whatever it is. I need to know, Snake. Come on, tell me. Please. We're friends, aren't we? So tell me, Snake. Please.'

Snake pretended to hesitate, pretended to wrestle with himself, pretended reluctance. *'Wellllll...'*

Cain was hanging on his every syllable. Yan-î too, thoroughly intrigued by now, was his mesmerised audience.

'The Tree. Right here above us, Cain. The Tree of the Knowledge of Good and Evil. The Tree of Knowledge, Cain. If you took the fruit of the Tree and ate it, your eyes would be opened. You'd be like God, Cain. You'd know good and evil, and you'd know for sure whether Glory was just stringing you along and it was Abel all along who's His favourite favourite. The Tree, Cain.'

Cain jumped back, shocked to his core. There was not a living creature who didn't know Glory's edict, who didn't know what had happened to Snake himself – the very Snake who was coiled now in front of him! – as a Consequence of the mere suggestion that the fruit be eaten, a quarter of a century ago.

'But Snake, the *Tree*! It's the Tree! It's the Tree of trust in our Relationship with Glory! It's the Tree that safeguards all Creation and keeps us in Relationship with Him! It's the same Tree that brought you the form you're in now! How *can* you suggest it?'

Snake shrugged, as if nonchalantly. *'See. I told you that you wouldn't be brave enough to do anything, that it was pointless mentioning it to you. What did I tell you? Glory's boy. Besides, look at me. You said it yourself. If I'm carrying the Consequence, then why am I alive, Cain? Surely if the Tree carried death, then I'd be dead, Cain, wouldn't I?'*

The logic wouldn't have borne close examination, but it didn't matter now.

'Glory's boy. But never Glory's favourite. Oh no. That would be Abel, wouldn't it? Glory's favourite favourite.'

Now Cain was baited. Hook, line and sinker.

And the Other snarled with gory anticipation. **At last! At last!**

Creation held its breath, and trembled.

And Cain reached out his hand and picked the fruit – that beautiful, precious, untouched fruit – and bit it, and passed it to Yan-î, who took it too, and ate. The fruit had a ravishing perfume. But the taste, now that they bit into it, was bland, insipid, tasteless, like nothing else in the Garden of Eden, like nothing else in the whole of perfect Earth. The juice dribbled in sticky globules down their hands, down their arms, onto their feet, in scarlet stains.

And Creation shuddered to its very foundations, and a rip appeared in the fabric of its being.

chapter thirty-one

'What have you done to us?'
(The Book of the Beginning 20:9)

They didn't *feel* any different. No lightning flashes of great power. No sudden growth in height. No sudden increase in radiance. If anything, it was everything *else* that seemed to grow more radiant – brighter and brighter, until they had to squint in the light. No, nothing had changed, after all. Snake had been both right and wrong. He'd been right when he'd assured them they wouldn't die. But… but where was the omniscience they'd been promised? Where was that assurance that Abel was not Glory's favourite favourite? Had this all been for nothing? Was the Tree just one huge practical joke, meaning nothing, representing nothing? Where was—? Cain looked at Yan-î, just as she looked at him.

… Oh. No.

Colour flooded their cheeks with mortification.

They were standing there. Naked. With nothing. No clothes. Nothing. Not even covering their genitals. Here in the open, for all to see, Cain's manhood dangling through his pubic hair, Yan-î's nipples dark on her golden breasts.

Their eyes widened as they both grabbed the nearest leaves and tried to hide the offending areas. Sticky juice treacled its way onto the leaves and dripped slowly onto their skin, red as blood.

'*Do* something,' hissed Yan-î to Cain.

'I can't,' he wailed, panicked. 'I'm not wearing anything.'

'Nor am I, Cain. So do something about it, you idiot. Find something; think of something. And stop *looking* at me!'

They turned to Snake, but Snake had vanished.

'Snake? Snake! Snake?!'

There was no answer.

'There's… there's the pocket we brought with us for the berries. You could use that for the moment. Till we make something better,' he said hesitantly, averting his eyes in horrified embarrassment.

Yan-î grabbed it from his hand and used it to cover her pubic area. But there was no belt for it, so she was forced to use one of her hands to keep it in place. It didn't cover very much. But it was larger than her slender hand. Slightly. Better than nothing, anyhow.

'If we go back to the Nest, we can... we can use some of the sewing stuff. There's a needle there, and some of that nice thread Dad's been using recently.'

'But... but they'll *see* us,' she spat.

'We'll go in quietly. Round the back. By Cedar's trunk. Most everyone will be in front, by the tables.'

They tiptoed back, taking advantage of every bush, every tree, every flower that offered camouflage, jumping at the slightest sound in case it was one of the others. One of the trees was a fig tree, and Cain, thankful for small mercies, hastily ripped a couple of leaves from it, not even bothering to thank the Tree as he did so, or apologise for his violence towards it. The leaves were large and tough, and sufficed to cover his pubic area. Cheeks flaring with pudor, he offered the other leaf to Yan-î, who took it with a scant nod and used it to hide her breasts.

Somehow they made it unnoticed to the clearing where the Nest had been built. But their hopes of slipping unobserved into the Nest itself stood no chance.

All Creation had heard the groan of the Universe; all Creation had felt the rip being torn in its foundation. And all Creation, it seemed, had converged on the Nest. Adam, his strong black arms white with flour up to the elbow where he'd been making some more bread, and Eve and M'burechet, almost breathless from their race up from one of the river's tributaries, where they'd been helping the youngest Beaver generation build their first dam, were already there. So was a milling of terrified animals, crying out for Glory, and come to their Lord and Lady for an explanation of what was going on, what had happened and what was going to happen.

There was an abrupt, shocked hush as Cain and Yan-î, squinting in the radiance and desperately clutching their leaves to themselves, skidded to a halt among them. Livid fruit stains drew all eyes.

Eve clutched Adam's arm in horror. 'Cain! Yan-î! Children! What... what have you *done*?'

chapter thirty-two

'They will grope about like those who are blind,
because they have sinned against the LORD.'
(The Ethiopian's Call 1:17)

Couldn't they see themselves? Standing there, naked, shameless, with all their bits on display? And calling *him*, Cain, to account? What business was it of theirs what he and Yan-î had done? Who cared what they'd done? It was just a stupid fruit, after all. Didn't even taste special. Yeah, so, they'd broken the Relationship. So what? It could be fixed. Everything was always fixed. One of the nestlings fell from a nest while trying optimistically to see if it could fly yet, and broke its wing? Glory would be there to heal it instantly, better than new. Or even catch it as it fell, to set it gently back among its siblings, unharmed. A sheaf of wheat got mistakenly trampled in a game of exuberant tag? His father would just tenderly stand it up again, and the bruise would disappear. So hey, big deal, they'd broken the Relationship. Get over it. It wasn't as though the fruit conferred any special powers, after all. And who were they to quiz him and Yan-î? Didn't they realise that they were all *naked*? He needed to tell them, before they embarrassed themselves, and him, further.

Besides, attack was the best defence. All he needed to do was direct their attention to their shameful ignorance, and in the distraction they could avoid the whole dumb issue of what he and Yan-î had done.

He felt like shaking them to bring them to their senses. He would have too, if it weren't for the fact that that would have entailed letting go of the leaves that were his own sole protection of modesty. 'You're *naked*,' he said with contempt. 'Can't you see that? Don't you have *any* shame? Standing there with no clothes on. You're no better than the Animals. Can't you *see*?' His voice rose almost to a scream with frustration.

His parents and the Animals exchanged looks of utter bewilderment. 'Cain, Dearheart, of *course* we're naked. Why on earth would we need to cover ourselves?'

'Because it's disgusting. It's... it's embarrassing. Can't you *see* that for yourselves?'

His parents looked at each other in bafflement. 'Cain, dear. What do you mean, it's embarrassing? Embarrassing for whom? Why? And why in Eden would these lovely bodies be disgusting? Glory made us. How could our bodies be disgusting, Dearheart? They're perfect. What *reason* would we have to hide parts of ourselves from view?'

Cain stamped the ground angrily. 'Fine. Have it your own way. Don't say I didn't warn you when Glory comes along and finds you *naked*. You'll see. I'm not staying around to watch. Come along, Yan-î. If Mum and Dad and M'burechet can't even *see* that they're naked, that's their lookout. Hey, Yan-î. Wakey wakey. You coming or not?'

He stomped off. The Animals, shocked, parted to let him through.

And with a panicked look at them all, and then at Cain's departing back, Yan-î clutched her leaves closer to herself and followed Cain.

chapter thirty-three

Their feet rush into sin;
they are swift to shed innocent blood.
They pursue evil schemes;
acts of violence mark their ways.
(The Book of the Far-Seer 59:7)

His. All his. At last.

He had been there at the fatal moment, had watched with all-consuming triumph through the idiot Snake's eyes as the usurpers allowed him and the reptile to steer them and all Creation to disaster. And then, after the deed was done, he had skulked in the bushes to watch those first priceless moments of realisation, the growing shame, the anger, the despair. Oh yes. He had feasted on that first dim realisation of the enormity of betrayal. He had fed on those emotions, soaked them up as the tribute due to him. Once, those first stunned emotions radiating from his prey would have been sufficient to keep him sated for an age, but now restraint was unnecessary. Now he would have the whole Earth to feed off. For the rest of eternity. His. All his. At last.

Already he could see the Earth restfully dimming. The Relationship was destroyed: Creation had been cut off from Life. Already its inexorable decay had begun. Already the crescendo of maleficent darkness was visible to him, seeping, suppurating, corroding Earth's veins. Tectonic plates crashed and groaned, hurricanes rose and battered the protesting land. Oh, but these were images he would carry with him until the end of eternity. The heralding of his reign.

Earth would be surrendered. Had to be surrendered, now that the Relationship was severed and Earth was defiled and no longer perfect. Now that Earth had been condemned by the dust-digger to Life's antithesis, death.

Power? Hah. Who had the power now? Who had the last laugh, if not he, the very same angel of light they had thought to punish by exiling from heaven? Oh, yes. And now Creation was his, all his. And the power that went with it. For eternity.

He needed to gloat. He wanted to gloat. He needed to be present at that final instant when Earth (fallen Earth! Wonderful, darkening, desecrated, decaying Earth!) was surrendered to him, to watch the ...*One*... Enemy finally acknowledge his supreme power. Oh yes.

The fact that he would simultaneously be witness to the incompetent Serpent's annihilation, and the dust-diggers' eradication... oh, that was simply the final touch, the delicious collateral victory, to be savoured throughout the aeons to come.

He steered the reluctant Snake towards the court of execution.

chapter thirty-four

The LORD takes his place in court;
he rises to judge the people.
(The Book of the Far-Seer 3:13)

The Nest clearing was deafening in its stricken silence. Not a hoof stamped, not a voice coughed, not a bee shook its wings.

Young Lord Cain. And Yan-î. Shatterers, desecrators of the Great Relationship. Authors of destruction. Their destruction. Creation's destruction. The shock felt paralysing, robbing them all of breath, of movement, of thought.

Out of sight, under a bush, Snake watched. The flames of retribution were extinguishing themselves in suffocating bitter ashes. Victory felt hollow. Only his foul inner guest thrilled with glee and drank in the scene, greedily. Yes. Oh yes. This was what he'd been waiting for.

He did not even retreat to Snake's knot when Majesty's radiance filled the dell, bathed them all, and took form, terrible in its holiness. Why should he? This, this was the moment he'd been waiting for. This was the ultimate triumph, whose consequences he would savour through the ages. The ultimate power was his now. Earth was his now, forfeited. His. All his. So that weak, pathetic ...*One*... was here to render verdict? Why should satan run from Him any more? He was the victor now, not that ...*One*... Oh, yes, this was the moment, above all others, for which he had schemed. Hide from the ...*One*...? No way. Not now. On the contrary. Let the ...*One*... see him in Snake's eyes. Let the Enemy ...*One*... know who had authored His defeat. Let the ...*One*... know who it was who patiently had guided Creation to its fall.

The Animals were still shocked, stunned, incapacitated.

Majesty did not ask them what had happened. They did not run to Him. They did not need to. All knew already, with every fibre of their being, what had been done. All had felt the tearing of Creation's foundations. All had heard Cain's words and seen the darkness.

'Cain,' He called.

And again. 'Cain.'

There was silence.

'Cain. Yan-î. Where are you?'

A muffled voice emerged from the undergrowth. 'Go away. We're not coming out. You can't force us.'

'Cain. Yan-î. Why are you hiding?'

'You know why. We heard you coming, and we were afraid. We're not wearing anything!'

'Cain. Yan-î.'

'We're *naked*! So go 'way. We're not coming out. You'd see us.'

I AM, Almighty, all-seeing Creator, shook His head with grief. 'Cain. Yan-î. Who told you that you were naked? Have you eaten from the Tree that I commanded you not to eat from?'

Yan-î's sulky voice sounded from the same bit of undergrowth. 'It's all Cain's fault. He's the one who gave it to me. Don't blame me. All I did was eat it. He did it. He picked it. It's all his fault.'

An indignant voice rose. ''S not my fault. Ask Snake. He's the one who tricked me.'

'Cain. Yan-î. Snake. There is no hiding in My Presence. I call you. Come.'

There was a rustle of leaves and the sound of a hissed, 'Stop pushing me. It's your fault. You go first. Ow!'

'Cain. Yan-î. Snake.'

Reluctant footsteps. The animals parted to let them through, like an inverted wake opening before the cause. Two sullen faces glared, and their owners came to a halt at Glory's feet, eyes scrunched, wincing in the radiance.

From beneath the other bush, Snake's jewelled colours wound their slow way to join them.

A stillness had descended on the clearing – no longer a stillness of shock or panic, but the stillness that comes when awaiting a verdict. *The* verdict.

chapter thirty-five

Judgement belongs to God.
(The Fifth Book 1:17)

The King of Righteousness grieved. A wave of the anguish of His heartbreak swept over Creation. And the other, whose tendril of consciousness in Snake's mind was absorbing every word, every nuance, rejoiced. At last!

'Ah, Snake,' Majesty whispered – but the whisper carried throughout Eden, into every ear, piercing every heart – 'what have you done, Snake? Instead of taking hold of My grace and turning back to Me in humility and repentance, you Chose to drink flattery that denied your responsibility for the Consequence – the Consequence you brought upon yourself. How often did I entreat you to come back to Me, Snake? Yet instead of choosing wholeness, you deliberately Chose your knot instead. Instead of choosing My truth, you knowingly Chose to listen to the lies that labelled your Consequence 'unjust punishment'. Instead of choosing to allow yourself to be healed in the love that surrounds you, you Chose to meet the deceiver every day, Chose to believe him, Chose to invite him into yourself. Did you think I did not see you, Snake? Did you think that because you met outside the boundaries of Eden, your Choice was hidden from Me? Your Choices have formed you, Snake; your Choices have brought Consequences. On you, and on all Creation.'

Majesty paused. Snake swayed uncomfortably. *Now! Now!* exulted his guest, anticipating the strike, the torture, the retaliation.

'This is the Consequence, Snake. Because you have done this, Snake, cursed are you above all the livestock and all the wild animals. You will eat dust all the days of your life, and there will be enmity between you and the woman. And now, Snake, look at me.'

Evil gloated in the frisson of triumph. Ah, this was the crowning moment. This was the moment when he would outstare the ...*One*..., the Enemy, to drink in His defeat! This was the moment when the ...*One*..., the Enemy, would finally be forced to acknowledge publicly the power now wielded by himself (his! all his!), and concede that

94

He had been bested by satan. This was the moment He would finally punish the reptile as it deserved for its incompetence. This would be the punishment overdue by quarter of a century.

Snake raised his eyes to meet Glory's.

And Majesty looked into the Serpent's eyes, to where Snake's guest exulted, and shone the spotlight of His radiance on the other's darkness. 'Hear this, then. I will put enmity between your offspring and the woman's. You will strike his heel. But he... he will crush your head.'

chapter thirty-six

A person's own folly leads to their ruin,
yet their heart rages against the LORD.
(An Anthology of Sayings 19:3)

How dare the ...*One*...? How *dare* He take the wind out of his sails, how *dare* He address him, not with meek submission, conceding eternal defeat, but a promise, a *threat*, of ultimate victory? How *dare* He? And how *could* He? He, satan, Lucifer, the destroyer, had won! Creation was his! Earth was his. Power was his. His, his, all his! For eternity! He, who had shattered the Great Relationship, who had cut Creation off from its Creator, he who had *won* — how *dare* the ...*One*... Enemy publicly humiliate him, publicly vow to crush his head? How *dare* He ruin that long-anticipated moment of ultimate triumph in this way? How? How? How? What about the Consequence of severing the Great Relationship, which made it impossible for the tainted, blighted, corrupted Earth to ever again be able to survive in the ...*One's*... presence? It was impossible! How *dare* He?

It couldn't be. It mustn't be. It daren't be true.

Yet it was that same Word that had created the Universe. The same authority. The same inexorability. How *dare* He?

chapter thirty-seven

*'Therefore this is what the Sovereign LORD says: since you have forgotten me
and turned your back on me, you must bear the consequences.'*
(Fragment: The Lord's Lament 23:35)

And now Majesty turned to the Man.

'It's not my fault,' burst out Cain. 'You said it Yourself. It's Snake's
fault.'

'You Chose to listen to him, Cain. You knew the terms. You Chose
to act. You Chose to eat of the fruit. You Chose to break our
Relationship. And with it, Earth's.'

'But it's not *fair*!'

'Not fair, Cain?'

Cain hesitated a brief second and then ploughed on. 'No. It isn't
fair. If You hadn't put the Tree there, then I couldn't have eaten from it.
So if You hadn't put the Tree there, I couldn't have broken the
Relationship. So it's *Your* fault that the Relationship is broken. So
making *me* pay a Consequence is unfair.'

'It is not in My Nature to be unfair, Cain. I cannot be unfair and
continue to exist. If I could be unfair, Cain, there would be no
Consequences, and therefore no freedom. I could warp and wrap
Creation to suit My whim, unstitch the fabric of the Universe to
pander to My favourites and wreak destruction on any who Choose to
use their free will to abandon Me.'

Cain pounced on the statement. 'There. You see. You said it
yourself. Free will! So I'm *allowed* to do what I want. And You said it
Yourself: You can't simply wreak destruction on me just 'cos I ate that
stupid fruit. That would be – what did You call it? Unstitching the
fabric of the Universe and un*fair*!'

'Cain.'

A belligerent 'yes' came from the young man.

'That's the whole point. I am not wreaking destruction on you for
using free will. The destruction is the *Consequence* of what you Chose
to do with your free will. Free will allows you to Choose as you wish –

but each Choice carries its Consequence. I AM, Cain. I AM Life itself. Choosing *not* Me is by definition choosing death. Death is the consequence of that choice.'

'I don't care. It's still Your fault. If You hadn't put that stupid Tree there, then I couldn't have used my Choice wrongly, could I! So it's *Your* fault. Don't blame me for Your mistakes, LORD.'

Creation flinched at each word from young Lord Cain's mouth. How could he? Wasn't it enough that he and Yan-î had eaten the fruit? What was he doing, condemning himself further?

'Be careful, Cain. Do not provoke My anger. There was no "mistake", as you call it. Free will cannot exist if there is no alternative to My way. Freedom cannot exist if I have removed all other options. If the Great Tree had not been there for you to choose to keep or to break our perfect Relationship, then free will would not exist. I offered you trust. Trust cannot exist if there is no option to betray that trust. Relationship cannot exist if Choice has been abolished. I created you to have Life, in all its abundance. But the Choice to accept or reject that Life is yours. I created you to love me as I love you, unconditionally. But the *Choice* – to accept or reject that Love – is yours. How could Love be love if it were coerced, extorted, forced? I created you to be in Relationship with Me. I did not create you all to be mere mindless drones, or slaves, lacking the option of Choosing to accept My Love, or to reject it.'

Cain rebelliously stabbed the ground with his bare toe. It did nothing to defuse his indignation. He winced at the light. His eyes were watering from it, even though he was still squinting. Why was the light continuing to get brighter, more painful? Was this just to make him suffer? He noticed that a few of the younger Animals, too, were starting to blink.

'Further,' Glory continued softly (but oh so unwaveringly, so inexorably!), 'when I formed Woman out of Man's side, Man... received responsibility. By "birthing" Woman, in a sense, as I had "birthed" Man, and as Woman, in turn, births all, Man received responsibility to nurture Woman, to protect her, to serve her, in the same way that I nurture, protect and serve Creation, and in the same way that mothers nurture, protect and Choose to serve their young. Yet instead of nurturing and protecting Yan-î, you led her to share your darkness. And between the two of you, you have condemned Creation.'

Cain gulped. He didn't feel it was fair that he was being given responsibility not only for his own act, but for that of Yan-î. Stupid girl. It was her own fault.

Memories flooded him: Yan-î as a tiny tot, following her eldest brother everywhere; Yan-î as a little girl, delightedly falling in with whatever her big brother suggested; Yan-î as a teenager, still joyfully endorsing with open-hearted admiration whatever the leader of the little group of two- and four-legged friends had propounded. And his own delight in guiding her, steering her, advising her, teaching her.

So instead of complaining that he should not be held responsible for leading Yan-î into sin, he asked in a small voice, 'Creation, LORD? *All* Creation?'

Majesty's tone softened a fraction. 'No. Not all. But the same proportion of Animals as is represented by you and Yan-î, Cain. As you and Yan-î are half the fruit of Eve's womb, so one half of all the Beasts' young is bound to you. One half of all the children, for you were their Head, and you have condemned them with your Choice. As the body must follow the head when the head leads, so all those of whom you are Lord must follow you. Not all, Cain. But half. And their descendants, for evermore. And all of Earth outside Eden. Already your sin has condemned My adored Creation, Cain. My cherished, My beloved children. Oh, Cain. Haven't you noticed how already those Animals whom you have condemned are beginning to struggle with My Light?'

There was a stirring in the great clearing as each individual looked around and saw eyes of those they loved blinking against the brightness. One half of the children. One half! Mama Bear fiercely, desperately, clutched both her cubs to her. Others around were reacting similarly.

'This is what is not fair, Cain: that you knowingly abused your responsibility as Head and chose to condemn your charges – the precious, flawless, beautiful charges who were under your protection – to destruction. You have condemned them. And their children. And their children's children.'

The weight of the Consequence. Cain did not want to meet the eyes around him. All this, for betraying his responsibilities, for his selfish destruction of the Relationship!

'Even the ground. Even Earth. And so, Cain, because you have severed the Relationship, cursed is the ground because of you. Because you Chose to break the Relationship, you have denied the ground my tending. And so, since the ground is cursed because of you, through painful toil you will eat of it all the days of your life. This is the Consequence, Cain, of your action. The ground will produce thorns and thistles for you, and you will eat the plants of the field. By the sweat of your brow you will eat your food until you return to the ground, since from it you were taken. For dust Man was, and to dust you will return.'

Grief paled the faces of all around.

chapter thirty-eight

You are not a God who takes pleasure in evil;
with you the wicked cannot dwell.
The arrogant cannot stand in your presence.
(Song 5:4-5)

Yan-î was weeping, silver teartracks glistening on her flawless cheeks, mingling with the vermilion stains on her chin, and dripping, unheeded, onto her hands that were still clutching the inadequate fig leaves. 'Not me, LORD, not me,' she whimpered. 'You said it yourself. Cain should have protected and nurtured me. It's his fault.'

Majesty shook His head with grief. 'Yan-î, Yan-î, have you not been listening? To each is the freedom and responsibility for their own Choice, and to each the Consequence. Love protects, nurtures, serves. Perhaps you could have stopped Cain, could have been My voice to him, restoring him, bringing him back before it was too late. Yet instead you remained silent when you saw Cain being taunted and tempted. You spoke no word when you saw him begin to rise to the bait. You made no sound of protest when you saw what he was about to do. You did not protect him. You did not serve him. You did not put your love into action. Inaction is its own action, its own Choice, and love without being put into action is… empty.'

Yan-î snivelled. 'But I don't understand why it's such a big deal,' she wept. 'Why can't you just ignore it and make everything go on as before? So we made a mistake. And you've taught us our lesson. So I don't understand why You have to punish us now!'

'Punish you?'

'Yes, of course You are! Punishing us. And I think that's the meanest thing You could do.' Hastily, she added, 'LORD.'

Wordlessly, Majesty pointed out a bunch of grapes on a nearby vine, hanging from a long stem. 'Yan-î', He said, 'look at this bunch of grapes hanging from its vine.'

She squinted at them through her half-closed eyes. The light was continuing to get brighter and more uncomfortable. 'Yes?' she asked dubiously.

'How often do you have to sever the stem before the bunch falls to the ground?'

'Well… once,' she said, uncertain as to where this was heading.

'Even so. And Creation is like this bunch of grapes. We were linked through the Great Relationship, in the same way that this stem keeps the grapes linked to its vine. And now, by deliberately setting yourself against Me and eating the forbidden fruit, you have severed our Relationship as surely as you would have caused the grapes to fall if you had cut through the stem. I am not punishing you, Yan-î. This is simply the Consequence. Our Relationship was woven into the fabric of Creation. You knew that. You chose to destroy it. Our Relationship was created Perfect, in Our image. You have brought darkness into it, imperfection. And that has destroyed it.'

'I don't understand,' she said sulkily. 'Why?'

'Imagine a pool of the purest water. Now imagine that beautiful crimson dye that Eve has created from the flowers. How many drops of dye would you have to add to the water before it was no longer utterly pure?'

She hesitated. 'One?'

'Yes. I AM that pool of purest living water. Imperfection cannot survive in me. I AM. I cannot be other. I AM who I AM. So long as our Relationship remained pure, you could abide in Me. Now that you have stained it, you cannot stay in Me. Not because I don't long for you to be able to, but because the stain could not exist in the force of My holiness. It would be utterly wiped out, obliterated by My holiness, and you would be destroyed with it because the stain is *in* you. Already Our radiance is hurting you: were it not for My hand placed on you to protect you, you would already be dust.'

'Then I'm sorry we ever touched Your stupid fruit,' she spat. 'Doesn't "sorry" count for anything?'

'Regret that an action has led to a Consequence is not the same as repentance from a broken and contrite heart for the act itself, Yan-î. You severed our Relationship. It is that stain that separates us.'

Yan-î stamped her foot in anger. 'But I tell You, it was Cain's fault!'

'Daughter of Eve. I created Woman out of Man's side. I did not create Woman from Man's foot, to be subservient to him. Nor did I create Woman from his head, to be his master. I did not create Woman from Man's hand, to be his tool. I created Woman from his side, to be his partner, his equal, his perfect complement in the Great Relationship. Yet instead of putting what you knew to be right first, instead of following My word, you willingly, knowingly, gave *Cain* the lordship over you which should never have been his, and followed his lead into sin. And thus the Consequence you bear is that your desire will continue to be for your husband, and he will rule over you. And because you have denied your body My life-giving tending, your pains in childbirth will greatly increase, and with pain you will give birth to children. And now...'

He paused. For a disturbance was swelling among the throng from the far end. Creatures great and small leapt back in shock and dread to make way for the two who now made their terrible way towards Glory.

It was Abel and Lion, with heads bowed and shoulders stooped from the load they bore – one on Abel's shoulders, the other two on Lion's broad back – with such heavy tread.

'Oh, Father,' Abel cried out. 'We can't wake them up! We can't wake them up! Lion said he'd seen some wonderful green pastures high up in the hills, and so we went with three of Sheep's most recent young to show them the way. And then... and then when we were there we felt Creation tear, and tremble, and the rocks above... the rocks above... crumbled! And fell on them, and crushed them, and we can't wake them up!'

His voice broke with the agony of grief, and all looked uncomprehendingly at the motionless, broken bodies carried by the two friends.

Death had come to Creation.

And God said to Snake and Cain and Yan-î: 'Behold the firstfruits of the Consequence you have inflicted.'

chapter thirty-nine

For the wages of sin is death.
(Letter of Justification and Salvation 6:23)

The Creatures, stunned, in shock, ripped in the deepest corners of their souls, milled uncertainly, torn between the longing to see and touch the remains of their friends, and the ephemeral hope that perhaps if they looked away, it would not be true.

The bodies had been gently, reverently, laid on the ground next to Abel and Lion's feet, on a little sward of moss and primroses. 'Children, it's alright to grieve,' said Father gently. 'It is right and proper that we acknowledge how much our friends meant to us, how much we will miss them. And this much I may do for you.' And He caressed the three broken, still bodies. Around the bodies, tiny violets opened up their shy petals next to the primroses, and a fern uncurled his fronds to give them shade. And where His hand had passed, the splinters of rock and dirt and shards of bone and blood were cleaned and mended, until it seemed that the three were merely sleeping.

The Animals mourned then, each in their own way, flinging themselves into Father's arms as He shared their loss with them. Some howled, some keened, some were silent, some laughed as they cried, remembering joyful times. The three silent (oh, so silent, so still!) corpses were nuzzled and stroked, kissed and gentled, their soft wool touched and caressed, as each creature bid goodbye in its own way and comforted others.

'*They're so still, Mummy. Can't they come and play with me any more? We were going to play hide-and-seek this afternoon!*' Wolf's youngest cub sobbed, and his mother licked his face and tried to put into words what she herself could barely comprehend.

The other, still watching through Snake's eyes, was avidly, triumphantly, exultantly drinking in the death and shock before him. **Death, his final victory.**

He did not see Spirit comforting each mourner, nor hear Her whisper to Ram and Ewe, 'Beloveds, Dearhearts. What you see here is just your children's broken casings. They do not need them any more. Do not fear. Glory has not lost them. He has hidden their spirits in His own heart.'

* * *

Yan-î and Cain, however, did not join in, did not approach the others. It wasn't that Yan-î wasn't sorry about the three young sheep: of course she was. They'd been her friends, after all, and had regularly given her some of their wool with which to weave. And it wasn't that she was trying to avoid the others: of course she wasn't. Why would she? All she'd done was eat that stupid fruit, and why should it be her fault that everyone else was over-reacting now? She'd just been keeping Cain company, after all, and now she was being punished for it. Even Cain was acting strangely towards her! After all she'd done for him! And everybody else who claimed to be her friends, and to love her!

And now, just 'cos of that one silly fruit, everybody was acting all sad and shocked and mournful, and now they were all fussing over those three sheep who needn't have been up in the mountains in the first place 'cos the Garden already had lots of green pastures, so really it must be their own silly fault that they were... were dead. Look at everyone! All clustered down that end of the clearing, all with heads drooping, all together. All *whispering*, it seemed to her. None of them were looking at her, but all at once she knew, she positively knew, that they were talking about *her*. And *whispering*, so she wouldn't be able to hear. She concentrated on listening, but it felt as though her ears were full of jam. She could hear noise, of course, but the voices seemed... muffled. Voices in Eden were *never* muffled. Why, she and her friends could communicate across the whole expanse of Eden just by thinking at each other and Calling and Hearing. But now... she could *see* Mama Bear hugging (or being hugged by?) Abel. But she couldn't... *Hear* them. She tried listening to others. None. No one. She couldn't Hear them! Now she *knew* that they were all ganging up against her. They'd all got together and were punishing her for the silly fruit. All this horrid whispering so that she couldn't hear them! Talking about *her* –

nasty, mean things. Well, she wouldn't stand for it. This dreadful light, and now her friends being horrid towards her. It wasn't fair. It wasn't *fair*!

'Stop it! Stop it! *Stop* it!' she screamed, stamping her foot for the second time that day.

Until that instant, the Creatures had almost forgotten the presence of the guilty threesome in the trauma of death's arrival. Now, however, hearing the anguish in Yan-î's voice, they turned towards the young Lord and Lady.

'*Little Lady?*' Bull Elephant asked in concern.

He'd been present at her birth. He'd rocked her to sleep in the crook of his trunk when she had been a baby. He'd blown water at her and bathed her when she was a child. He'd lifted her onto his back and carried her through the length and breadth of the land when she was a teenager. But now Yan-î couldn't hear him. He was *whispering*. Just like the others. On purpose, so that she wouldn't be able to hear. He was mocking her, that's what he was doing.

'Stop it! Stop it! *Stop* it!' she yelled at him, and burst into tears of fury.

The Animals were bewildered. Why was Yan-î screaming at them? At Bull Elephant, who, as everyone knew, doted on her?

Mama Bear and Monkey drew near to her now. 'Yan-î?' they asked uncertainly.

But Yan-î couldn't hear them either, and screamed louder.

Eve approached. 'Yan-î?'

Even Eve sounded slightly distant, but at least Yan-î could understand her. She threw herself, sobbing, into her mother's arms. 'Make them stop,' she begged through her tears. 'Make them stop mocking me. Make them stop *whispering*. Make them stop saying mean things about me!'

'But, darling, no one's whispering. No one's mocking. No one's saying mean things about you.'

Yan-î pushed Eve away. 'Stop it! Stop it! *Stop* it,' she screamed. 'Stop pretending. Of *course* they are!'

Eve and the friends looked up helplessly at Glory. 'What's wrong with her, Father? What's wrong with her? She seems convinced that everyone is whispering!'

Majesty hugged them sadly. 'The stain is growing. She cannot hear you or understand you properly because the Relationship is broken. It is no longer safe for her or the others to stay in the Garden. Soon even My hand on them will not be sufficient to protect them. Already they are suffering – see how they cannot bear the purity of light here? If we do not help them now, it will blind them, and after the blindness, the stain would kill them when it comes into contact with My holiness. They have to leave the Garden.'

He approached Yan-î and Cain. 'It is time, little ones. It is time. You have to leave. You cannot stay here any longer. You need to go with the Creatures of whom you are Lord and Lady, and take them to where they will be safe, out of the Garden, away from My direct Presence, which you can no longer survive with the stain in you.'

Even *His* voice sounded distant, whispery, like rolling thunder, though they could still make out His words.

'But we're *naked*,' said Cain, desperately.

'Yes,' He said. 'I know. There is one more thing I need to do.'

Majesty, King of kings and Lord of lords, went and knelt in front of Ram and Ewe, still standing together by the limp forms of their three daughters. 'Ewe, Ram?' He called softly.

They raised their eyes to Him. *'They're not coming back, are they, Father?'* they said. It was a statement rather than a question. *'This is just their... their... casings, as Spirit said, isn't it?'*

'Yes, Dearhearts,' He said.

'But Spirit said... She said that...'

'That I have their spirits hidden in My heart. Yes, Beloveds. I do. While I AM, they will be remembered. I know every curl of their fleece, every lash of their eyes. I know where their favourite corner of pasture is. I AM when they took their very first wobbly steps up in the meadow by the waterfall; I AM when they were lambs and went swimming in Eve's pools of dye by mistake – do you remember how long it took before you all managed to get the colours washed out?! I AM when they gave their first wool to Adam. Their spirits are safe, Beloveds, treasured in My heart.'

They breathed in His peace. *'Thank you, Father,'* they murmured. *'But... but it just seems so... so pointless somehow. They're just... lying there. And their... their death... hasn't counted for anything. Hasn't achieved anything.*

Their sacrifice... doesn't seem to have brought anything, made anything better.'

'Ah, Beloveds. Would you like it to?'

'Yes, Glory. We would. Is there... **Is there something that could redeem** *their deaths, give it purpose, make something good come of the tragedy?'*

Glory paused. 'Yes, Beloveds, there is. Cain and Yan-î need to leave the Garden, together with their portion of the children – yours and every other Creature's. But outside the Garden... outside the Garden it is no longer perfect, now that the Relationship has been broken. It will get cold outside now. And Cain and Yan-î do not have your beautiful warm pelts to keep them warm. They are indeed naked.'

Ram and Ewe looked at Him. *'Our daughters' wool?'* they asked.

'More. If you are willing.'

The two Sheep looked at each other, and then back at Him. *'They do not need them now, Father. You know that best of all. Their bodies are just... their casings. They do not need their casings now. Yes, Father. You may. Thank You... for making their deaths count for something, Father. Thank You.'*

'Ah, Beloveds. Thank *you,*' He said sadly and in humility. 'But it will not be pretty. Now that the Relationship has been broken and My perfect Creation has been stained, there will be more deaths. I need to teach Cain and Yan-î what to do, so that they will be ready and not let the deaths be wasted. Do you understand? You may not want to watch.'

'We understand, Father. But we... we owe them this. We owe it to them to watch, owe it to their lives to see that their deaths not be wasted. We will watch, Father, if we may.'

'Yes, Beloveds. That is your right, to choose.'

He called Cain and Yan-î to Him then, and showed them how to skin the carcasses, cure and tan the beautiful hides. 'Do not let these deaths be wasted,' He said to them, when they wrinkled their noses in disgust and tried to look away. 'Honour this sacrifice, for it is paying your debt, not theirs.'

He consumed the bodies in refining fire then, so that where they had lain, there was now only the finest, most silvery of ash. 'Till the ash into the soil,' He instructed Adam and Eve and Abel and M'burechet, 'so that even their ashes will bless the soil and make it richer.'

And then He made the three supple, beautiful pelts into clothes for Cain and Yan-î. A buttersoft tunic for Yan-î, together with comfortable baggy trousers ('You will want these for when it gets cold, to put on your legs under your tunic'). And trousers and a shorter tunic for Cain. Finally, He made a cloak for each of them, with the beautiful soft wool still attached as a lining. The clothes were so beautiful that they could almost forget the price which had been paid.

And then it was time, and He led the Fallen out of the Garden, to where His radiance was dimmer and their eyes no longer hurt. 'You cannot enter the Garden again,' He warned them. 'It would kill you. The stain is too deep in you. Do not attempt to enter it again.'

And it seemed to them that His voice was the roar of a waterfall, the thunder of a great storm.

'Who cares about Your stupid Garden,' they said bitterly. 'Everyone's mean there. All we did was eat that stupid fruit.'

chapter forty

Your enemy the devil prowls around like a roaring lion looking for someone to devour.
(The Fisherman's First Letter 5:8)

What sort of punishment was this? Where was the torture that he himself would have devised if he had been the ...*One*...? Mere *exile*? To infest *his* Earth? Mere mortality, instead of instant, agonising execution? That ...*One*.... That namby-pamby so-called Ruler!

And not even condemning *all* of Creation, merely that half of which Cain and Yan-î were head! When it should *all* have been *his* by now. His, his, *his!* And *threatening* him, satan, with that impossible, unacceptable, unimaginable prophecy!

No. He would not believe it.

And meanwhile, mere mortality?!? Given the whole Earth? Call that punishment? That was not punishment. That... that was *reward!* With the Earth that should by rights be *his*, his, all *his!*

But then again... that vermin... was now cut off from the ...*One*... Enemy's Life, protection, perfection. Condemned by their own idiocy to toil and pain and mortality. Ohhhhh... Now that he thought about it... *now* he could see possibilities. Oh, yes, this could be fun. Would be fun.

Crush his head? Oh no, he didn't think so. Still... No. He pushed that thought aside. It couldn't be. It mustn't be. It daren't be true.

And in the meantime he had all of fallen Creation as his playthings, to feed off, to plague and torture, accuse and deceive. And kill. Death, his final victory. Oh yes. This... was going to be fun.

end of part one

interlude: revelation

Eden, which had felt so full in the days before a single youngling was born, now felt bereft, desolate, empty now that only half the younglings were there.

It was not just numbers. It was not simply that half of the great Family had been lost, exiled out of Eden: each of the Unfallen felt that there was a ragged chunk of their own hearts missing, as if part of themselves had also disappeared. It was the Great Grief, and all felt muted.

And now they had been called together for a Great Council, under open Heavens. Every one of the Unfallen had been invited to attend if they so chose, and everyone had so chosen. Not the tiniest puppy or the youngest nestling was missing. Before the Fall, such a gathering would have been filled with the excitement and joy of the Great Dance; today their hearts were too heavy. Even the angels shared their grief. Even the angels seemed subdued.

'Children,' He called, and His radiance filled the Council, outshining the sun. 'Beloveds.'

Adam stepped forth, with Eve and Abel and M'burechet by his side. 'Father?'

'Yes, Dearhearts.'

'May we... can we... could *we* take Cain and Yan-î's places?'

Father gently shook His head. 'No, Dearhearts. You cannot. Would you condemn the rest of Creation too?'

'But... but...'

'I know, Beloveds. I know. That is why we are here today.' He addressed the throng. 'Beloveds... what we have seen is the Consequence of damaging the Great Relationship. We have seen the effect of that stain. We have lost... so many.' The pang of collective mourning swelled and rose from all, reliving yet again that rip as they saw their children, their friends, their siblings, traipse out of Eden for the last time, reliving the helpless agony of watching the others' eyes dim against the Light.

'We have seen those we adore grow blind and deaf to us. We have shared the horror of the firstfruit of that stain, knowing that those were

111

merely the first deaths, not the last; knowing that that is what awaits every single one of the Fallen, now that the Relationship is broken, now that they have cut themselves off from My Life.'

Someone sobbed, as the full heartbreak of what they had before only dimly comprehended now came crushing down on them in the enormity of realisation.

'For death is the consequence of Cain and Yan-î's Choice, and this Consequence has stained all over whom they are Lord and Lady. I cannot be who I AM and remove that Consequence of their free will without destroying free will itself, and becoming a despot, other than I AM. I cannot unravel the fabric of the Universe to pretend that the Consequence need not exist. Sin has entered the world through Cain and Yan-î, and death through sin, and in this way, death will come to all the Fallen, and to all their seed. I AM life. Apart from me is *not*-life: apart from me is death. Death is the Consequence. Death is the price.'

A chill ran through the assembly.

Ewe and Ram stepped forward, their delicate hooves treading daintily on the ground. *'But… Father…?'*

Majesty's radiance enveloped them. 'Speak, Dearhearts.'

'You said… You said… You said that You had hidden our daughters' spirits in your heart.'

And Glory's joy washed over them, washed over all the Unfallen. 'Yes, Beloveds. For death… death does not have the final victory.'

A gasp, a swell. *'Did He say…?' 'Did I hear…?' 'Does He mean…?' 'But…!'*

And the first shy bud of hope returned to their hearts.

'Yes,' He said. And the sound of that word made Eden tremble and the stars dance. It thrummed the lowest chords that even the rocks could hear, and soared on the highest flight of light in the spectrum. It was the most dread syllable in all Creation, and the most joyous. 'Yes,' He said again.

*'But **how**?'* they cried. *'How, Father? How?' 'How, Glory, how?'*

'By paying the Price,' He said. 'By redeeming that Price. By paying for death… with death.'

There was a stunned, shocked silence.

'We don't understand, Father. How…?'

And the Godhead said, 'Through Ourselves. Through My Word. My Word, made flesh. My Word, unstained, giving Himself as the perfect sacrifice. My Word, to redeem the Fallen. My Word, to reign victorious over death itself by accepting upon Himself the debt which is not Ours to pay. My Life, to bring the Fallen back into Relationship.'

And now the Unfallen noticed Redeemer, standing at Father's right hand: the Word, who had always deferred to the Father, as now Father was deferring to Him. The Word, potentiality to come, present since before the dawn of Time, but never before truly noticed by Eden's children, now seen in His radiance. Triperson Godhead: Father, Word and Spirit; three, yet one, as the three strands of a cord are distinct yet one. God Himself, offering Himself to redeem Creation. God Himself... to... to *die?*

'No, Glory! That price... is too high! Father, let me go in your place!' 'No, Father, let me!' 'Let me!' 'Let me!'

'Children,' He said, and they quieted.

'Beloveds, I know. And I thank each one of you. Each one of you... each one of you is ready. Each one of you would take My place. But you cannot. You saw how the stain consumes the Fallen. If you were to go, you too would be consumed, inexorably. And your sacrifice would be for nothing. Trust me, Dearhearts. This is the only way.'

'But ... how? When...?' they asked.

'That is the Divine Mystery, Beloveds. When the time is right. At the pivot of History, when Fallen Man is finally as ready as can be to accept My grace. Later, Dearhearts. Later. And you will be witnesses to it. I AM, to redeem all time – past, present, future. But for now... for now, just remember, when you see the darkness on the Earth, when you see one after the other of the Fallen succumb to the darkness and to death, to evil and destruction, when you grieve over the Consequence... for now, just remember, Beloveds. Death will not have the final victory. For I AM. And my Redemption will not be by unravelling the fabric of the universe, but by meeting the Consequence on its own terms and taking that load onto My own shoulders, to pay the debt that is not Mine.'

And now joy filled them with renewed awe, and the Great Dance began again, richer, deeper, sadder, more wonderful than ever before.

Holy, Holy, Holy.

part two

chapter one

'Anyone who does not listen to him will be completely cut off from their people.'
(The Deeds of the Sent 3:23)

Cain woke up and rubbed his eyes. He'd had a horrible dream, a dreadful dream, an extraordinary dream. He'd dreamt that he and Yan-î had done something too terrible to even contemplate, that they'd destroyed the Great Relationship, that Glory had gently but oh-so-firmly and terribly been unable to undo the damage, the damage *he*, Cain, had caused! He'd dreamt that he and Yan-î and all the Creatures under their headship had been forced to leave Eden, that it had become too bright for them.

He shuddered. He'd never had a nightmare before: no one ever had in Eden. He'd have to ask Glory about it later that morning. Glory would be able to explain it. Glory would be able to comfort him. Glory…

… was to blame! It wasn't a nightmare. It had really happened. The LORD, the dread LORD, terrifying LORD in all His unbearable radiance – *He* had condemned them. He had exiled them. Cain wasn't in Eden any more, could never go back. And it was all… *someone's* fault. Snake's. Yan-î's. The *LORD's*. Not his. It wasn't his fault. It couldn't be his fault. Couldn't. Wasn't. How could it be? He remembered now. And now they were *here*. Outside Eden. Punished with a Consequence. It wasn't fair. Well, he would show them all. He didn't need the LORD. His gifting was Harvest, so he'd show them all. Grow the grain, harvest the grain. Simple.

He stretched and sprang up from where he'd been sleeping: a soft bed of hay and sweet-smelling bracken under a spreading cedar. He noticed Yan-î still curled up asleep a few yards away but decided not to wake her. He didn't particularly want to talk to her this morning, not while her role in his unfair punishment was so raw in his memory.

This place that the LORD had led them to last night... was actually rather beautiful, he admitted rather grudgingly to himself. If he hadn't known better, he would have thought he was still in Eden. A gentle, sunlit meadow ran from the cedar under which he stood to a slight incline at the far end, graced by fruit trees and a silver birch. Higher up, he could make out a few larches, and a bassar tree full of its gloriously savoury fruit which tasted so delicious when cooked. He could hear the unmistakable sound of a little brook, and beyond that the deeper sound of a small weir.

Not bad, he conceded grudgingly. Now to show them all that he could manage just great by himself.

He Called Wild Boar's young to come and till the field.

But Wild Boar's young didn't appear, didn't answer. Didn't... hear? But... but... but how was he to till the field in that case?

Perhaps, he thought optimistically, it was just a temporary glitch in Creation. What with last night's exile and all. Wild Boar's young just needed time to adapt. Yes, that would be it. Or perhaps they mistakenly thought that *he* was to blame and were punishing him as well. He'd just have to go and find them to straighten things out and explain that it wasn't his fault at all, just everyone else's, and then everything would be fine again.

Well, in the meantime, the meadow still needed tilling. If Wild Boar's young were out of hearing, it didn't matter. He'd just Call one of the other Creatures who liked snuffling in soil, get them to come and do Wild Boar's job until he could sort out whatever the problem was. Only he couldn't think of any offhand.

Perhaps some of the burrowers, then? Rabbit or Mole or Badger? But they were silent too.

He could see one of the young cows grazing at the bottom of the field. Ah, wonderful – she'd obviously come to bring him some milk for breakfast! Perhaps she'd know whom to ask about the tilling. Or give him news on where to find Wild Boar's young.

He Called her. Unaccountably, not even she answered! This was really just too unfair. Well, he'd just walk up to her and ask her face to face. That way she couldn't pretend not to have seen him.

He marched up to her. 'Cow!'

Still she continued to rip up mouthfuls of lush grass, apparently oblivious to him.

'Cow?' He slapped her gently on her flank to draw her attention to him. It worked! She lifted up her head and gazed at him with her long-lashed brown eyes.

'At last!' he exclaimed in relief. 'Do you know, I was beginning to think that…'

'Moooooooo.'

He looked at her, dumbfounded. 'Cow?'

But she only looked at him without particular recognition, and mooed again.

chapter two

A friend loves at all times.
(An Anthology of Sayings 17:17)

They'd been observing Cain and Yan-î from the lookout mound near the heart of the Garden. 'Just to make sure that they're alright,' Eve had somewhat unnecessarily explained.

The mound was really just a little hillock, but the Garden was such an even expanse that all the Creatures used it as a vantage point when they were looking for their friends, able as they all were to focus on any point at any distance.

This morning, of course, it was the Fallen who were uppermost on everyone's heart, and the hillock had seen a progression of loving eyes follow the well-being of the exiles. *'Have you seen...?'* *'Have you seen ...?'* *'Oh look! That's Blackbird's daughter, that is. Look what a beautiful Nest she's already made!'*

Inevitably, though, it was the young Lord Cain and Lady Yan-î who had drawn the most concern.

'Are they going to be alright?' they'd asked Glory, and in the same way that He'd responded to that question years before, when Snake had brought the first Consequence upon himself, so now He replied gently, 'That's up to them to choose. We cannot force another's heart choices. We can only love them.'

And now they watched, baffled, as Cain tried to Call the animals. *'Why can't he simply Call them?'* they asked, and Glory explained sadly, 'It's part of the Consequence, Beloveds. One of the first things to be lost is the wholeness of our communication. They have become deaf to each other. That is why they thought you were whispering yesterday: they cannot Hear us any more. Or each other.'

They'd seen Yan-î wake up and join Cain. They'd observed the pair's first efforts to milk the young cow: the first easy caress, expecting out of long habit that the milk would flow, followed by the puzzlement, the determination and the effort. There 'd been universal delight when the young couple's efforts finally brought forth the rich frothy reward. *'That's our children,'* had agreed Mama Bear proudly with Elephant Bull, and as usual blithely indifferent to genetics. *'Quick learners, both of them!'*

'Yes, but they urgently need a gourd or a pot in which to put the milk,' had pointed out Monkey, who was sitting on top of Elephant's head for the even greater vantage point the added height gave him. *'There's an awful lot of milk splashing onto the ground when they're trying to drink it straight from her udder. And look! It's mixing with the dust and getting all over Yan-î's hair as well. Can we bring them one, Glory?'*

'Of course you may, Children. It is only they for whom it is no longer safe to enter Eden. You yourselves may go out and come back in as you choose. Only... be careful, Beloveds. The Fall has destroyed much. It is not only their Hearing that they have lost. Even their Sight has been warped, you will find. The stain has entered their hearts. Do not... do not let yourselves be wounded by their anger. It is not truly directed at you. It is merely directed away from themselves.'

chapter three

Excel in this grace of giving.
(Tackling Issues Part II, 8:7)

Naturally, every Creature wanted to be among those visiting the young Lady Yan-î and Lord Cain on this first day. The Bees wanted to take some honey along. Wild Boar wanted to help till the field, *'Since my own Fallen children can no longer hear him Call.'* Mama Bear just wanted to give them a hug. The Dogs simply felt that they needed to be there. Lion was sure they'd need his strength. Monkey wanted to share some beautiful bananas he'd found that morning. Little Grass Snake wanted to remind the Human pair of sunny days stretched out together in friendship by the bathing pool. Elephant was sure that...

'Stop,' said Eve firmly, laughing. 'There'll be a chance for all of you! But remember how Snake needed a little time and space to adjust to his new form when he brought the first Consequence on himself? It may be that Yan-î and Cain do too. So perhaps for this first visit, it should be just Adam and me. Yes, alright, Mama Bear, I guess you're as much their mama as I am! Is that right, Glory?'

Father agreed gravely that perhaps a smaller party rather than the whole of Unfallen Creation might indeed be a gentler visit for Cain and Yan-î.

'But we can still bring all your gifts and love to them,' pointed out Adam, and set about marshalling the bounty that immediately flowed in for delivery. 'Remember it's only Eve and Mama Bear and myself carrying it, though! Perhaps if we emptied out that gourd first, it might make it lighter,' he added tactfully, as Camel knelt in front of him with an enormous container of water on his back. 'They have a lovely stream of clear water just next door to them,' he explained at Camel's crestfallen look. Camel cheered up immediately and offered to bring some bales of straw along to add to the pile.

In the end, it was a well-laden threesome who set off to visit Yan-î and Cain. Mama Bear had elected to walk on all fours (*'I can carry more on my back that way,*' she'd explained), and now balanced a small pyramid of wonderful goodies on her back, carefully strapped down by Eve so that they wouldn't dislodge during the walk and prove uncomfortable for Mama Bear. Adam and Eve themselves had filled bags and pockets, packs and gourds with other delights and were carrying them on their backs and in their arms, and even a few on their heads.

The Unfallen watched their progress with high anticipation. '*It'll be so wonderful for the young Lord and Lady to receive our gifts!*' they exclaimed joyfully.

chapter four

Lead out those who have eyes but are blind,
who have ears but are deaf.
(The Book of the Far-Seer 43:8)

It was Yan-î who first spotted the little convoy making its way towards them.

'Look, Cain,' she exclaimed, a wave of excitement washing her heart. It had been a long day already, and her muscles were complaining about the harder work to which they had been put. Simply milking young Cow had been strenuous! And then she'd had to wash her hair – all gummy from the dust-and-milk mixture that she'd succeeded in getting on it – in the little pool under the weir, and the water had been *cold*, not sparkling hot like the springs next to the Nest! And the new garments that the LORD had made for them were wonderful in protecting her modesty, and beautifully comfortable, but she had to admit that they were also more... complicated... than wearing nothing. One had to be more careful about not spilling things on them, for a start, as she'd discovered to her rue when she'd had to wash the tunic to remove the same dust-and-milk mixture that she'd got on her hair from trying to drink the milk straight from the udder. And she didn't even yet have any of that beautiful jasmine-scented cream that Eve and M'burechet loved making, which made bathing such a delight. Tomorrow, she promised herself. Tomorrow she'd find the plants and make some for herself.

So seeing the threesome approach – she couldn't quite make out *who* it was from this distance – for some reason her eyes weren't able to focus over long distances at will today – was a delightful and welcome surprise. Perhaps it was some of the Animals, come to apologise for this morning's silence. That lumpy shape in the middle – that might be one of the younger Elephants, perhaps? She wasn't quite sure what species the two slightly top-heavy slenderer figures might be, but they'd soon be close enough to distinguish, she was sure.

The visitors drew closer. 'Why, it's Mum and Dad!' exclaimed Cain in astonishment. 'And… and do you think that creature in the middle is… Mama Bear? What on earth is she carrying?'

But he did not sound as overjoyed as she might have expected.

'Should have guessed they'd be along to lecture us,' he muttered by way of explanation, and suddenly Yan-î's own excitement was dampened as she reflected that Cain was probably right.

But as the threesome drew closer still, the purpose of their visit became immaterial. 'I don't believe it!' Cain stormed. 'Look at them! *Look* at them! I *told* them yesterday! How… how *dare* they? It's *disgusting!*'

Yan-î's eyes followed his gaze, and she too reddened. 'Perhaps they…'

'Oh, shut up, Yan-î. You know as well as I do. They've done it just to spite us. Just to show that they don't care what we think. It's disgusting!'

He strode forward and bellowed at the oncoming party. 'How dare you?! Go away! Go away! How dare you? It's… disgusting!'

The three visitors halted in mid-step. They were close enough now for Yan-î to be able to see the looks of bewilderment they exchanged.

'Cain? Yan-î?' they asked uncertainly.

'Who else would we be?' yelled Cain. 'Who else do you know who's been punished like this for something that's not even our fault?'

The figure in the middle – Yan-î was certain now that it must indeed be Mama Bear, though a Mama Bear so laden with things that it was hard to recognise her – seemed to whisper something. Or grunt. Whispering, again! thought Yan-î. So she hadn't simply dreamt that horrid, mean behaviour yesterday…

The three appeared, however, to be awaiting a response to the grunt, so Yan-î called out with annoyance, 'If you want to ask us something, you'll have to stop whispering. How do you expect us to Hear you if you're just whispering mean things between yourselves?'

There seemed to be another whispered conference between the three, and then Adam translated the answer to Cain's rhetorical question. 'Mama Bear,' (Ah, so it *is* Mama Bear under that load! I was right! thought Yan-î) 'was simply saying that the answer is half of Creation. In terms of who's suffering the Consequence for something that isn't their fault, and that you of all her cubs should know that.'

122

'I don't care. How dare you come here like that? How dare you? It's disgusting! Go away!'

The threesome had drawn nearer. 'Cain, darling, what do you mean? What's wrong? Why are you so upset? We thought you'd be so glad. All the Creatures have…'

'How can you just *stand* there and pretend you don't know perfectly well?' screamed Cain. 'You're… *naked*! It's disgusting! Go away! I don't want to see you. You're not wearing anything!'

Mama Bear seemed to grunt something again, and this time it was Eve who translated. 'Mama Bear says that we're wearing all these gifts that we've brought for you from the Anim—'

'Shut up! Shut up! Shut up!' Cain roared. 'Just *stop* pretending! I know perfectly well that Mama Bear didn't say anything. Don't you think I have ears of my own? I'd have Heard if Mama Bear had said anything to us. All she did was grunt! Didn't she, Yan-î?'

Yan-î confirmed his declaration with a nod.

'So shut up and *go away*,' resumed Cain. 'And don't come back until you're properly decent!'

'We'll just leave the gifts here then, Dearhearts, shall we?' asked Eve, distressed at her son's obvious strain. 'They're from all the Anim—'

'Just go! Go! *Go!*'

'And *stop* all your horrid whispering!' yelled Yan-î at their retreating backs, and burst into tears.

And with saddened hearts and heavy tread, the three returned with their gifts to Eden.

chapter five

But when grace is shown to the wicked,
they do not learn righteousness.
(The Book of the Far-Seer 26:10)

Their progress had, of course, been monitored with high anticipation and then growing dismay by all the friends in Eden, and the threesome were surrounded by everyone the instant they got back into the Garden.

'Why?' 'Why?' 'Why?' was the clamour.

Eve and Adam and Mama Bear tried to answer. 'It's like Glory warned us,' they explained sadly. 'They seem... they seem to be getting increasingly deaf – they couldn't hear Mama Bear at *all*, could they, Dearheart?'

Mama Bear sighed heartbrokenly, and shook her head. '*And I thought they'd be so happy,*' she said disconsolately.

'And the thing they seemed most upset about was our nakedness!' exclaimed Adam, still astonished.

'*Did they ask about the others? Do they know that young Cheetah just gave birth? Do they know...?*' but the threesome shook their heads sadly.

'No. They didn't seem... that's to say, there wasn't really enough time, but I'm sure they... well... I'm sure it was just this funny thing they've got about nakedness that distracted them,' said Adam.

Eve suddenly brightened up. 'I know,' she said. 'If it's so important to them, why don't we just *make* some clothes? That way they won't be distracted! And then we can deliver everyone's love properly! All your beautiful, wonderful, precious gifts to them!'

The idea was greeted with sheer delight by all.

'Er... *what do you think they want us to wear?*' asked Mama Bear hesitantly.

They considered this carefully. '*They seemed to be trying to hold those poor little fig leaves in different places yesterday, didn't they?*' asked Elephant Bull. '*Do you think that has any significance?*'

The question was enthusiastically debated for a few seconds before the Humans and the Creatures agreed that there probably had indeed been some significance to the placement of the leaves.

'*Breasts?*' asked Monkey.

Dog pointed out that Cain had breasts too, if only nipples, and that *Cain* hadn't been covering up that area.

M'burechet suggested that perhaps the salient point was precisely that: Cain's nipples were smaller than Yan-î's breasts. It seemed a plausible suggestion, though they were unsure what relevance size might have to pudency.

'And genitals,' said Abel. 'They both seemed terribly worried about their genitals.'

This, too, was given careful thought, and all agreed that the two Fallen Humans had undoubtedly seemed fixated about keeping their genitals hidden, though nobody could think of a logical explanation.

They brought their deductions to Glory. 'Yes,' He said. 'That's what they were attempting to hide. Their genitals and Yan-î's breasts.' But He didn't choose to explain why.

Eden exploded in a frenzy of creativity as Adam, Eve and Mama Bear were suitably decked out in attire befitting the King, Queen and honorary Foster Mother of Creation. For Adam, the birds wove together some feathers, carefully snipped to size – the eyes of the Peacock's feathers to cover his scrotum, and a brilliant cascade of tiny feathers sewn together to make a veil for his penis – and for Eve and Mama Bear a glorious concoction of flowers, which honoured the offending parts while nevertheless hiding them. Getting the outfits to stay on was a little more tricky, until Woodpecker suggested gluing them on with some amber tree sap. Mama Bear claimed that the tree sap made her itch, but cheerfully admitted that it kept the flowers in place.

The Creatures were thrilled with the results of their labours. '*We never thought you could look more beautiful,*' they confessed with admiration, '*but these... these "clothes" look lovely on you! Oh, won't young Lady Yan-î and Lord Cain be touched by the care you've taken!*'

And the threesome, gifts once more strapped to them, set back out to the beautiful place Father had given to Cain and Yan-î.

And returned again to Eden, still laden. 'I'm not sure. For some reason they still seemed upset!' explained Adam, utterly baffled. 'They said we were mocking them!'

'And they still can't Hear me,' added Mama Bear, who was now forlornly eating her unappreciated beautiful outfit and trying to lick the tree sap off her glossy black fur. It had matted the fur together and was proving harder than expected to clean off. She asked Glory for help, and between them every last trace was removed.

The Creatures added diaphanous veils to the original costumes, made from the shed skins of little Grass Snake's family, meticulously stitched together. They added some palm fronds for musical effect. But those, too, were rejected by the two affronted young Fallen Humans, and Mama Bear cleaned herself a second time with Glory's help.

'We don't understand,' the Creatures said to Glory. 'We're covering everything that seems to offend them. Why are they still offended, Abba? How can we make them happy?'

'It's called Shame, Beloveds. As the stain is deepening, so their shame is causing them to see the pure as impure. It's not just their genitals now; it's anything that reminds them of their genitals.'

Leaves and feathers were added to cover bottoms and backs. Mama Bear now resembled an ambulant feather cascade. 'I'm catching the feather veils under my paws with every step I take. I'm scared I'm going to tear them. After all the effort you've put in!' she protested worriedly, and the scarlet boas were shortened until they no longer tripped her up.

Apparently it was not sufficient to mollify the Fallen pair. 'They still think we're trying to mock them!' exclaimed Eve. 'And they said we were too gaudy. And not respectable. They were most insistent about that. Not respectable. And they were even ruder about Mama Bear's clothes.'

'Poor little cubs,' sighed Mama Bear. 'They still haven't let us give them all their beautiful gifts! They've been without them all day! And they do seem so terribly upset about this nakedness thing. I just wish we could make them happier.'

'Let's just try one more time this evening, Dearhearts,' suggested Adam. 'It would be so lovely if we could give them their presents this evening before they start feeling – what was it Glory called it? – chilly. Otherwise,' he conceded with a resigned shrug, 'we'll try again tomorrow. Eventually they're bound to be satisfied, don't you think?'

The prospect of the beloved youngsters not allowing themselves to receive their gifts until the morrow renewed everyone's enthusiasm for discerning what *would* be acceptable.

'What if we scrapped everything we've done so far,' suggested Adam slightly sadly, for the 'everything so far' represented so much precious love and care, 'and tried to think of something different. Something that they'll find less gaudy?'

'What does "gaudy" mean, Lord Adam?' asked one of the Unfallen Lambs.

'I think... I think it means gloriously colourful,' he replied. 'But it might mean something different to them,' he added hastily, all too aware after the day's futile treks that Fallen definitions might be diverging from his own.

It was one of the Peacocks who came up with the idea. *'Perhaps they mean they want you to look like my beautiful Peahen?'* he asked. *'Her gentle, lovely mottled brown that blends so perfectly into the ground?'*

'And the garments that Glory made for them – those tunics. Perhaps that sort of styling would be acceptable to them?' suggested Monkey.

'How are you going to get a tunic to fit **me***?'* asked Mama Bear. Elephant Cow suggested making something out of grass, *'like the thatch on Lady Eve's Nest. Simply draped over you.'*

They couldn't really find many brown leaves in Eden, apart from Copper Beech's, and there was a limit to the number of brown feathers that the Birds could really spare, so in the end the tunics were an amalgam of feathers and leaves and hay, expertly woven together by the Weaver Birds. They were slightly itchy until Rabbit suggested lining them with soft petals and some of her own belly fur (*'Lord Cain and Lady Yan-î won't be able to see them under those tunics, so they won't be offended'*), and all agreed that the finished products were resplendent in a lovely gentle mottled way, like Peahen's plumage.

And this time, it appeared, the clothes were acceptable. At least sufficiently acceptable for the loving threesome to be given grudging permission to hand over the gifts.

'But why is Mama Bear dressed up?' they were asked. 'So ridiculous! She's an *animal*. Why have you given *her* clothes?'

And: 'I can still see your *legs*, Mother. And your *knees*! And your *hair*! You can't simply have it on display like that! It's... it's... not *decent*! Look, Yan-î has hidden *hers* away in her tunic this evening.'

'I'm going to use some of that wool you brought from the Sheep to weave myself a proper covering for my hair,' she explained proudly to Eve. 'That way it'll be decently covered.'

Eve tried to ask what it was about nakedness that seemed so terrible to them.

'You're no better than an *animal* if you're not wearing anything,' they told her. 'It's disgusting.'

'But you just said that Mama Bear shouldn't wear anything *because* she's an Animal,' said Eve, now thoroughly confused.

'That's different,' Cain said. 'Besides, the LORD wouldn't have given us garments if it was right to be naked. So that proves that nakedness is shameful. And disgusting.'

'I thought... I thought Grace made them garments because **they** *thought that nakedness was terrible, not because He did? And because He said they'd need the covering now that they were Fallen and were having to leave the Garden?'* said Mama Bear.

Eve translated.

Yan-î pulled a face. Nothing could convince her that Mama Bear was truly speaking: now that they were so close to one another, it didn't even sound as though Mama Bear was whispering. It just sounded like a guttural grunt.

'Of course He didn't,' she snapped. 'Cain's right. The LORD gave us garments because *we* know better than you, because *we* have the knowledge of good and evil. And nakedness is *evil.*'

And to emphasise her point, she hugged her tunic around her and threw her cloak on for good measure. Her garments... made from the skins of her friends. The friends... whose death she had caused.

The threesome kept their visit brief. Something about their Fallen children's arguments made them feel tired and saddened. But at least they'd succeeded in finally handing over the beautiful, precious gifts. And they promised they'd be back again soon.

'Don't let that animal get dressed up again,' they were told. 'It's a mockery of everything that's right. She's just an *animal*. And now that we've explained to you what decency is, make sure we can't see your knees, Mother. Or your hair.'

chapter six

Teach me knowledge and good judgment,
for I trust your commands.
(Song 119:66)

They were walking hand in hand in Hand that evening along the beach at the southernmost tip of the Garden. Mama Bear mooched along beside them on all fours, with Adam's arm slung companionably across her broad shoulders. The sky still glowed with dusk's last tinges, and they could hear the soft rush of bubbles as each wavelet lapped gently at the shore and receded again.

They'd undressed as soon as they'd moved out of Cain and Yan-î's sight and carefully folded the garments, made with so much precious love, to use the next time they visited the pair. Now the lightest of warm breezes caressed their bare skins and gently ruffled Mama Bear's pelt.

'Is it true, Abba?' Adam was asking Father. 'That our nakedness is evil? They said that since they'd eaten from the Tree of the Knowledge of Good and Evil, they *know* it is.'

'Ah, Beloveds,' He answered. 'How many times have I told you how We created the world! And do you remember, Dearhearts, what I judged when I saw all that We had made?'

Eve smiled shyly. 'You saw... You saw all that You had made, and...'

'Yes. And...?'

'And... You saw that it was good.'

Father gave her an extra hug. 'Just "good", Dearheart?'

She grinned happily up at Him. 'No. You saw that it was *very* good.'

'Yes, Dearheart. I saw all that I had made, and it was *very* good. *You* are very good. *You* are beautiful, precious, wonderful in My sight.'

'So... so... we're not being evil when we rejoice just in being as You made us? We're not offending You? It's just that... Cain and Yan-î seemed so convinced...'

'Beloveds,' He turned to them gently. 'Ask yourselves this: when you were sitting there with Yan-î and Cain... to what extent did their conviction glorify Me? To what extent did their garments make you feel overwhelmed anew by My joy, awed anew by My glory, exalted anew by My grace, wooed anew by My love, and humbled anew by My majesty?'

'We didn't, Father. We didn't feel those things,' confessed Eve. 'But we wondered whether perhaps that was because we weren't wise enough. Because it *was* the Tree of the Knowledge of Good and Evil that they ate from, so we feared that maybe You *would* prefer us to wear clothes and that we'd been offending You all this time!'

Father laughed uproariously and whirled around with them as lightly as a feather dipping and dancing in the breeze. Fireflies sprang into being at the music of His voice, and delicate little bats carolled enraptured in the twilight air.

'Ah, Dearhearts!' He cried. 'Did you really fear that I would not have told you if you were doing something that offended Me, something that might mar our perfect Relationship?'

'But the Tree...'

And now He spoke gravely. 'Dearest ones. The Tree... is indeed the Tree of the Knowledge of Good and Evil. But it does not confer omniscience, all-knowingness. And without omniscience, how can you truly Judge? How can you Judge, how can you properly weigh good and evil if you do not understand the heart of things? Cain and Yan-î have indeed eaten of the Tree's fruit. And now everything they see, they judge. But their judgements are based on what little they perceive, and what little they perceive shrinks even further as they trap themselves in what they have judged...'

He paused, and then continued, 'Already you have seen how they are becoming blinder and deafer, how their eyes are drawing ever inward to centre on themselves instead of on others. Already you have seen how their eyes have dimmed and they can no longer stand in My direct presence. They ate from the Tree, and they judge. But *because* they judge with neither fullness of understanding nor omniscience, so their conviction that in fact they see everything and have the Right to judge everything will continue to grow.'

The three Unfallen digested this in silence for a few minutes. Their footsteps on the sand glistened in the starlight, and from the Garden's woodlands they could hear a distant choir of nightingales adorn the evening air with their songs.

'*So something can seem Good to them simply because they benefit personally, rather than because it is truly good? Or something can seem Good to them because they have convinced themselves of it, without knowing its entirety? And something can seem Evil to them simply because they do not benefit personally from it, or because they do not understand it, rather than because it is necessarily truly evil?*' queried Mama Bear eventually. '*As though I had judged that tree sap evil just because it clogged my fur?*'

'Yes,' He answered simply. 'I AM. It is my Nature to be who I AM. I AM life. I AM goodness. I AM light. I AM righteousness. I AM holiness. I AM love. I AM joy. I AM Creator. I AM... I AM Judge. I AM. I AM who I AM. Apart from me there is none of these, and it is the absence of these which defines evil. Just as without light there is only darkness. And so whoever attempts to measure good and evil simply with their own parameters is measuring with false scales.'

Eve hesitated. 'I'm not sure I understand, Abba. It's... too wide and too deep for me, I think!'

Glory smiled. 'Imagine trying to measure an ocean by a single drop of water, Beloved. The drop of water will tell you many things. It will tell you that the ocean is salty. That it is wet. Perhaps it will even carry a grain of sand within it. But judging the entire ocean from it – its size and depth, where its currents run, and where its proud waves must halt? Will that single drop map all water's journey from the springs of the sea, or tell you what swims in the recesses of its briny depths? Will it reveal to you where sleeps the Leviathan of the deep or show you a coral reef through a dolphin's eyes? And even if you were to judge the ocean not by the drop of water, but by the expanse you could see to the horizon, would that enable you to measure it in its entirety?'

'Ohhhhhh,' said Adam slowly. 'So judging the ocean from the drop of water... is fine as far as it goes, but it can never be the full picture, and therefore never the true Judgement?'

'Yes, Beloved. But Cain and Yan-î, having eaten from the Tree, now believe themselves equipped to judge the full ocean from the drop of water. And sometimes they will even convince themselves that the drop of water *is* the full ocean.'

'I'm glad it's You doing the true judging, Glory,' said Eve softly. 'It'd be too big for me!' And the air rang with the foursome's laughter.

'*But You did make garments for them, Father,*' pointed out Mama Bear a little while later. '*Why?*'

'Ah, Dearheart,' He said. 'Love meets you where you are, not simply where you should be. They were naked and ashamed. And,' He added sadly, 'they have no fur to keep them warm. Now that they have destroyed My perfect balance and brought the stain to My perfect world, they will need those extra layers.'

chapter seven

Greater love has no one than this: to lay down one's life for one's friends.
(The Record of Grace 15:13)

Above them, the dusky sky had deepened to the richest velvet, and their steps slowly drifted back in the direction of the rest of the Garden, the soft sand still warm under their toes, and the scent of the sea gradually mingling with the fragrance of flowering acacias.

A shape detached itself from some bushes and approached them. In Glory's lambent radiance, they could see that it was one of the younger Unfallen dogs. They welcomed her, and for a few minutes she thumped her tail in bliss as Adam and Glory petted her with the ear-rubs that she particularly adored and which were her portion.

She'd come with a petition.

'Speak, Braveheart,' He encouraged her gently.

She looked up at them. *'Glory… You know… You know already all that's in my heart. May… May I? May I?'*

'Ah, Beloved. Do you know what you are asking? Do you know the cost?'

She gazed at Him. *'But they need me, Glory. They need me. I know that my brothers and sisters went out from the Garden with them — but none of them is with them now! I know I can't go in their place. I know that the stain will envelop me. I know…'* and here her mental voice quavered a moment, and her head drooped, *'I know that I will never again be able to come Home here to You, until I have returned to dust and You have gathered me into the secret place of Your heart. But… but they need me, Glory. We've been watching them all day, and they're so… they're so alone now that their Sight has dimmed…! Please, Father. May I? May I? May I be with them, may I remind them, even in their blindness, of unconditional love?'*

'Yes, Dearheart. You may. And this I Speak over you: that you and your seed will find My joy even in the most humble things. You will find My joy in a fall of leaves, in a day-old scent, in a puddle and in sunshine. You will find My joy in your Human's gaze, My joy in a gentle word. Even when all else has faded from your memory and the

Consequence has robbed us of our Relationship, yet you will feel My touch, and My joy in your heart. You may go, Beloved. With My grief and My delight, My joy and My blessings.'

He breathed on her. And she touched noses with Mama Bear and nuzzled the Humans' hands. Then she set off, step steady and tail held high, to go out from Eden, out from the Garden, to serve with joyful sacrifice the Fallen Humans who needed reminding of unconditional love.

Love meets us where we are, not simply where we should be.

She did not look back.

chapter eight

'The godless in heart harbour resentment.'
(Torment of a Patient Man 36:13)

It was not simply the milking which was harder. *Everything* was more difficult now. Everything was different. Everything was... not right. Wrong. And it was all Snake's fault. Yan-î's. The LORD's. The Tree's.

It was the smallest things which were the worst.

Take beards. In Eden, he and Dad and Abel could simply elect to grow fur around their jaws, or be smooth-chinned. Mostly they'd stayed fresh-faced. But here... here he had no control over it. It just... grew. By itself. Already the stubble was making him itchy and uncomfortable. And he had no idea how to resolve it. Perhaps the little obsidian knife that Dad had brought for him from the Garden yesterday? Yes, that might work.

Several cuts and a considerable amount of newly minted invective later, he decided that for the time being he would pretend it didn't itch and go for the beard option.

But his most recent challenge was... voiding. Before, in Eden, wherever and whenever they voided themselves, Glor... the LORD made it be instantly absorbed into the soil, and where it had been, new flowers would nod, or new moss would carpet the ground. Clean. Beautiful. Simple.

But *now*...

Cain looked with disgust at the pile he had just created. Not to put too fine a point on it, it... stank. Reeked. Ponged. And it didn't disappear.

He prodded it gingerly with a stick. It still didn't disappear. On the contrary, bits of it... stuck to the stick.

Eeeuuwwwch!

Something needed to be done about it.

Out of long habit, he Called one of the burrowing Creatures. Perhaps they could bury it. The Creatures didn't Hear, didn't come.

'Yan-î!'

She'd been teasing out some of the wool the Sheep had sent to them on Mama Bear's back the day before, and strands of wool were still on her fingers and in her hair. One strand even fluttered from an eyebrow until she brushed it away with a frustrated arm. 'Yes. What?'

He pointed.

'That's revolting, Cain. Get it away from here.'

'But...'

'It's your mess. I'm not clearing it up. And it can't stay here. *Do* something about it. Do something about it a *long* way from here.'

'But...'

'I'm trying to comb the wool, Cain. You know, the wool which Monkey and his family and Glor... the LORD... always used to help comb before? The wool which I wouldn't have needed to be teasing out if *you* hadn't broken the Relationship and got us punished? Clean it up yourself, Cain. It's your fault that we're here in the first place.'

Torn between the injustice of being blamed for the Fall and the pressing need to get the steaming pile of his voiding removed, Cain settled for a tight-lipped seethe.

He used some leaves to gingerly scoop it up.

'And don't just sprinkle some earth on it, Cain. That stuff needs to be *buried*. A long way away. Yeuch!'

In the end, he settled on the end of the field furthest from the cedar tree where they'd camped out these past two nights.

But the issue wasn't going to go away. Voiding was unavoidable.

'You'll have to dig a pit,' Yan-î reasoned. 'A *deep* pit. So that we can use it quite a bit before you fill it in and dig the next one. Downwind.'

'Why me?' Cain asked, astonished.

''Cos I'm still combing the stupid wool. And 'cos it's your fault that we're here, Cain, having to do all this. Your stupid fault. *Your* stupid fault. And it's not fair!'

He tore some strong, wide strips of bark from one of the trees to use as a tool like one of Mole's paddle-paws for shifting the soil. Fortunately the soil was rich and soft – the most perfect earth for growing crops, he knew – not heavy and filled with clay or sand. But digging the privy trench was still hard work, work that was all someone else's fault in the first place.

136

And to add insult to injury, digging introduced him to yet another Consequence. He sweated.

And not only did he sweat, but the sweat, too, started to smell.

It was all just plain wrong. And it wasn't fair. Eating that stupid fruit hadn't been his fault. It was all Snake's fault. Yan-î's. The LORD's. The Tree's. If the Tree hadn't been there in the first place, Cain wouldn't be here now.

It wasn't fair.

And even the water in which he was washing himself now was cold.

It wasn't fair.

chapter nine

His eyes watch in secret for his victims;
like a lion in cover he lies in wait.
He lies in wait to catch the helpless;
he catches the helpless and drags them off in his net.
(Song 10:8-9)

Oh yes. This was fun. Drinking in the emotions boiling off the two Fallen Humans. All that wonderful anger. The resentment. The self-deception. The recriminations. And he wasn't even having to prod them along — they were doing it all to themselves!

It was still unfair, though. That namby-pamby ...*One*... should have *punished* them. Killed them. Allowed His holiness to simply consume their sin, and them with it. And instead, what had that ...*One*... done? Protected them! Led them to a perfect land! Provided them with *everything* they needed: shelter, water, food, rich and fertile soil, help. *Meddling.* Where was the justice in that? Justice, he decided, was needed. He was a firm believer in justice when it suited him.

Idly, he looked at the honey bee he'd plucked out of the air. He'd been intending to pull its wings off it, slowly, to revel in its tiny pain. But what if... What if he simply... *tweaked* it instead? Corrupted it, fed it some of his own anger, changed it? Stripped some of that ridiculous fluffy fur from around its neck. Ripped away its Knowledge of how to make honey. Drip-fed it with rage. And now... ah yes... now came the best. A retractable sting in its tail. Oh yes. *Wasp.*

Who said that evil was not creative? When there were so many, many ways to corrupt and destroy, ravage and spoil the horror of perfection? Of course, he could never create anything from scratch. Only Life could do such a thing — and Life was the opposite of himself. But why would he need to, when he could simply distort and debase and rot what was already?

Small. That was the key. Small and aggravating. Small and deadly perversions of Creation. Small and constant, to wear his victims down without their realising it, without drawing their attention to him. Oh yes.

chapter ten

[Grace and love] are a honeycomb,
sweet to the soul and healing to the bones.
(An Anthology of Sayings 16:24)

She'd at long last finished teasing out the wool. Her fingers were stiff and sore, and there was a painful shiny red bump on one of them where it had been rubbed too much. She wasn't sure what it was, but it hurt. It would not be the last blister, but it was certainly the first.

Her back ached, too. Aches were new. And horrible. It wasn't fair. It was all Cain's fault. She stretched, looked out beyond the cedar where she'd been sitting. South. South-west. Towards… No. She wasn't going to think of the Garden. It hurt too much.

But something was approaching from that direction. Not yesterday's ambassadors. Something smaller. She squinted, trying to make out more clearly what it might be. This… this dimming of her sight was disconcerting, frightening. Just two days ago she could focus on whatever she wanted, anywhere she wanted, and see the tiniest butterfly emerge from his cocoon, the smallest blade of grass. And now… now she strained to see anything beyond a few miles away. Even big things. Like Mama Bear yesterday, piled up with all those welcome gifts. She'd had to get within six or seven miles before Yan-î had been able to discern her identity! It wasn't fair. And now this shape… this shape, too, was still too far to resolve itself into recognisability.

Yan-î waited impatiently for the creature to draw closer. Perhaps it was bringing more gifts from Eden. She hoped it was bringing some of that jasmine-scented cream for washing herself. Even if the water here *was* cold… Or something for her hair – her beautiful, glossy, jet-black hair which fell in a smooth curtain down her back. Or had done before she'd realised how wrong it was to be naked and have her hair on display… Her sore fingers and aching back ensured that today at least she would not be weaving the snood to keep her hair covered, and meanwhile her crowning glory formed a layer between her skin and the tunic. Strange how, before she'd understood how wrong it was to be naked, her hair had never irritated her bare skin. But now that it was sandwiched between the same bare skin and the tunic, the friction was uncomfortable. But at least it was no longer on immodest display. And perhaps the gifts that the Creature, whoever it was, was bringing, would include a nice balsam for her hair. It was only right that they should send gifts, she reflected, to make up for their horrid, mean behaviour towards her when that silly fruit was eaten.

She amused herself imagining what other gifts might be arriving with the visitor. The approaching shape seemed to be a smaller size than yesterday's visitors, so the gifts would be smaller, of course, but perhaps all the more precious for that. Unguents and tools and spices, she expected. And perhaps her beautifully carved wooden comb. Yes, that would be nice.

The shape drew nearer, and now at last she could make out what it was. One of the dogs, it appeared. That made sense, she supposed, though if they'd sent a larger ambassador it could have borne more gifts for her and Cain. Typical, she thought. They realise they've overreacted over just a stupid fruit, and send gifts in acknowledgement of their horrid mean behaviour – and then they go and choose one of the dogs to bring them, who can hardly carry anything at all! Not like Bull Elephant. Bull Elephant could have brought *everything* with him that they wanted. Even some stones to build an oven, perhaps. *And* he could have helped to build it. She sighed long-sufferingly. Ah well, perhaps the Unfallen would work that out for themselves tomorrow. And meanwhile she supposed that she should be graciously forgiving towards their stop-gap ambassador.

She squinted. Not because she couldn't see the dog yet – it was now well within perfect sight range, only four or five miles away – but because (she rubbed her eyes and squinted even harder to double-check) she couldn't actually believe her eyes.

Yes, it was a dog. But... but it was carrying... *nothing*! Nothing at all. Nothing whatsoever!

So what on earth was the point of sending it?

A horrifying thought struck her. Perhaps they weren't intending to send any more gifts at all! Perhaps yesterday... perhaps yesterday had simply been a one-off, and now they'd already forgotten all about her. Yes, that would fit in with their horrid, mean behaviour the other day.

Typical. All they could think about was themselves. She and Cain had been gone less than two days and already Eden had forgotten them. Selfish, horrid, mean Unfallen. And after all she'd gone through, preparing herself to be graciously forgiving. For what? For nothing. Just one single dog, and not even bringing any gifts.

Well, if that was the case, she'd show them how little she cared. They could stuff their rapprochement. She wasn't going to be the first one to give in. Especially since none of this horrid thing was her fault.

Yan-î turned her back to the approaching dog and pretended to be very busy again with the wool, in a way that didn't actually require her to touch it with her blistered hand or bend her creaky back. She reassured herself that it was a very convincing show of nonchalance.

She didn't even yell to let Cain know of their impending visitor.

* * *

The young dog was almost there now. It would have been such a short walk yesterday, when steps were light and distance insignificant! But now she'd walked through the night, and for the first time in her life was starting to feel a tiny bit weary. It was the Stain, she supposed, intimating the mortality she had chosen of her free will. Yes. It had been a long walk. In some ways, a lonely walk, accompanied by the pang of loss at turning her back on Glory and the Garden and her friends, though with the blessing of Glory's love still warm in her heart. Yet the loss mingled with the joy of her approaching... *home*coming, and the closer she got to young Lord Cain and Lady Yan-î, the more that anticipation transcended the loss. Lady Yan-î and Lord Cain *needed* her. And she would love them. She would be there for them. She would listen to them when they were unable even to listen to themselves. She would accompany them, serve them, obey them, adore them. Love them.

She could see Lady Yan-î. Lady Yan-î had been watching her since she'd first noticed the young dog's approach. But now for some reason Lady Yan-î had turned her back to her. Yan-î was pretending to be busy. The young dog knew that it was just pretence, knew by the set of the shoulders, even disguised as they were by the unfamiliar clothes. But it didn't matter. It was Lady Yan-î, who needed her.

She had arrived.

She wagged her tail. *'Lady Yan-î. I'm here. I'm here. I'm here for you! Oh, it's so wonderful to see you again. We miss you all so much, you know.'*

But Lady Yan-î did not, could not Hear, and did not turn around.

'Oh, Lady Yan-î! We were so glad that in the end we were able to get our gifts to you yesterday. You should have heard Cow! She was so pleased that you'd be able to drink **her** *milk from a proper beaker instead of trying to drink it straight from her daughter's udder! And the Beavers are cutting some more wood for you that the Trees have given! And...'*

But Lady Yan-î was still not listening.

Talking was obviously not going to do the trick. Poor, beloved Lady Yan-î, to be so deaf so soon! It must have come as such a shock to her, leaving her so bereft!

The young dog danced around until Lady Yan-î was facing her. *'I know you can't Hear me any longer, beloved Lady. But I'm here! I'm here!'*

'Oh, go away,' snapped Lady Yan-î. 'I don't know why you bothered to come. Is this everyone's idea of a joke? Ha ha. Some joke. When here we are, stuck where the water is cold and none of the Animals helped me comb the wool, and my fingers hurt and my back aches and everyone is being horrid and mean and it was just a stupid fruit and it wasn't even my fault!'

'I'm here! I'm here! Oh, dearest, dearest Lady! We all offered, you know. We all asked if we could take the places of the Fallen under the Consequence. We love you so much. But Father... oh, Lady, if you only knew how much He loves you! If only you knew what sacrifice of love He and Redeemer and Spirit have Chosen! Ah, Lady, if you only knew!'

'Go away, I said.'

'But I'm here... I'm here to serve you and Lord Cain. Look, Lady. I can help you! Ask me anything, and I will try to do it for you! Look, Lady! See how strong I am?' She picked up a stick lying under the cedar. Fortunately not the same one that the young Lord Cain had used that morning. *That* was now buried at the other end of the meadow, together with the offensive pile. *'Look, Lady, I can even fetch firewood for you!'*

Yan-î glared at the dog. She'd told it to go away. Twice. And now it had brought her a stick and dropped it at her feet. What was this? Some kind of apology for forgetting to bring any gifts? One measly stick, just picked up from under the tree?

'I said, *go away*,' she yelled. 'Are you so stupid that you can't even understand two simple words? *Go away!*'

The young dog took a step backwards.

'Yes, that's right. *Go away*. And take your stupid stick with you! Who cares about your stupid stick?'

She flung the stick away as far as she could, sat down, and burst into tears again. It was all so unfair! So mean!

The dog retrieved the stick. Brought it back. Dropped it back at Yan-î's feet. Sat down on its (her!) hindquarters. Waited, tongue lolling daftly out of her mouth. *'I've brought it back, dearest Lady. I'm here. I'm here. I can help. I can be here for you.'*

Yan-î opened her eyes and sniffed miserably. 'Go *away*, I said. Can't you take a hint? Go *away*! Leave me alone! And *take that horrid stick with you!*'

The dog cocked her head on the other side, but stayed where she was.

Yan-î picked up the stick. It was slippery where the young dog had had it in her mouth. Yeuch. She hastily moved her hand to the other end, which was still dry.

The dog thumped her tail on the ground. A small cloud of dust rose in motes where her tail had drummed the grass. *'Yes, Lady. Pick it up. See? Firewood. I can fetch it. I can help!'*

Yan-î threw it again, this time in a different direction. Stupid dog. Why wouldn't she leave Yan-î alone? Perhaps this time she'd get the hint. 'Go away.'

The dog bounded after the stick, leaping into the air with all fours to catch it before it touched the ground, and trotted back proudly, stick sticking out from both sides of her muzzle.

She didn't drop the stick at Yan-î's feet this time. She pushed it into Yan-î's hand instead. Somehow, Yan-î managed to get the slippery bit. Again. Dog slobber. On her hand. Oh, this was just great.

The unfairness of it all rose up again, intensified.

And the Enemy watched. Yes. Yes. Anger, that's what was needed. More anger. Delicious anger. Feed that anger. Feel that anger. Use that anger. Let the anger control you. Let it take you. Raise your hand; hurt the creature next to you. Rage. Hate. Hurt. Hurt. Hit. More, more!

And Yan-î's hand clutched the stick, raised the stick, the slobbery stick, and for a moment the self-pity was transformed into rage against the slobberer. Blind, unthinking rage, wanting to lash out, hit out, hurt...

'Woof!' said the dog, and waited, eyes bright, for Yan-î's reaction.

Yan-î paused. The blind instant of wanting to lash out, beat the dog, hurt the dog, lifted. And throwing the stick wasn't having quite the reaction she'd demanded.

The dog laid its front paws flat on the ground, bottom sticking up and tail wagging wildly. Actually, the tail was succeeding in wagging the bottom at the same time.

'Yes, Lady! Yes! The stick is for you! For you! For firewood! Oh, beloved Lady! I can't go on my knees for you, but look! I'm trying! See! And I give you my heart and my allegiance, Lady!'

'Woof!'

It was just too absurd. Here she and Cain were, stuck in the middle of nowhere, forgotten by all Creation, punished by the LORD for something that wasn't her fault, and this... this *dog* came here, without any gifts, proffered a slimed stick from under the cedar, and now had her bottom waggling madly in the air, woofing! Yan-î was determined not to let go of her righteous anger. She had every right to be upset. She was not going to smile. She was not. Absolutely not. *Not.*

But it was just too comical.

A giggle escaped her.

And the giggle became a chuckle, and the chuckle became a laugh, and the laugh became free. 'Oh, you stupid dog,' she said between gasps for mirth-filled breath. 'You stupid, stupid, *stupid* dog. Do you have *any* idea how ridiculous you look?'

And the young dog bounded and bounced, capered and woofed, and washed away the teartracks on her Human's face, with kisses. *'I'm here. I'm here. I'm here!'*

chapter eleven

A friend loves at all times,
and a brother is born for a time of adversity ... [but]
Haughty eyes and a proud heart –
the unploughed field of the wicked – produce sin.
(An Anthology of Sayings 17:17 & 21:4)

In the morning, a somewhat larger contingent of the Unfallen turned up to visit the Fallen youngsters. Wild Boar and Sow had brought most of their Unfallen offspring with them. (*'We need to get on with that field, so that they can grow a crop and harvest!'*)

The Weaver Birds had also accompanied them. (*'The sooner we help them weave a roof for their Nest with the straw Camel sent, the better!'*)

A couple of the Cats had come along to visit the young Dog and play with her.

M'burechet had come because she thought they might like some music after two-and-a-bit days of hearing none. And to help her sister make some of the cleansing creams that she knew Yan-î wanted. Just the day before she'd put the finishing touches to a new one containing rose essence and a touch of mint to leave the skin feeling all tingly, and she was certain that Yan-î – and indeed Cain! – would love it as much as Abel and Mum and Dad had.

Abel had stayed behind because he and some of the Goats were working on creating a new cheese. 'But hug them from me, and tell them I'll be along later this afternoon!'

The three Humans had painstakingly dressed themselves to ensure that the Fallen pair would not feel hurt or upset or disturbed or insulted. 'Love meets us where we are,' Glory had said, and it would not be loving to ignore the youngsters' distress. Mama Bear had *not* dressed, for the same reason. She grinned mischievously at the Humans. *'Isn't it wonderful that sometimes Love means doing what we prefer doing anyhow?! That tree sap itched, and the thatch-tunic made me feel hot!'*

Eve laughed and patted her tunic, which had duly been lengthened to cover her knees. 'Yes. But I'm so glad that this helps them feel more at ease. And think of how much precious love went into making these garments – I'm as honoured by these clothes as I was when the Birds made our wonderful coverlet for us!'

Adam exchanged a loving glance with her, and agreed.

* * *

It was the young dog who spotted them first, and she bounded across to alert her Humans. Cain was sitting hunched, staring morosely at the meadow he needed to till. Given the deafness of the Wild Pigs to his Call, he'd come to the conclusion that he would have to do something about it himself. But using the bark shovel that he'd made to dig the privy hole hadn't quite worked.

It was most frustrating. He'd gone on all fours and tried to push it in front of him, to mimic the snout action of the Pigs when they helped till, but all that had happened was that the shovel kept on digging itself in, and he'd got his nice tunic all dirty. And his knees kept sinking in, making uneven pockmarks next to the gouged holes which were *supposed* to be a furrow.

So then he'd tried going on all fours and crawling *backwards* while dragging the shovel. That, at least, had the advantage that the shovel didn't catch in the soil so much. On the other hand, the few yards of furrow he'd managed to create were anything but straight. And the soil kept piling up between him and the shovel, and his tunic got even dirtier, and surely the LORD hadn't created him to crawl backwards on his hands and knees pulling a piece of bark towards himself with every slow, laborious crawl-step backwards.

And then the piece of long-suffering bark had broken. Cracked into a dozen irreparable pieces. And he couldn't find a similar piece of bark with which to replace it.

And to rub salt into the wound, even that tiny length of furrow that he'd so painstakingly created was far too shallow.

It had never looked that hard when the Wild Pigs had been doing it so enthusiastically.

And it wasn't fair.

So now he was sitting glaring at the meadow. There *had* to be a way of mimicking the Wild Pigs' perfect furrows. Even without the Pigs – who were probably having a laugh at his expense in Eden right now. Along with everyone else. Jeering. As if any of this had been his fault! How dare they? It wasn't *fair*.

It was one thing for Yan-î to have become more reconciled to the behaviour of the Unfallen, just because that stupid young dog had made her laugh, but *he* wasn't going to be taken in so easily. First that business with his parents and the Bear mortifying them with their disgusting nakedness, and then with the costumes which had so clearly been designed to mock them. And then yesterday's complete absence of gifts, followed by the calculated insult of sending just the single dog, with not a present on her. He'd told Yan-î so as well, and she'd agreed, of course.

But she'd still continued to pet that dog, and grin idiotically every time the creature had woofed and nuzzled her.

But *he* hadn't let himself be hoodwinked by the dog's affection. The fact that she was sweet and loving and funny in no way diminished the insult that Eden had clearly tossed at them. Well, if this was how the Unfallen showed their love, then it clearly wasn't worth anything. Especially given the fact that *everyone* could see that the Fall hadn't been his fault. It was Snake's. And Yan-î's. And the LORD's. And the Tree's. *Everyone* knew that as well as he did – knew how unjust this horrid punishment was, punishing him for what wasn't his fault. So if this was how the Unfallen behaved, *even* though they knew perfectly well that none of this was his fault, then he didn't need them. He and Yan-î would manage on their own.

And now the same stupid dog was barking at him excitedly and acting as though she were trying to tell him something. Running back and forth between him and the cedar, and then pointing with her muzzle and entire body, back in the direction of the Garden. But if she wanted to tell him something, why didn't she just Tell him instead of barking? This silence from all the Animals – and their deafness – was just another calculated insult, it seemed.

But just to quiet the silly creature, he looked in the direction she appeared to be indicating.

Nothing, just as he'd thought.

He threw a small stone at her, to shut her up. She dodged it, and continued barking and pointing. 'There's nothing there, you stupid dog,' he growled at her. 'See?'

But she continued her shenanigans, and now at last he could just make out a tiny cloud of dust. It was only seven or eight miles away – how strange that he'd missed it before. His eyesight had always been perfect.

The cloud grew slightly bigger, and now he could finally see that it was caused by an approaching group. 'How did you see that when I didn't?' he asked the young dog crossly.

She didn't answer, of course. Affectionate as she seemed to be, she was still part of the Animals' conspiracy to stay silent. But perhaps Yan-î had been right, even if only by chance. The dog might be useful, it seemed, if she could spot things before him. Though he still didn't understand how he'd missed seeing the approaching crowd.

No, not a crowd. A horde. A horde of creatures, approaching from Eden, come to mock them again, no doubt. How dare they?

chapter twelve

In return for my friendship they accuse me.
(Song 109:4)

Yan-î had been drawn by the young dog's noise to where Cain was on the lookout. Together they watched the approach of the visiting party. As it drew closer, they could see that there seemed to be a lot of merriment among the group. Sounds of laughter, snatches of song, dancing. And assorted grunts, squeals, and other... *animal* noises. A party in all senses.

But Cain and she weren't included. Excluded. Outcast. Forgott— a damp black nose thrust itself into her hand, pulling her back. Oh. Not forgotten. And it was true, the group was heading this way. Still, she was no longer *part* of it. No longer part of the party. A wave of yearning tugged her heartstrings.

The young dog (young dog? Young dog? Surely she could come up with a Name for her. A name all her own. Doggy? Woofey? Wooley? Wally? No – none of those) nuzzled her hand again, and Yan-î stroked the soft head. 'Stupid dog,' she said affectionately. 'But at least you're here, aren't you?'

The young dog (Barker? Darling? Darley? M'Darley, since she was a she-dog? No... still not the right name...) licked her hand. Almost as though she understood, Yan-î thought, even though she could no longer Hear. Strange, that.

Beside her, Cain grunted. She could see his anger mount, even as she watched. She could see the tensing of his muscles as they bunched under his skin, see the darker flush climb up his neck to his jaw, see his hand clench into a fist, his knuckles whiten...

'How dare they,' he hissed, 'bring along even more of them to mock us now. Oh, and typical. Look, isn't that M'burechet as well? Come to gloat as well, no doubt,' he added bitterly. 'Wasn't it enough to mock us and to insult us and to punish me? And now they've all come along to watch. Great. Look at them! They're going to trample my precious field! Destroy my furrow!'

'But, Cain, you haven't really *got* a furrow yet.'

'Shut up. That's not the point. The point is that they're going to destroy it.'

'But, perhaps…'

'I said, shut *up*,' he rounded on her, snapping, snarling, face suffused with scarlet fury. 'What do you know about anything? It's your fault we're here anyhow, so I'd be very quiet if I were you. Go away!' he yelled at the approaching party. 'Go away!'

The visitors slowed their approach, and even the animals seemed to quieten. 'Dearhearts?'

'I told you to go away. Go away. We don't need you here. We don't want you. Go away. Stop mocking us.'

'Mocking you?'

'And stop repeating what I say. Go away!'

'But, Beloved, we thought you might like—'

'That's rich, coming from you. You *thought*, did you? That *we might like*, did you? You should have *thought* of that before you punished me for something that wasn't even my fault. You should have *thought* of that before you mocked us. You should have *thought* of that before you insulted us yesterday by sending just this one stupid dog without even any gifts. You *thought* we *might like*? That's the final straw, that is. Go away!'

'We came to *help*, Dearhearts. Help till the field and everything!'

Cain snarled. 'Oh, rub it in, will you. I'll wager you've been laughing yourselves silly there in your stupid Garden, watching me try to do it all. Gloating. Well, here's some news for you, *dear*hearts. We don't need you. We don't need your help. We don't need your patronising. We don't need your mockery. We don't need your insults. We don't need *you* at all. We're just fine here. We're managing just great. Aren't we, Yan-î?'

'Actually, Cain, I…'

'Who asked you for your opinion, Yan-î? Shut up. I'm handling this. Go away!' he roared. 'Go away! I don't want to ever see any of you again! *We* don't want to ever see any of you again!'

And slowly, sadly, the Unfallen turned and retraced their steps, while Yan-î sobbed on the young dog's shoulder, and Cain went back to glare at the uncooperative field.

chapter thirteen

'The mirth of the wicked is brief,
the joy of the godless lasts but a moment.
Though the pride of the godless person reaches to the heavens
and his head touches the clouds ...
Though evil is sweet in his mouth
and he hides it under his tongue,
though he cannot bear to let it go
and lets it linger in his mouth ... [yet]
Surely he will have no respite from his craving.'
(Torment of a Patient Man 20:5-6, 12-13, 20)

At last. At last the... *meddlers*... had been sent packing. And he hadn't even needed to do anything! The idiot Fallen had done it all themselves, and he'd simply been able to feast on all those tasty angers and paranoias while they did so.

It was so much easier when they did it to themselves. Now that that so-called Relationship had been destroyed once and for all, he could simply sit back and reap it all. So much easier than the work he'd had to put into engineering the Fall in the first place. Incompetent reptile... He wondered idly what had become of the Snake. Crawled into a hole somewhere, no doubt, to shed tears as well as his skin. Well, no matter. Now that he had these mud-men, these dust-diggers, to feast off, these... *humans* made in the image of that ... *One*... Himself, the small fry were just... tidbits.

Ah, this was what true power was about.

It was never enough, of course. No matter how much he feasted off their roiled emotions, no matter how much he thrilled to watch their self-destruction, their diminishing and shrinkage from what they had once been, the darkening of the world, it was never enough. He had assumed that once he had pulled Creation and the mud-men down into the darkness, that yawning nothingness, death's devouring vacuum, with himself, he would feel sated. But it was never enough, never enough. The darkness, the hunger, the emptiness, the *need* to destroy and corrupt and hurt, gripped ever greater, all-consuming. The darkness... the hollowness... still swallowed... everything.

But he had power now. He would continue to poison them, continue to feast off their rotted relationships, continue to sneak and steal and grubby their tiny joys, twist and sully and debase all they had, and he could enjoy himself. He would never leave, never cease. Watching from the sidelines, pouncing, accusing, destroying, dragging down into his darkness, septic suppuration. Power! It was his. All his. For all eternity. Finally, he would feel sated.

Wouldn't he?

chapter fourteen

Because of your great compassion you did not abandon them in the
wilderness.
(The Royal Cupbearer's Saga 9:19)

'I don't understand,' wept Eve in Abba's arms a short while later.
'They're not *seeing*. Young Dog gave herself to them, and they think
we *sent* her! They think we *sent* her, Abba, as though she were our
property, our slave! How can they not *realise*? We didn't send gifts
yesterday because anything we would have sent would have been
such worthless trinkets compared to the awesomeness of what she has
given them. Yet they haven't even *looked* at her properly; they haven't
even *realised*! All they can see are the trinkets! And they're hurting so
much. They need us so much. But they're not allowing us to be there
with them, for them! Oh, Abba, what do we do now? How *can* we help
them if they won't allow it? How do *You* stand it, Father? How do You
stand it when Your Creatures whom You made in Your image reject
Your love, reject You? How do You bear the broken Relationship with
them?'

Father was silent a moment. 'I don't,' He said simply. 'I can't. I can't
bear it. I... abide it, because it is their Choice, their free will, which I
gave to them for all time. But We can never bear it. I can never simply
pretend that I am indifferent, never simply brush it aside. We can
never bear it. We can never simply abandon them to their
Consequence. That is why, when the time is right... when Fallen
humankind is at last able to understand grace, Redeemer will... pay
the price for them.'

'Oh, Father... Will... will that rescue all of them?'

And Abba once more fell silent. 'No, Dearheart,' He said at length.
'Not all. Only those who Choose to accept My grace. We will pay the
price, but it will still be Man's Choice to take what We have paid for. I
can never, *will* never, trample on free will. That is the power I have
given to you: the power of free will. I can never, will never, rescind it.
But My heart is broken every time the Fallen use that power to hurt

themselves by Choosing not-Light. And there will never be a minute, a second, an instant that I stop Loving them, or that I am not beseeching them back into My Light, into wholeness, into Life. I AM, eternal, beyond Time. Yet there will never be a time, within Time itself or out of it, when I can bear our broken Relationship.'

'So what do we *do* now, Abba?'

'Continue loving them, Dearhearts. Continue loving them.'

chapter fifteen

My help comes from the Lord,
the Maker of heaven and earth.
He will not let your foot slip –
he who watches over you will not slumber;
indeed, he who watches over [Creation]
will neither slumber nor sleep.
The Lord watches over you –
the Lord is your shade at your right hand;
the sun will not harm you by day,
nor the moon by night.
The Lord will keep you from all harm –
he will watch over your life;
the Lord will watch over your coming and going
both now and for evermore.
(Song 121:2-8)

He was watching over them, of course. How could He not? His love for them was deeper than the deepest ocean, higher than the highest mountain, greater than all imagination. His love for them transcended all, would *always* transcend all. His love for them... was His very essence. And there were still things He could do without infringing their free will, or overriding the Consequence. He could summon a breeze to carry the fragrance of an alpine meadow to the nostrils of a young Fallen chamois who had been about to head in the wrong direction, towards the sea instead of towards the mountains, and so turn it around to face the right way. He could rustle a bush to attract a young Fallen leopard's attention, and so ensure that she took a step to the right to miss the sharp thorn which would otherwise have caught her unwary paw.

And He could ensure that a certain branch that had been broken up in the hills and which just happened to be a useful size would be carried down the stream and be brought to rest there, just there, by a little weir, next to those rocks, by a little bank which just happened to have a wonderful little stretch of clay...

chapter sixteen

And from your bounty, God, you provided.
(Song 68:10)

Cain was scowling. It was all very well telling those Unfallen prigs that he and Yan-î were doing just fine. It was quite another resolving the challenge of how to actually achieve that claim.

He'd abandoned the meadow and its (so far invisible) furrows for the moment, and was harvesting some of the abundant fruit from the trees at the far end, up by the little silver birch, below the larches and the bassar tree. He had to admit that there was a nice variety of fruit here. It was just as well, really, since until that blasted meadow was tilled and sown, there would be no harvest of any of the lovely grains that had arrived on Mam... the bear's back. It was so unfair!

The air was warm, and some of the crickets had started zithering away. He could hear the little weir tumbling its water from the pool above it to the frothier pool below it, and closer still there was the comforting buzz of some honeybees, darting between the flowers. He tried Asking them for some of their honey, but apparently they too were in on the conspiracy of silence, and didn't reply. Let alone bring him any honey. It figured. Typical. Everyone was punishing him, and it hadn't even been his fault. Why wouldn't anyone understand that?

One of the buzzes was getting closer. Perhaps making eye contact would work better with the bees than it had with that stupid young cow. He could hear the bee just behind that leaf there. Strange – he didn't recall having seen any clusters of blossoms there, only the ripe plums that he'd just been picking. No matter. On the contrary, how nice that it was coming to him rather than forcing him to try and find it elsewhere.

He pulled back one of the leaves.

There.

Odd. He'd never noticed a bee quite like that before. Sharper looking, with a longer waist than he recalled seeing. Not that he'd ever really paid attention to the Bees before, he had to confess. He'd always simply Asked them for honey and then enjoyed the golden treat. The Bees themselves – like the other livestock – had always been more of Abel's thing: he seemed to enjoy spending time with them just for the sake of spending time with them. Personally, he'd always preferred the *happening* things like Harvest, orchestrating it all so that each Harvest was more splendid than the one before. But Harvest, he was just beginning to suspect ruefully, would not be quite as much... *fun*... now that the only one left to direct in the orchestrating was himself...

The sleeker-looking bee was still busy, apparently, and oblivious to his presence. It was eating the fruit. *His* fruit! This was getting stranger and stranger. It was time for them to Talk, and not just about the provision of honey any longer.

He stretched out his hand and caught the creature in it. He could feel the feather-brush of its wings as it beat against the cage of his hand, and hear it bzzzz louder in protest. Angrily. Angrily? Since when did the gentle Bees get angry? But *this* one... this one definitely sounded angr— Ow!!!!! His hand was on fire. His hand had been stabbed with molten hot metal. His hand had been sliced. Stabbed. Hurt. Stung. *Ow!!!!!!!!!!!!*

He opened his hand. The... bee...? – the whatever-it-was flew off furiously, to attack another of his fruit. And his hand... his hand, it appeared, was still attached. From the pain, he would have been unsurprised to discover that his hand had been burnt to a cinder, but there wasn't so much as a scorch mark. Only a tiny indentation centred on a nasty red bump which continued to swell as he looked at it, and a fiery pain which he was certain was hotter than the most white-hot blaze ever produced in Dad's ovens. He needed... water. Water to quench the fire. Water to douse the flames which seemed to be enveloping his hand from where he'd been stung.

He abandoned the bag of harvested fruit. The nasty bee-thing had made a beeline for it. Cain swore, but left it to its feast. Some things – hands, for instance – were more important than fruit. Carrying his injured hand with his other, as though it were truly in danger of falling off or exploding or something, Cain legged it for the little pool above the weir.

And the enemy gloated. Yes. Yes! Power. Pain. Ah, the triumph!

It didn't take the fire away completely, of course – how could it, when the fire seemed to be *in* his hand? But it did seem to ease it a little, and the bump appeared to have stopped swelling. Just as well, or he wouldn't have been able to even see his thumb any more, let alone use it. How dare that... that bee-thing sting him? When all he'd been intending to do was to Talk to it, demand to know why it was eating his fruit and request some honey? How dare Glor... the LORD allow such a thing to happen to him? To him, Cain, young Lord of half Creation? Well, half *Fallen* Creation, but it came to the same thing given that those Unfallen mockers were taking it easy in their Garden where all they had to do was Call and Creatures answered. It wasn't fair!

He withdrew his hand from the water – for the first time glad that it was cold! – and was bitterly sucking the fleshy base of his thumb where the wasp had attacked him when he spotted it. A branch. A long, forked branch, with two lower branches sticking out at right angles to the upper fork. A branch which had somehow got itself wedged between two rocks just before the water went across the weir. A branch which... if he just... if it could just... Yes. So simple! All he would need would be some kind of harness. Yes. Surely that would do the trick? Now all he needed to do was to retrieve the branch.

But he was wearing his tunic.

And if he were to get in the water, his tunic would get wet. And cold. And uggghy. He knew. He remembered all too well what it had felt like after he'd washed off the dirt from his failed furrows.

But on the other hand, there was no one here to see. Surely it wouldn't matter if he stripped off first? Nobody would be any the wiser, and his tunic would remain dry.

He splashed through the cold water and triumphantly collected his trophy. So they thought he needed their help, did they, the condescending prigs, to till his field? Watch this, then, and see! He'd show them!

The air was wonderfully warm. Hot and sticky, almost. It dried him off quickly and he hastily dressed again. There was an indefinable new quality to the air which he couldn't quite place. It was as though it were slightly thicker, somehow, pressing in on his head. No matter. He had his prize.

Still sucking his thumb where it had been stung by the wasp, Cain went to retrieve the fruit he'd dropped, and to smugly show Yan-î the solution to all their problems.

* * *

Back in the garden, they were celebrating, jumping up and down and hugging each other. 'Oh Father, he *found* it! He found it, just as we hoped he would! Oh, Spirit, thank You so much for whispering Your inspiration to him!'

'*Did You organise the wasp as well, Glory?*' asked Mama Bear, who had a particular fondness for honey and was rather alarmed by the prospect of her Fallen cubs, both two- and four-legged, encountering another wasp and mistaking it for a bee if they chose to gather the sweet elixir.

'No, Beloved. I do not cause evil. But I *can* turn intended evil into unexpected good.'

'*Speaking of evil, Glory... I thought... I thought young Lord Cain was convinced that his nakedness was evil? So why... why did he strip off then, to go into the water?*' enquired a rather puzzled Dodo. He'd had more difficulty than most in understanding why the Fallen Humans needed clothes in the first place, and now that he'd finally understood that their nakedness upset them terribly, there was young Lord Cain baring all again. It was very confusing.

'Ah, Dearheart! He stripped off because it was convenient, and he thought no one could see him.'

'*But I thought... I thought it was the nakedness itself which upset him, which he felt was wrong?*'

Glory smiled gently. 'Yes, Dodo. But you will see that Fallen humans sometimes allow their convictions to evaporate when those same convictions get in the way of what they want to do.'

chapter seventeen

'In repentance and rest is your salvation,
in quietness and trust is your strength.'
(The Book of the Far-Seer 30:15)

Only five days since they had triggered the Consequence! Only five days since they had eaten that stupid fruit! It felt so much longer. She could scarcely remember what it had been like before they came here, before her universe had constricted to the cedar, the meadow, the fruit trees, the brook and the weir. Before she had been cut off from the perfect fellowship in which she'd grown up: the easy laughter, the joy-filled work, the intimacy of communion with all around her – bird, beast, Human, angels, LORD. Had there really been a time when her fingers had not been sore, her back hadn't ached? A time when Cain and she delighted in each other and in all around them, when there had been no anger or loss, no seething silences, no... guilt?

Had there really been a time when all that had been as constant as the air itself, so ever-present that she had simply taken it for granted, so trivially thrown it away?

And yet it seemed as though it had been some other she who had lived that life, some other Yan-î who had been so free, so joyous, so... stupid. Surely it must have been someone else, some terrible, terrifying stranger who had wantonly destroyed the Relationship, and condemned not only herself, but all those Creatures of whom she was Head? Surely it must have been someone else who had brought... death to them all. She herself, it felt, had always been here, measuring existence by how many strands of wool she'd teased out with blistered hands, and by the slow, slow creep of shadow's fingers – shortening, lengthening, circling each tree, each blade of grass – that marked the passing of the day.

Even the scorned visits of the Unfallen had been highlights in her day, she recognised now, too late. And now... now Cain had told them to go, and never to come back. And she had stood by silent, passive, acquiescent, while he cut them off from all those she loved. All those who... who... loved *her*. Loved her... loved her *despite* what she had done. Had continued to love her... *despite* her rejection of them. What was it that the LORD had said? Inaction is its own action. She had not tried to recall Cain to himself before he ate the fruit. She had eaten the fruit herself from that same passivity. And now... now, when despite all that, the Unfallen had continued to love her and visit them... now her inaction had cost her even that.

And all she could feel was numbness.

A forefoot gently pawed her arm. Young dog (M'Marley? M'Parley?) gazed at her with limpid eyes. *'I'm here for you. I'm here for you.'*

Yan-î hugged the creature. 'Stupid dog. What made you come here, I wonder? Great Lord and Lady of Creation we are, Cain and I, condemning you all. You should have left us to what we deserved, don't you know that?'

The young dog wriggled in Yan-î's arms to stretch up and kiss the tip of Yan-î's nose with her long, soft pink tongue. *'I'm here for you, Lady Yan-î. I'm here for you.'*

'Ah, Dog... I don't know how you manage it, but,' she smiled into the trusting eyes (M'Farley? M'Sar... no, hang on. M'Farley. M'Farley. It sounded warm and lilting, like the breeze that had breathed on the rows of ripening grain in Eden. A gentle sound, for a gentle soul...), 'but I feel less... numb when you're here, did you know that? I wish we could Understand each other. Wish I knew if you understood...'

She laughed as the young dog thumped her tail.

'Well, I know you can't now 'cos we all seem to have gone deaf – but I'd swear you did sometimes! So then,' she looked down with mock seriousness at the furred face in her arms, 'how would you feel about being called M'Farley? It's not a Naming, of course, 'cos you already have that: you'll always be a dog. But how would you feel about having another name that's all your own, eh, M'Farley? Since we can no longer simply Call each other and Talk!'

Woof. Woof. Woof. Tail thump, thump, thump.

'Well, I guess that settles it then. M'Farley it is. What say you, M'Farley, to leaving that stupid wool for this morning and going on a walk? Walk? Walkies?'

Woof! Woof! *Woof!*

They ran, then, revelling in the sunshine and the day, thrilling in the beauty around, exploring their new home, laughing in each other's company. Since that first stick had made her Lady laugh, M'Farley found another, all thoughts of firewood forgotten, and brought it to her Human to throw, and she chased it and retrieved it, for as long as her Human had energy and joy to do so.

They went up, past the bassar tree, past the weir, following the brook up into the foothills of the mountains rising up in the distance (was it really only five short days ago that such a distance would have seemed close, trivial, a mere afternoon's gentle lope?) and back again to the weir. Yan-î was covered with a sheen of perspiration, and M'Farley was panting.

They flopped down in the dappled shade by the pool. Yan-î washed herself in the deliciously cool water, and M'Farley noisily lapped a refreshing drink. And then they sat, four-paws leaning against her precious two-legs, to watch the water run and burble over its stony bed, collect in the pool, and then slip – so smoothly! – with its glossy, glassy surface over the weir into the pool below.

This was where Cain must have found that branch about which he was so excited, thought Yan-î. Those rocks over there must have been where it had jammed. She hadn't quite understood what he intended to do with it, but he had assured her that it was all very simple. Something to do with harnessing the branch so that it trailed behind and made furrows. How lucky, she thought, that it had landed just here. Perhaps the LORD hadn't forgotten them, after all. But no, of course He had. She'd destroyed the Relationship, after all. It was just luck, then, that had brought the bough there.

M'Farley whined and nuzzled her.

Then again... the Unfallen... M'Farley herself... Was it possible? Was it possible? Just maybe? That the LORD too... might... might still remember them, love them, despite everything, despite all they had done, despite all *she* had done?

M'Farley woofed and thumped her tail.

'Silly dog. What on earth are you barking about, eh? It's not as though you can still Hear me! Come on, it's time we started heading back to the... the Nest. *Our* Nest.'

She pushed herself up off the ground where they'd been resting. Her hand skidded slightly on the compact, slippery surface, and she almost sat down again with a thump. Mud? No, not mud. Clay. Clay? Clay!

Heart thumping with excitement, she took a closer look at where they'd been sitting. All along this bank was clay. Beautiful clay. Perfect clay. Clay of the finest quality. Clay of the sort that she'd spent hours forming, shaping, tooling when she'd been in Eden. Clay that could be made into wonderful sculptures, beautiful shapes. Clay that could be made into… anything – pots, dishes, bricks.

All they needed now was fire, and a kiln to cook them in.

He couldn't hear her, of course, she was sure. But, 'Thank You, LORD,' she whispered in her heart.

And unheard by her, all the angels echoed her words, and Grace rejoiced.

chapter eighteen

They close up their callous hearts,
and their mouths speak with arrogance.
(Song 17:10)

It turned out, of course, not to be quite as simple as he'd first assumed. That, Cain thought darkly, was turning out to be a rather universally applicable assessment.

Still and all, today's work had been worth it. Let the condescending, patronising prigs back in Eden see that and take note!

Admittedly, he had probably given them cause for sniggers when he had *first* tried out his idea. Strapping the branch to his own back did permit him to walk up and down the field in straight lines. But the branch had simply bounced up and down, like some strange wooden tail sprouting from his shoulders, and had merely followed the contours of the soil rather than carving its way through it and throwing up furrows in its wake. Except for when the lower fork, which he'd trimmed and sharpened, snagged on something and jerked him back painfully. And even when it wasn't snagging, it hurt his shoulders. Pain, Cain, decided, was decidedly unpleasant. He didn't like pain. Pain was... unfair.

He'd even tried padding the fork. He'd found some nice wool under the cedar tree where Yan-î had been sitting and had wound it round the symmetrical ends of the bough where it would otherwise have rubbed a sore on his shoulders. Cain had found two piles of wool: one was rather higgledy-piggledy, and was clearly in the same state in which it had been when it was given. It would have been fine for his purposes for the little plough, but he would have had to waste a little time getting the padding even. But the other pile had been teased out already, and was much simpler to use. Much more... efficient. Efficiency, Cain had decided, was something he enjoyed. It was all part of orchestrating. His own time, energy and effort were the most precious, since he was the one paying the price for those. So using the ready-teased wool was also efficient.

A small voice deep inside him suggested that Yan-î might be a tiny bit upset at his cavalier commandeering of her painstaking work, but he dismissed the thought airily. Yan-î would understand how precious his time and energy were, and would be impressed by his wise husbanding of them, and by his consequent efficiency. Besides, he reasoned, he was preparing the furrows to benefit *her*, too – not just himself. He would plough the furrows and sow the seed, and then in a few days' time the harvest would be ready for her to collect. More efficiency: he would have done all the hard work of ploughing, and so as soon as the grain had ripened, Yan-î could do the job of the Creatures who had always reaped the crops. Easy.

Meanwhile, padding the ends of the bough helped. But did not solve. His shoulders still hurt – though less than they had before he'd had his brainwave of using Yan-î's wool – and the branch still bounced behind him. But then he'd thought of roping the young cow into it. Without her permission, of course, but he was, after all, her Lord, and entitled to use her as he saw fit, particularly since she was continuing to play dumb in this unfair conspiracy of silence, pretending not to Hear. By guiding her, they walked in a nice straight line, and the actual work of dragging was now done by the young cow rather than by him. All *he* had to do was walk behind her, the sticking-up branch in his hand to guide his ard in a straight line, while its trimmed twin bit into the soil. That, in Cain's eyes, was a *much* more satisfactory arrangement. It was almost like it had been in the Garden, before they'd so unfairly punished him, where he had Called on each animal to do its part while he orchestrated.

Using the cow spared his own shoulders, so it was more efficient. Just like using the ready-teased wool. And meanwhile... behold, a furrow! It was so simple!

Yes. Today's work had been worth it. He couldn't wait to tell Yan-î and bask in her admiration. And meanwhile, he was hungry. He hoped that she'd prepared something special for dinner, to celebrate his triumph. It was hard work, being efficient, and he'd earned himself an appetite.

He left the young cow to fend for herself, though he had the foresight to hobble her so she wouldn't be able to wander off in the night. More efficiency. He wouldn't have to waste time tomorrow looking for her.

chapter nineteen

'A voice is heard in Ramah,
mourning and great weeping,
Rachel weeping for her children
and refusing to be comforted,
because they are no more.'
(The Prophet's Oracle 31:15)

They'd watched Cain in growing bewilderment and concern that day. Mama Bear was almost frantic. *'I don't understand,'* she said. *'Is that what dying is like, Glory? Is my cub dying? Oh, Glory, surely the Consequence can't kill him yet? Please don't let him die, Glory. Look! He must be dying! Look!'*

It wasn't that he was botching the ploughing. On the contrary, they had all marvelled at the speed with which he had grasped the concept and put it into practice. No. He was doing all the right... actions... to follow up on Spirit's inspiration. He'd created the plough he needed – that rudimentary ard – and the young cow was pulling it, and the meadow already had a couple of beautiful furrows, perfect trenches for the seed.

It was the way he was taking those steps...

He'd started by forcing the gentle heifer into the ard's harness with harsh words and some nasty slaps...

'Perhaps it just looks harsher than it is,' suggested Gazelle desperately. But they all enjoyed the same perfect Unfallen eyesight, and all knew that it had been as harsh as it had appeared.

And then he'd simply annexed the precious carded wool when the uncarded wool would have served his purposes admirably.

'Perhaps he doesn't realise what carding it cost Yan-î?' asked one of the Cats, who was always meticulously washing and grooming her own fur and knew how much effort even that took. But they had all witnessed the hours – days! – of aching labour and blistered fingers that the wool had demanded – and all knew that Cain, too, had seen it.

And now he had hobbled the young cow without even ensuring that she was surrounded by lush grass to thank her for her help. *'Perhaps he's intending to feed her later?'* asked one of the Rabbits, whose own feeding schedule for her babies was to visit them only at night. But they had all seen the care with which he had ensured she was hobbled (*'But **why** is he imprisoning her, Glory? She hasn't done anything wrong!'*), and they knew that if her welfare had mattered to him, he would have lavished the same care in ensuring that she was well fed. And he would have hobbled her less tightly.

Glory turned His face away for a moment. 'Yes, Beloved. Cain is dying. But not physically. Not the way the firstfruit Fallen died. Cain's dying... is his Choice.'

chapter twenty

*Why is my pain unending
and my wound grievous and incurable?*
(The Prophet's Oracle 15:18)

She'd been so certain that Cain would rejoice with her over the clay, so
confident that he would share her joy and excitement and have his
spirits lifted by this proof of Abba's grace, that her steps had soared to
match M'Farley's on their return to the Nest.

And, 'Just wait 'til we tell him you've got a *name* now, M'Farley!
Oh, isn't this just such a wonderful day!'

But: 'Where've *you* been? What made you think it was ok to just
swan around all afternoon while I was working? How could you?
How dare you? Did you think you can just do nothing all day? And
just look at you! Covered in mud. Are you so stupid that you can't
even see that you're dirty? Or just so lazy? What? Have you gone deaf
and dumb too? Oh, shut up. Why isn't my dinner ready?'

But there was no fire and there were no gifts of food from Unfallen
friends, and the fruit he'd gathered earlier had been scattered and left
for the wasps – and it was all, apparently, her fault.

And when she burst into tears upon discovering his appropriation
of her precious wool, he rounded on her, snarling and livid at her
ingratitude and lack of appreciation for his efficiency. How dare she
create such a scene, he demanded. How dare she? It wasn't as though
she couldn't card some more. She was a selfish ingrate, that's what she
was, only thinking about herself. And now she should just shut up.
Shut *up*, did she hear, because his head was hurting and *he* had spent
the afternoon working and needed some peace and quiet now, and
how dare she make such fuss about nothing? Lazy slut, that's what she
was – hadn't even prepared dinner, when that was the very least she
could do when he'd spent the day slaving away.

And the air was close and stifling, and the skies were lowering in
angry shades of billowing coppered grey that had never existed

before, until the baleful light sank into an angry twilight, and the new clouds gathered and mounded and heaped and finally exploded in lashings of noise and whippings of lightning and thundering of raindrops.

And they had no fire.

And they huddled under the cedar while M'Farley buried her muzzle under her paws and whined and whimpered in fright at the terrible noise as this new thing, this storm, raged around them.

They came together, then, for the first time since they had left Eden. But it was urgent, ungentle, unjoyous; a desperate defiance, a hollow act, a joining of bodies but none of souls.

And the Unfallen grieved, while the other... gloated.

chapter twenty-one

Keep me safe, Lord, from the hands of the wicked;
protect me from the violent.
(Song 140:4)

'Look, Mummy. Isn't she beautiful!?' Shemid was sitting at Yan-î's feet, cuddling his most prized lamb, seven-year-old fingers dimpling as he stroked her extraordinary silky wool. 'Do you think Abba would like this wool, if I offer it to Him?'

The lamb chose that moment to headbutt his chin to get more attention. Shemid rewarded her with a tighter hug and some assiduous head-scratching. M'Farley, sitting on the other side of Yan-î's feet, thumped her tail contentedly.

Yan-î smiled at her second son. 'Yes, she is, isn't she?! And yes, I'm sure He would. Your uncle Abel does the same, you know. Do you remember Uncle Abel, Shemid? You look just like him, you know.'

Shemid pondered a moment, and beamed. 'I was only little then, wasn't I? I was only six the last time he came. With Auntie M'burechet and Granny and Grampa and some of the Animals. And they brought Irad and me some presents, didn't they? And Auntie M'burechet played some lovely music, didn't she?'

'That's right, Shemid. Well done.'

Shemid was quiet for an instant. 'Mummy, why was Daddy so angry at them? Was he angry 'cos of me, Mummy? Why did he shout at them and tell them to go 'way again? Was it my fault, Mummy? Why haven't they come again since then? I'm ever so much bigger now, Mummy. I'm seven now. Seven-and-a-half, really, 'cos my birthday was a whole month ago. I promise I'd be good if they came!'

Yan-î scooped him up – lamb and all – into her arms and held him as tight as she could over her near-term belly. Her unborn daughter kicked in response to the pressure, either in protest or greeting. 'No, Sweetheart, you didn't do anything wrong. Daddy… was just being Daddy, Sweetie. You know how he is whenever he thinks of them… Daddy and I did something very… naughty and very stupid before you were born, Shemid. And so we had to leave the Garden. We couldn't stay there. It was our own fault. And Daddy… Daddy's still mad at everyone except himself for that Consequence. So… I… I don't know if they'll come again. They tried so often, you see. They still love us so much. But Daddy sent them away every time.'

'Why, Mummy?'

'Oh, Sweetheart, maybe when you're older you'll understand.'

She buried her face into the back of his neck and breathed in the clean smell of freshly washed-that-morning little boy. A little boy who was indeed the spitting image of his Unfallen uncle, in both looks and character. A reminder which did not, unfortunately, endear him to Cain, nor make more likely the prospect of the Unfallen being made welcome when they attempted their progressively more infrequent visits. Cain found it trying enough to see that uncanny likeness to his Unfallen brother on a daily basis. Being visited by the original of that face, and by the other Unfallen, was something he found utterly intolerable.

The woven hanging which curtained off the doorway was abruptly pushed aside, letting in a blast of the hot early-summer air, as her boisterous firstborn came in search of her. 'Mummy! I'm hungr—' Irad's voice tailed off as he caught sight of the little tableau – mother, brother, lamb and dog. Thoughts of food were temporarily shelved by the more urgent emotion of jealousy. 'Mummy, why is Shemid here instead of working with the sheep?'

'He was keeping me company, Sweetie, while I carded some more wool and prepared it for spinning.'

'Well, it's not fair. *I've* been weeding the vegetables this morning. *I've* been working.'

Yan-î laughed and opened up her other arm to include him in her hug. 'I'm sure you have, Sweetie. And I'm sure you've done an absolutely wonderful job of it too, haven't you?'

Irad was momentarily mollified.

'Shemid here worked as well, you know. In fact, he only came in about half an hour ago, to show me his little lamb, and then stayed to keep me company.'

Irad stiffened again, and then looked at the lamb with grudging admiration. A covetous gleam lit up his eyes. 'It's nice. Shemid, is it for me? I want it.'

171

Shemid looked at their mother for support. She smiled at him with her eyes and dipped her head almost imperceptibly to give him permission to stand his ground.

Shemid shook his head at his brother. 'No, Irad, it's not for you. I was showing it to Mummy 'cos the lamb's so beautiful that I want to give her wool to Abba.'

Irad's face took on an all-too-familiar look of petulance. 'I want it. Give it to me. I'm going to tell Daddy that you called the LORD that name. You know he told you not to.'

Shemid shook his head again.

Irad wheedled. 'Oh, come on, Shem. You've got so many others. All I'm asking is for this one. It's not as if the LORD even knows or cares about them. *He* won't know. Oh, come on, Shemid.'

Mutely, Shemid signalled 'no' again.

Ten-year-old lungs rent the air with frustrated volume. 'Daaaaddy!'

A pounding of heavy footsteps outside. 'Irad?'

Irad produced some suitably important tears. 'He won't give it!'

'Give what?'

'He won't give his lamb to me. An' I asked nicely, Daddy. And I want it and he won't give it. *And* he called the LORD "Abba". That's disrespet... disrespes... disrespectful, Daddy, isn't it? You said so yourself, that we weren't to call Him that no more.'

Cain rounded on his second son. 'Why won't you give it to your brother, Shemid? I've told you before you need to share. Now give it to him. Now. *Now*, I said.'

Shemid's lower lip was starting to tremble. 'But...'

'Don't give me any "buts", young fellow. I told you to give it to your brother. Now. And what was that about calling the LORD "Abba"? I've told you before: We won't have any of that irreverence here. He's no "Abba" of ours any more, since He drove us out of the Garden. He's not our Father any more. And *certainly* not our Daddy. How dare you be so disrespectful? You will address Him as the LORD. And keep Him out of this conversation. What on earth has He got to do with this wretched lamb anyhow?'

Irad piped up spitefully. 'He said he wanted to give its wool to the LORD!'

Cain whirled and landed a heavy back-handed slap on Shemid's cheek. 'How dare you? Since when do the sheep belong to you, to

172

decide what to do with them? Your job, young man, is to look after them. But they are *not* yours. How dare you? Now hand it over to Irad. Now, I said!'

Shemid valiantly tried to hold back the tears starting to leak out of his eyes, over the blazing print left by his father's hand, and Cain rounded on Yan-î. 'And you! It's *your* fault he's talking such rubbish. How dare you? How many times have I told you to shut up about them? It's bad enough the brat looking like that... that *prig* without your filling his head with such stuff.'

Yan-î kept quiet. Too many times had the worst arguments started this way. Speaking... would simply exacerbate the situation. This way... this way, perhaps he wouldn't hit out at her. Or the boys. Or not as much at any rate.

Their daughter, alerted perhaps by the raised voice, or by the thumping of Yan-î's fear-raised heartbeat, kicked again at the womb wall. Only another few weeks before the birth. And that was another grim prospect on the horizon: the pain of childbirth. Something else that the Unfallen would never know. M'burechet's children, and Eve's, continued to be born without pain or effort. But for Yan-î, this would be the third time. Third child, third labour. She quailed at the thought.

Cain mistook the reason for the flinch. 'I'm talking to you, woman. Look at me when I talk to you. How many times have I told you?'

It was too late. When the conversation took this turn, Yan-î knew what to expect. And sure enough, when she raised her eyes, Cain interpreted the look as defiance, and roared at her for daring to go against his orders, for not showing him proper respect, for not knowing her proper place, while the boys cowered in the background and the dog shivered, tail between her legs, under the chair.

And then, inevitably, that too became her fault: 'Now look what you've made me do! Why do you force me to lose my temper?' And then she had to be 'punished' for that, too.

It could have been worse. Irad at least was spared, today, and went off, half-tearful, half-gloating, with the prize lamb in his arms and his father's gruff hand on his shoulder.

And in her womb, the baby stirred, unharmed. Cain had not lost his control to that extent.

She prayed he never would.

chapter twenty-two

There is a time for everything,
and a season for every activity under the heavens:
a time to be born and a time to die.
(The Old King's Wisdom 3:1-2)

Seventy years. Only seventy years since their Fall. Only seventy years since they had eaten the forbidden fruit and condemned themselves and half of all creation to distance from the LORD. And to mortality. Only seventy years. It felt like an eternity, and yet it felt like only yesterday that they had been led, blinking, from the blinding dazzle of Unfallen Light, out of Eden.

Time, Yan-î reflected, had not improved her husband's moods. Or character. Even though Abba had blessed their land, blessed their work, blessed their family, Cain still seemed blind to those blessings, still determined to see ugliness everywhere, and to blame all but himself for the perceived injustice of the Great Consequence.

It had not made for gentle decades.

And yet their tribe had prospered. The land they had been given required hard work to till and weed, and crops no longer ripened in days as they had in Eden. Yet the soil was fertile, the harvest plentiful, the livestock abundant, and the weather kind. The children had children, and those children in turn were starting to have children. Her eldest great-grandchild was already fifteen, already proud of the first faint fuzz on his chin and his deeper tones.

And Cain... loved her still. In his way, she thought. In his way. He couldn't help his rages, she reasoned. And perhaps sometimes it *was* her fault for provoking him. Perhaps he was right. Perhaps if she weren't so stupid, and selfish, and pathetic, she could have done something. Could have done something to prevent that first fateful folly, could have saved them and the half of Creation of which they were the Heads. So perhaps it was her fault, after all, that Cain got so angry. After all, he loved her. Didn't he? He would never say such things to her if they weren't true, for how could anyone say such dreadful things to anyone – let alone to someone they loved – if they weren't true? And he was always so sorry afterwards, for hitting her and screaming at her. Always promised it would be the last time, that he wouldn't have done it if she hadn't provoked him. If the plough hadn't broken... If that grandchild hadn't destroyed Cain's tunic that morning... If Shemid hadn't deliberately infuriated him by wanting to sacrifice that prize wool to the LORD... If such-and-such a daughter hadn't been spotted walking around in the fields with her hair indecently uncovered, or her ankles showing, or – horror of horrors! – her skirts tied up out of the way and showing her knees... If... If... If... There was always an if. Always a reason why Cain's fury had been justified. Always a reason why in the end it came down to being Yan-î's fault. Never his.

Small wonder, then, that most of her boys had adopted their father's attitude towards her, and, by extension, towards their sisters, their wives, their daughters. Small wonder that the girls grew up cowed, trained to obey, trained to accept that this was right and normal, whatever the infrequent visits of the Unfallen showed to the contrary. Small wonder even that so many of the younger ones acted as though their own power lay in petty, destructive gossip, in little viciousnesses, in manipulation and bullying of those who in turn were weaker than they.

Not Shemid, though. Shemid still seemed to carry a spark inside him, a reminder of how hearts had been before she and Cain had thrown it all away with that forbidden fruit. Shemid... was still gentle, still... had that soul's glow he'd kept since earliest childhood. Shemid still brought the day's treasures to show her, still set them aside for Abba, for the LORD of whom she'd told him, for whom his heart hungered. Shemid, still shy, still single... still earning his father's – and brothers' – wrath when discovered squandering such firstfruits to their terrible God.

She sometimes wondered how they squared it all up to themselves, these menfolk of hers: this terrifying LORD, author of iron rule and power, fearsome and all-seeing, who yet apparently wouldn't notice whether something was the best of the crop or the least of it. A terrifying, terrible God who occasionally had to be appeased with pompous gestures, whose rule was grudged, and who counted merely the action, not the spirit behind the action. It was not the way she

175

remembered Glory. Not the way she recalled their perfect Fellowship, His joy in the tiniest leaf, His care for His smallest creature. Their God... did not chime with her memory of His joy and laughter and love, His abounding grace. It did not equate with that final memory of Abba leading them out of Eden with tears, to protect them – *them!* – she and Cain and the Fallen half of Creation! – from His own presence. His Holy presence, which the newly Fall-flawed vessels of their bodies could no longer have survived.

They were like clay, she meditated, drawing from a lifetime of potting. Long years of kneading clay to expel air, of clearing up shards of exploded pots when a fatal imperfection had nevertheless slipped in, had taught her that much: put clay that contained impurities in a kiln, and it would not, could not, survive the heat. How much more with Glory then: in the face of His Absolute Holiness, how could they, Fallen flawed vessels, have survived had He not placed His covering over them until they could get out of Eden, away from the glorious terribleness of His presence?

Her thoughts turned back to Shemid. It always grieved her that, alone of her sons, Shemid – the best of all of them! – should be the one who had not yet married and started his own line.

'The thing is, she'd have to be pretty special, Mum,' he'd once told her. 'I love you, and I love Abba even more, though I know I'll never meet Him. And my wife... my wife would have to share that love. Share my heart, in all senses – know that she is not being short-rationed, *and* herself love Abba and you with the same joy. She'd have to be someone... well, someone with whom the whole was greater than the sum of our parts. Someone with whom I could become a... bigger person than I can ever be on my own, and the same for her. Like... like Granny and Grandpa, who seem to love each other more deeply every time we see them. Maybe one day. We've still got plenty of time, Mama. We're still so young! Don't worry. I'll bring you grandchildren yet! You'll see. And even Dad will love them. And all the more for having waited so long for them!'

And then he'd gone off, back to his flocks, whom he treated with more care and gentleness and respect than his father or siblings would ever have permitted, had they known. To them, Animals... were just

176

animals, after all. To be used – for their fur, their work, their wool, their milk, their skin. For their ashes, to fertilise the soil.

Ah yes. Time. Plenty of time, still. Perhaps Shemid was right. She was only ninety-five, after all. Still in the prime of her youth, though she'd had the shock of discovering her first grey hair that morning, and Shemid was only sixty-seven. Time enough for him to find someone. Even those who weren't as biased as she might be, being his mother, had commented on how strong and intelligent and handsome he was. And tall. Well, not the tallest, perhaps – a few of his brothers and cousins were several inches taller than he – but nevertheless a strapping lad at seven feet tall. Time enough. Still, it would be so lovely to see him settled with someone special. Perhaps one of his nieces. One of Irad's brood, maybe – what was that lass's name – that gentle, doe-eyed girl with the joy-filled laugh? Abi, that was it. Yes, perhaps Abi. She wondered how she could engineer a nice coincidental meeting for them...

chapter twenty-three

Since no one knows the future,
who can tell someone else what is to come?
As no one has power over the wind to contain it,
so no one has power over the time…
(The Old King's Wisdom 8:7-8)

But Abi married someone else, and Shemid was still single, unhurriedly trusting that when the time was right, Abba would allow him to meet that one special woman.

M'Farley, who had slowly aged, white-muzzled but beautiful as ever, died. She was a mere hundred and one years old, faithful to the end, and left an aching hole of loss in Yan-î's heart. In Cain's too, could he only admit it – the sharp reminder of the Great Consequence terrifyingly heavy to him. Even though he'd never had quite the close bond with the dog that Yan-î had had, M'Farley had nevertheless been with the two of them since the first days after their Fall. He was used to seeing her limpid eyes follow him, to hearing her tail thump in welcome, to feeling her cool snout nuzzle his hand in greeting. He was used to her unquestioning and unconditional love. And now… now she was gone. She had not taken up that much space physically, yet their home felt resoundingly empty in her absence, the air itself incomplete without her. And if she had aged, and died, and gone – then it brought home in unwelcome clarity that they, too, eventually, would die.

It was terrifying, this inexorable, unstoppable march of time. The great-grandchildren had grown up and the first few had children of their own. The family units were moving further afield, carving new holds for themselves, tilling new land, building new homes to house their swelling ranks. Yan-î had discovered a second white hair in her glossy crown of silky black, and Cain… today Cain had discovered one of his own. His first.

He had not been amused.

He'd come in to show it to her, in a rare moment of companionship. 'It's white!'

'Yes, dear.'

'But it can't be white! Why's it white, Yan-î?'

Yan-î laughed, a merry peal of notes, as she took in her husband's woeful face. 'We *are* over a hundred, Dearheart. About a hundred and thirty, by my count, actually. Well, *you* are. I,' she sparkled mischievously, 'am only a hundred and twenty-five. Look, I found *my* second white hair this morning! I guess this is what's called mortality!'

Cain hurrumphed. 'Are you sure?' he asked plaintively. 'You sure it's not just dust or something coating it? Or... or a bird dropping? Or something?'

Yan-î assured him that bird droppings were rarely so selective as to coat a single hair.

'Well, you'd better pull it out, then.'

'Pull it out? Why?'

'Because. Just because. It... it doesn't match the rest of my hair, that's why!'

She reached up and fondly ruffled his glossy brown curls, noting that the faintest of lines now creased the skin by his eyes. 'Well, why don't *you* pull it out for yourself, then?'

Cain dimpled at her, his great grey eyes sparkling. He caught her by her waist – still slim, still lithe, though she was no longer quite the girlish beauty she had once been. Oh yes. It was for moments like these that she loved him, adored him, lived for. Moments of shared confidences, of friendship. Moments when she knew he needed her, trusted her. Moments like these, which made the abuse, the deprecation, the apparently automatic belittlement, all irrelevant.

'Oh, go on. Please.'

Yan-î rolled her eyes with amusement and carefully took hold of the offending hair. 'Are you sure? No one else will notice it, you know! It's just part of you!'

Cain growled.

Yan-î tugged.

Cain yelped.

He glared at the hair, now lying innocently in Yan-î's palm. And then, averting his eyes from it, as though that tiny reminder that they were mortal were too painful even to contemplate: 'Burn it!'

Just then, a hubbub outside came to their ears. One of the dogs –
M'Farley's descendant – had given tongue, baying excitedly to alert
the settlement to visitors, and now one of the children, Methushael,
dashed in, closely followed by one of his youngest sisters. 'Elder-gran!
Elder-gran! Guess who's comin…'

His enthusiasm abruptly braked as he spotted his great-great-
grandfather standing there with Yan-î. Cain's allergic reaction to
mention of the Unfallen was known to all the family, though it had
been a couple of years since their last abortive visit.

Cain's mood promptly lost its evenness. There could only be one
reason for the child's abrupt halt in outpouring. 'Who?'

'They… *They* are, Elder-grandfather. Your… your parents. And' – in
a rush – 'your other brothers and sisters. And… and… a few animals.'

The lad's voice tailed off as Cain's face darkened. 'I… think I'll go
now, Elder-grandfather. Um… see you later. Um… bye, Elder-gran!'

The boy sketched a brief reverence in his patriarchs' directions, and
scarpered, trailed by his sister.

Cain whirled towards the doorway, fists clenched. 'How. Dare.
They.'

chapter twenty-four

I will weep in secret
because of your pride;
my eyes will weep bitterly,
overflowing with tears.
(The Prophet's Oracle 13:17)

The visit... had not gone well. More precisely, it had gone... even worse than usual.

Oh, they'd tried, as they always did. They'd dressed up in garb that even Cain and his sons could not fault for modesty. (But how was it, Yan-î wondered, that even under those heavy coverings, she could still make out their *joie de vivre*?) They'd brought gifts for Cain and Yan-î, gifts for the children, and the children's children, and the children's children's children, each gift lovingly thought of and crafted and tailored to its intended recipient's tastes and interests. M'burechet and Eve had snatched a few seconds with Yan-î, to hug her and bring her up to date on news from the Garden, and translate Mama Bear's grunts into loving regards and delight at Yan-î's ever-expanding tribe.

But the Heavenlight glowing from their faces seemed more painfully dazzling than ever before. And – most unforgivable of all – the Unfallen were, of course, untouched by time. Living in Eden, still in perfect Relationship, still eating from the Tree of Life, and forever exempt from death and mortality – that consequence of sin and distance from God – they bore no hallmarks of the passage of time. Yan-î's face had seemed scarcely altered since that far-off day of the Fall, but next to her twin, she seemed aged, her skin-tone saggier, her figure heavier. Cain's berry-brown skin had seemed touched oh-so-lightly by the first lines, the first intimations of mortality – yet next to Abel's lustrous, ever-young features, those whisper-fine engravings on his face seemed like ponderous creases.

And the men had followed their patriarch's hostile example, standing in glowering, stiffly serried ranks. Some, braver than their brethren, had relaxed sufficiently to mutter an embarrassed 'Thank you' for their gifts, but most sneered, growled, and spat at the givers and the gifts. Later, when the Unfallen had left, each present would be surreptitiously picked up, dusted off, and jealously guarded. But for now, the men showed their disdain and outright anger, and the women hung back, clustered together, fearful of provoking their menfolk's anger by appearing too eager for the welcome gifts, or appearing too curious about their cousins, of whom fragmented rumours and legends were told.

Appearances counted. And so the men bristled with antagonism. How dare the Unfallen rub it in? How dare those patronising prigs think that distributing largesse would make up for the hardships to which they'd abandoned the Fallen?

And how dare they show their faces, those hatefully beaming, sempiternal faces, today of all days, here where mortality had inflicted its first white hair on Cain?

Even their language, now, seemed designed to insult them: the courtesy, the kindnesses, the endearments, the... the *correctness* and articulacy of their speech – all of it felt calculated to shame the Fallen, whose language now so often reflected anger and bitterness and indifference to intended structure. For language, too, had deteriorated, the further men got from the Word which had given birth to all Creation, and the deafer they had become to that perfect communication between Heaven and Earth, Man and Beast, Creator and Created, which still hallmarked all the Unfallen. How dare the Unfallen show them up even with the beauty of their words?

Only Shemid, alone of all the men, stood unbowed to peer pressure. He gazed at the visitors, heart leaping, drinking in the light that shone from the Unfallen. His strong hand lightly resting on the head of a young bullock, he was storing every precious moment of their visit in his heart. As a Fallen man, he would never be able to see Abba face to face, never be able to withstand the full power of utter Holiness, but he could see Glory's glow on his Unfallen cousins, and that was cause enough for worship. It was as Yan-î had told him: they were still loved, still individually known by name. Despite the Fall.

It earned him a vicious kick from Irad, and a pulverising glare from his father, but the disapproval did not, could not, dint the deepness of his joy.

chapter twenty-five

There are those who turn justice into bitterness
and cast righteousness to the ground.
(The Book of the Peasant Prophet 5:7)

Cain raged.

It was the final insult. He would make them pay. Prigs! Sanctimonious do-gooders! All their talk of love... Where had their love been when he had been so unfairly kicked out of Eden? Where had their love been when he'd been so unjustly punished for such a trivial disobedience? Where had their love been with each hard-won inch of land, in the tilling and the sowing and the harvesting, in the building and the digging and the firewood cutting? Where had their love been all these years of hard labour? In the blisters and the sweating and the smells and the storms and the changing of the seasons? Reminding him of their kinship, that he was their son, their brother, Lord Cain of old, beloved of the LORD... Hah! Mere words, he knew.

As far as he was concerned, they had ceased to exist when they turned their backs on him and exiled him. They were dead to him. Hypocrites one and all. All their offers of help, their attempted visits, their gifts... *he* wasn't fooled. *He* knew it was all mere condescension, to rub it in and laugh at him, to judge him, to sneer at him. And now they'd come again. He just *knew* they'd come only to vaunt their agelessness, their facile lives. They'd come, he knew, to show off, to remind the Fallen that in Eden all their work (work!? hah! as if they had any idea what honest work might be!) was aided by the LORD and all Unfallen Creation. Small wonder they found the energy to smile, to dance, to sing, to invent new and wonderful things – trinkets and toys and tools and musical instruments – while he and his children were forced to labour. And to grow old. And die.

While they... those... *prigs*... would continue, strong and young and perfect, timeless. Feasting on the labour of all Creation. Feeding on the fruit of the Tree of Life... and oh, continuing to rub it in. *They* would never age, never die! How dare they mock him, knowing how age was already tingeing his hair, making its mark on him?

He would make them pay. Somehow.

And the other, the tireless enemy, always on watch to taint, to destroy, to corrupt, sneaked a seed of an idea into that fertile mind. These humans, swarming and multiplying and squatting on the Earth that should by rights be his... what sweeter mischief than to set them against the Unfallen and the Great ... *One*... Enemy Himself? These Fallen mud-rats were so easily nudgeable, malleable to his ideas! Their emotions so deliciously roiled...

And the idea took root, germinated, grew...

Ageless, were they? Banishing the Fallen from Eden, under pretext of protection? What rubbish! All that talk of love, when they wouldn't even share the most obvious thing. Not couldn't: wouldn't. Hogging it all for themselves. Deliberately keeping the goodies for themselves, that was all, so that they could look down their patronising noses at Fallen man's efforts to wrestle a living from the ungrateful soil. Fallen man. Mortal man. Why, he should have thought of it before. He knew how to strike back. Sanctimonious prigs. Ageless, huh? Just wait. Conquering mortality would, after all, be simple.

It was time to strike back at Eden.

chapter twenty-six

They encourage each other in evil plans …
they say, 'Who will see it?'
They plot injustice and say,
'We have devised a perfect plan!'
Surely the human mind and heart are cunning.
(Song 64:5-6)

He wouldn't strike at the LORD, of course – that would be hopeless, and wrong. (In his nightmares he still remembered that terrible, thundering, awe-filling voice, the implacability of sentencing.) So of course he wouldn't strike at the LORD. He simply wanted to reclaim at least a part of what should by rights have been his, that was all. And his children's.

He called a few of his sons together. Some of the more stolid ones – feet on the ground, practical, obedient. The ones who could see the logic of his idea, who would be quick to grasp the advantages for themselves that far outweighed any possible dangers. The ones who, like himself, could see through the sweet-talking Unfallen, could understand that the *real* motive behind their attempted visits was simply to rub everything in, while not sharing the one thing that would be useful.

'What keeps them immortal?' he demanded. 'It can't just be the LORD. He has better things to do. Of course, you never saw Eden, so you wouldn't know. But let me tell you, lads, the real reason we're not living in Eden any more. They were jealous, that's what it was, that I – and your mother – ate from the Tree of the Knowledge of Good and Evil. *We* became like God, knowing good and evil, and the others couldn't bear that. So they exiled us 'cos they were jealous.'

'I… I thought it was 'cos you disobeyed the LORD and broke the Great Relationship?' ventured one of the sons.

('Smart alec. I'll have to watch out for that whippersnapper,' thought Cain. 'Thinks he's got a right to contradict me, does he? I'll have to see about taking him down a notch or two. Teach him some proper respect for me.')

But aloud, he laughed. 'Don't tell me you've been listening to your mother. She's just a stupid woman. A dumb female. What does she know? She can't see what's right in front of her eyes. Just believes every stupid lie they've ever fed her, that's what. But there, what can you expect of a mere female, eh? They belong in the homestead, to cook for us and look after the brats. You can't expect them to have brains as well, son. Thinking is for us men. Not them! You got that?'

He elbowed his son in the ribs with what he felt resembled a jovial nudge. ''Sides, think of all the times you young rogues didn't show *me* proper respect, answered me back, even disobeyed me when you was younger? Well, I didn't go and exile *you* for that, did I? Clobbered you round the ears, maybe, but I didn't go and drive you out of the homestead, did I, and tell you never to show your face again? Well, then. Doesn't make sense for your mam and me to have been kicked out just 'cos we ate one tiny forbidden fruit, does it?'

He watched his reasoning sink in. 'Nah, I'll tell you what it was. Jealousy, pure and simple. Jealousy, 'cos *we* knew, and *they're* too cowardly to join us. Too cowardly to taste from that Tree. And I'll tell you another thing, too, while I'm about it. D'you know what's standing next to the Tree of the Knowledge of Good and Evil? Hah! I'll tell you, lads. It's the *real* reason they kicked us out, you know, 'cos they were afraid of us, and jealous of us, and they didn't want to share it now that we're better and cleverer than them.'

He lowered his voice and looked at each of them in turn, capturing their eyes for dramatic effect. 'No, lads. I'll tell you what's standing next to the Tree of Knowledge of Good and Evil. It's what keeps them permanently strong and young, is what. It's the Tree of Life! And *this*, lads, is what we're going to do about it.'

He sketched out his plan.

'So you see, it's easy,' he concluded. 'And only fair. Why should they hog the whole Tree to themselves, eh? All this talk about love for us, and they can't even share one measly fruit, one measly tree. It's not as if we'd be *harming* any of them. *Or* the Tree. Just taking what's due to us, is all. They can't expect us to carry on living and working out here and getting *old* and *dying* when all it needs is for one measly little fruit to make the playing field a little fairer! They're just jealous, is

186

what. And you know I've always taught you to share, haven't I? Well, it's time *they* shared. So, lads, who's with me?'

The men shared a look with one another, then, one by one, raised their hands.

'All right, then. Let's do it tonight, then, while half of them are asleep. Now remember, lads, bring along some heavy cloths. And enough rope. And a bag, for the fruits we're going to harvest. It's time to get some of our own back. I'll see you here just after sundown.'

chapter twenty-seven

The fear of the Lord is the beginning of knowledge,
but fools despise wisdom and instruction.
(An Anthology of Sayings 1:7)

The logic, as far as Cain was concerned, was impeccable.

What kept them out of Eden, apart from the sentence laid down by the LORD? Just the light – that confounded light, that dazzled and hurt.

But it's easy to shut out light. You just close your eyes to it. And take turns to squint and lead the way so that no one gets permanently hurt by it.

What kept the Unfallen immortal? Just a fruit, was all. What kept the fruit out of reach? Just the light, was all. And blind obedience up to now. For what? For nothing. Just 'cos the Unfallen were selfishly, jealously hogging it; just 'cos the Unfallen knew that the Fallen were better than they. Wiser, braver, 'cos he and Yan-î had dared to eat the fruit from the Tree of Knowledge of Good and Evil, and the Unfallen hadn't. And for that, well, they'd been punished good and proper. Out of all proportion to such a trivial act. It wasn't fair. And hogging the Tree of Life all to themselves, to boot. Well, time to put an end to that.

chapter twenty-eight

Fools mock at making amends for sin,
but goodwill is found among the upright.
(An Anthology of Sayings 14:9)

The Unfallen watched in alarm as their beloved descendants approached the eastern side of the Garden, lashed together in single file, all but the current leader blindfolded.

If it hadn't been so serious, there would have been something rather lovably humorous about the sight. A row of men, roped together, twelve with blindfolds, being led by an increasingly dazzled and uncomfortable thirteenth. From their manner, it appeared that they were doing their utmost to walk with exaggerated caution. They seemed to believe that their advance might somehow thus escape notice from the Garden. Thirteen grown men tiptoeing with knees arching up in overblown care, hissing hushes at each other with every step, and apparently blissfully unaware of the racket that thirteen such sets of pssttings and shushings made.

There were a few other slight flaws in their plan, too. Such as the fact that they hadn't practised that type of roped-together motion before – let alone blindfolded... If their aim had been to resemble a row of cats stealthily stalking a dancing leaf, velvet-quiet and intent, the *actual* effect was... a little more uneven. Well, perhaps more than a little. A lot more uneven. An *awful* lot more uneven. More like... a clumsy row of children's spinning tops all crashing into each other, dragging each other in different directions, treading on each other's heels, falling over, tripping, swearing, jerking backwards on the rope, blaming each other, and arguing about who would swap places with the leader next, and when. *Noisy* children's spinning tops...

It was not a quick procession, nor a brief one. They had, after all, been walking for hours, and the closer they came to Eden's boundaries, the more exaggerated their attempts at stealth. And the more, apparently, they convinced themselves of that stealth's success.

The potential for merriment, though, was eclipsed by their watchers' concern for them, as the little group so laboriously drew nearer to the out-of-bounds Garden. 'But… don't they *know*? Don't they *realise*? Doesn't Cain *remember*?' asked Eve worriedly. Glory, standing beside her, shook His head sadly.

'No, Dearheart. Cain has convinced himself – and them – that their mortality is simply a result of no longer having access to the fruit of the Tree of Life. He has chosen to forget that mortality is the Great Consequence of breaking the Relationship with Me, who *am* Life. I AM – and whoever is in Me shares that Life too. He is mortal because, being divorced from Me, he and all Fallen Creation, are therefore divorced from Life itself. Separated from Me. The wages of sin… are death.

'Death… is the unavoidable Consequence of no longer being in perfect Relationship with Me. It is the Great Consequence, which We cannot alter except by paying that price Ourselves. And even when We have paid the ultimate price, still it will not be sufficient to lift mortality off the Fallen. It will only ensure that death does not have the *final* victory.

'Cain has chosen to forget that I cannot alter the Great Consequence of his having broken our perfect Relationship. Instead… he has fooled himself, and them, into believing that the Tree of Life is the answer to their mortality. But the Tree is merely one expression of the Life I share with you, and it cannot bridge the divide. It cannot overturn the Great Consequence. It cannot repair the Relationship. Only Redeemer can restore that, at the turning of the times, by paying the debt which is not His to pay. The Tree… the Tree would not give Cain what he thinks he needs.'

They watched as the would-be raiders took another tumble. One of the younger sons swapped places and protective head/eye-scarves with the current leader, and strode off to show how much better he was at leading the group. The group, not having his sight, nor therefore his confident momentum, wasn't quite prepared, and their stolidness was an immovable brake on his rope. His resulting whiplashed return caused them, yet again, to fall over themselves. The hissed hushes were not getting happier.

'But Abba… they're coming here. They'll… they'll *die* if they enter into the presence of Your Holiness. You set the boundaries around Eden to *protect* them from straying too close by mistake. Oh, Father, what are we going to do? How can we save them? How *can* they believe that it's simply a dazzle in their eyes that's the obstacle to their setting foot here? How *can* they not realise that it's the darkness in *them* which would not permit them to survive one moment in the presence of Your purity?'

Glory hugged them. 'You already know the answer, Dearhearts. They find it easier to fool themselves and blame us all than to take responsibility for the Great Consequence they brought upon themselves and upon their half of all Creation of which they were the Heads. They have convinced themselves that they are outside this Garden as punishment, rather than for their own protection so that they may live long and prosperous lives instead of dying instantly when their darkness meets my Light. Blaming others… is so much easier than humbly acknowledging their sinfulness and accepting grace. And jealousy is always convinced it's others' fault.'

'Will they die, Father, when they step into this place again?'

'Yes, Beloveds.'

'Can… can we stop them?'

'Yes, Beloveds. But they will not understand. They… may never forgive you. Or Me, for keeping them out. Can you accept that? Do you understand the cost, if We save their lives this evening? They will convince themselves that you are jealous of them, that you are selfishly choosing not to share My Life, which *they* threw away. You have been rejected each time you have sought them out, Beloveds. Do you understand that this… this will make it even worse?'

'They already *have* convinced themselves of all of that, Abba, haven't they, though?' asked Abel sadly. 'You told us Yourself: the one thing You cannot do is force their free will. It's their freedom, their choice, to believe whatever they choose about us. We can tell them and tell them and show them it is not so, but it is their freedom whether to open their eyes to see that or not.'

'Yes, Dearheart.'

'So… so it doesn't matter about us, Abba. *We* know we love them. *You* know we love them. Yan-î and Shemid know we love them… So… just save them, Abba, please?'

191

And the LORD placed on the east side of the Garden of Eden cherubim and a flaming sword flashing back and forth to guard the way to the Tree of Life.

And the men returned to their homes, hearts filled with rancour, and the conviction that they had been barred out of jealousy. For, they argued, the LORD God must have said, 'The men have now become like us, knowing good and evil. They must not be allowed to reach out their hands and take also from the Tree of Life and eat, and live forever.'

Three measly fruits, to plant and grow into Trees of Life for themselves, to overcome mortality. That's all they'd wanted. All they'd planned. All they'd dared. Three measly fruits, which no one would ever have missed. And now barred forever.

Ha! All that talk from the Unfallen about Love. Funny how the *facts* were very different, wasn't it? Hypocrites! Misers! Jealous, useless scum. Two-faced patronising prigs! Three measly fruits from the Tree of Life to lift the curse of mortality, and they wouldn't even share *those*...

Somehow, of course, it was all Yan-î's fault again, when Cain got home.

The bruises took two weeks to disappear.

The hurt took longer.

chapter twenty-nine

He refreshes my soul.
He guides me along the right paths
for his name's sake.
Even though I walk
through the darkest valley,
I will fear no evil,
for you are with me;
your rod and your staff,
they comfort me.
(Song 23:3-4)

Eden was not accessible as a target for the men's frustration. Someone had to become the focal point for their resentment. Someone, for instance, whose attitude reminded them most of the Unfallen.

The someone, of course, was Shemid.

He wasn't quite sure who had started the nastiness, or what he might have done to deserve it. He hadn't been part of the unsuccessful raid, of course – his father had judged him too goody-goody ('It's bad enough having an Unfallen brother without my own flesh-and-blood *son* aping him!') and had pointedly not included him in the council of war. Indeed, Shemid had known nothing of it until after the fact. But whether it was that deliberate exclusion or something else which had catalysed the present unpleasant atmosphere, he didn't know.

What he did know was that he was finding it difficult to deal with. The animated chatter which broke off abruptly into hostile silence the moment he entered a room, the snide comments, the deliberate snubs... Sometimes it was so bad it almost made him laugh – he found he was developing a fair streak of black humour which permitted him to see the ridiculousness of the situation. All the same, it was not easy when his voice was ignored in conversation, as though he were non-existent; when any suggestion he made in discussions about the livestock went apparently unheard, yet was rapturously approved when one of his other brothers or cousins repeated the identical suggestion mere minutes later...

He confided in Yan-î. 'I'm... I'm really struggling, Mum. I don't know how the Unfallen cope, always being rejected, being treated as dirt every time they try to visit us – even though they only ever bring us good things and never retaliate for our nastiness towards them, but only love us and love us and love us. I... just don't know how they do it, Mama. *They*'ve been loving us forever, and here I am, struggling after just a few days!'

He bowed his tall head onto his mother's shoulder, and she held him wordlessly for an instant, before cupping his face in her hands. 'I know, Beloved. I wish... I wish there was something I could do to make it easier. But there isn't. The only thing we can do is... is ask Glory to give us the strength we need to get through it.'

Shemid took a deep breath and grimaced wryly. Together, they sat down on the pile of cushions in the corner of the room, where the afternoon sunshine streamed down in a golden glow of dust motes from the window above. 'Yes, I know, Mum, I know. I know. And He does seem to, doesn't He!? But... it helps just being able to talk about it with you, you know.' He sighed with frustration, and then gave a wry bark of mirth.

'It's so... daft, you know. It's as if Dad and the rest of them have built a whole structure out of some invisible fabric of warped logic. It's as if... as if they've decided that because they can't get into Eden to nab those fruits, that makes everything *Eden's* fault. And they seem to believe that if it's Eden's fault, then *that* somehow shows that the Unfallen are hypocrites. And so then their logic seems to argue that if the Unfallen are hypocrites, then they're liars. And if they're liars, they're selfish monsters.'

He shook his head at the surreal mental pyramid of escalation, and continued enumerating his deductions. 'And then it seems they think that since the Unfallen are in perfect relationship with Abba, then anyone else who worships Him must *also* somehow be a liar and a hypocrite and a selfish monster just by association. And since they know that I've always sought Him and loved Him, just from what I've seen and what you've told me and from how the Unfallen are... it's almost as though they've decided that I need to be punished and... and put in my place for "being" a liar and a hypocrite and a selfish

194

monster! And it's just so... *silly*! But at the same time... oh, Mum, at the same time it's so *hard* to not let *their* treatment of me affect *my* treatment of them! It's so *hard* not to start thinking of ways of getting my own back on them, you know, or to ask Abba to somehow punish them! It's so *hard* to Choose still to love them irrespective, just like I see the Unfallen Choosing every time Dad sends them packing!'

He took a deep breath. 'I know... I know. At some stage they'll get over what they see as this snub from the Unfallen. At some stage things will go back to normal. Dad will rant and roar at me when he catches me putting aside the best for Abba. Irad will take his cue from Dad and mock me, and the others... well, the others will just go back to being the others. But I'm *used* to that. I can live with that. At least it'll just be normal for this family, not this horrid atmosphere we're living with at the moment!'

He fell silent for a moment, and then his face suddenly split into a broad grin, white teeth gleaming, and a wholly mischievous glint in his eye. For a moment the look of strain vanished, replaced simply with laughter. 'But oh, Mum, I confess that at times I've entertained myself with dreaming up ideas of revenge-by-crude-practical joke... Can you picture the ringleaders' faces if, oh, say, someone were to smuggle some fresh cowpats next to their beds just before they woke up, for them to step into? I could feed my beautiful ladies a pottage of dried skunk cabbage the night before, to make their pats smell *really* vile, and then... Can you just imagine it? Or... how 'bout spinning some fibre using fur from one of the long-haired dogs, and using the fibre to weave a cape for them to wear in wet weather... Mmmm, wet-dog smell on *top* of being soaked through!'

He caught her eye and chuckled. 'Well, I never said that my daydreaming was *practical*, did I?!'

They looked at each other, and laughed.

The laughter was good.

The laughter hurt.

Shemid looked at Yan-î sombrely for a moment. 'He's taken it out on you again, hasn't he, Mum?'

It was a statement rather than a question.

Yan-î lowered her eyes, started to dredge up an excuse.

Shemid touched her hand lightly. 'Don't, Mama. Don't try to excuse it. I know what he's like. Did... did he hurt you very badly?'

195

Yan-î half-shrugged a shoulder. 'Oh, Mama, I'm so sorry. There I am, going on about my silly little challenges, and you… I don't know how you bear it.'

She looked up at him at that, and a smile briefly lit her beautiful almond eyes. 'He's a good man at heart, Beloved. You should have seen him before our Fall. Young Lord Cain, tending the fields and the vineyards, the orchards and the paddies, in the company of Glory. He was wonderful, you know. It's only since our disobedience that he's become so bitter and angry. But he's still *him* inside it all, you know. Sometimes I see him – the real him – in something he says or does. He does love me, Shemid. He's just… forgotten how to remember it, somehow. And I know he loves *you*, Shemid, deep inside himself. I think… I think he treats you as he does because he's afraid, Shemid. He's afraid of you because you remind him of who he used to be before he allowed himself to become so resentful. And… and… I can't explain it, Shemid. I still believe *he*'s in there, somewhere, the *real* Cain, and one day he'll find his way back out of his darkness. And… I want to be there on that day, to welcome him back… You'll see, Dearheart. You'll see.'

'Mum, you're wonderful. You know that, don't you? You're a very special lady. Whatever Dad or Irad may tell you when they're angry, just remember that, ok? Personally, I'd be relieved if you left him. Because I don't know what Dad has done to deserve you, but I hope he comes to his senses soon and starts appreciating you!'

They touched foreheads gently, and then Shemid heaved himself up powerfully from where he'd been sitting. He stretched, his great seven-foot frame filling the corner of the room they were in.

'…and meanwhile, thanks so much for listening, Mama. I needed to get that off my chest, you know. I do tell Abba, you know. You've told me that He hears and sees everything. So I know that He must hear what I say. But… But it's not the same, Mum, is it? I wish… oh, I so wish that I had lived in the Garden, been able to see Him face to face, that I knew His voice and felt His hugs. Instead of this… this silence, *believing* He hears me but not *knowing*…' He hugged her tenderly, careful now not to make her wince.

'I'll be fine, Dearheart. Truly. You know how fast my bruises always heal! Now go on, shoo!'

Shemid grinned. 'OK. Thanks, Mum. And now… I have my little ladies waiting to be milked. It's time I got back to them, or I shall have some very unhappy ewes and nanny goats out there! Did you want a gourd of milk, by the way? I noticed you're running low on curds at the moment. I'll bring it round after I've finished for the evening – I've still got to shear a couple of them as well before I can call it a day.'

He strode out, whistling, to return to his rounds. Yan-î, left behind, whispered a quick 'Thank You' to Glory for Shemid, and prayed that Abba might somehow let some of His Light leaven the black moods of her other menfolk, and the reflected venom of their wives, to make life easier for all those around.

chapter thirty

The fool says in his heart,
'There is no God.' ...
The Lord looks down from heaven
on all mankind
to see if there are any who understand,
any who seek God.
All have turned away ...
But there they are, overwhelmed with dread,
for God is present in the company of the righteous.
(Song 14:1-3, 5)

It was all very well for Dad to rant and bluster about what he thought of his Unfallen relatives, thought Irad. But what if the Unfallen weren't simply hypocritical snobs? What if... what if they finally got *angry*? What if they turned out to be *powerful* hypocritical snobs? What if the abortive raid finally tipped them into anger, after all these years of putting up with abuse every time they tried to visit and bring gifts? What if... (and here Irad's heart quailed) what if... what if *this* time... the LORD was angered? It was one thing for Him to put cherubim and a flaming sword to guard the Garden. But what if... what if He decided to *punish* them as well!? By all accounts, He'd been pretty mean to Mum and Dad when they'd eaten just one fruit from that other Tree. What if this time He got *really* angry? I mean, thought Irad, just think what *Dad* would have done if he'd caught wind of some of his sons trying to filch something from him. Yes, Cain would have set up some sort of guard to prevent them from succeeding. But you could bet your last crumb that he'd have thought up some way of teaching them all a lesson afterwards as well. He'd be *angry*. Angrier than usual. And that wouldn't bode well for the foiled plotters.

So what if the LORD and the Unfallen were like that? Stood to reason, really, that they would be.

Perhaps, thought Irad, he should try to curry some favour. That way, when the LORD hit everyone with a great bolt of lightning, He might at least let Irad off with something not quite so deadly. Or painful.

What was it his pathetic brother was always talking about? Offering something to the LORD, that was it. Well, if Shemid could suck up to the LORD by chucking something at Him, then so could he.

Let's see. What would make a good bribe? Hmmm. Well, strawberries were always popular with everyone, so the LORD probably liked them too. Besides, he currently had a glut of them which would go to waste anyhow if he couldn't get rid of them. No point in taking something Irad actually needed – it wouldn't make any difference to the LORD anyway. What was He going to do, come down and eat the things? It wasn't as though any of them had ever seen Him except Mum and Dad. (Well, and except the Unfallen, of course. But they didn't count.) Or seen Him do anything. Seemed to Irad that He'd kicked out the Fallen and then forgotten about them, whatever that stupid mother and brother of his said to the contrary. Though the failed foray might just have brought them back to His notice... which was why a little mollification was needed now to show willing and lessen any sentence... But the offering... nah, it was just for show anyhow. It was the gesture that counted, and it wasn't as if He was going to do anything with whatever was offered. It would all go to waste anyhow, and surely the LORD wouldn't approve of wasting *good* food that the kids needed.

Irad grabbed a couple of hampers of slightly overripe strawberries and set off for a distant corner of the fields where his father and brothers wouldn't spot him toadying up to the LORD.

chapter thirty-one

Blessed are the pure in heart,
for they will see God
(The Tax-collector's Tale 5:8)
[but]
a bribe corrupts the heart.
(The Old King's Wisdom 7:7)

Irad morosely surveyed the pile of clearly decomposing strawberries. There. He'd always known that his mother and Shemid were wittering nonsense, and now here was the proof. The LORD wasn't a factor to worry about – just some irrelevant, distant being. Clearly, He didn't even have the power to reach out and take the offering.

What made Irad feel angry was that he'd allowed himself to be taken in by his mother's and brother's constant stories about how the LORD was actively watching over them. *And* that he'd allowed himself to be spooked by the thought and worried that he might be in for some punishment. *And* that he'd wasted a couple of hampers of perfectly good (well, almost perfectly good. Good enough for jam, perhaps, at any rate) strawberries on the LORD. *And* that he might have been spotted in his moment of madness by one of his teeming relatives. And all for nothing! The strawberries just lay there, rotting.

So much for his attempted bribery. Not that it mattered, anyhow. The fact that the strawberries were all putrefying where they lay was enough to put his mind at rest. He was safe. He'd got away with it. The LORD wasn't going to get involved. And there would therefore be no comeuppance from the other night. Cherubim and a flaming sword? Well, who cared about that? It wasn't as though they'd ever set foot in the Garden before anyhow, so what difference did it make now?

The important thing was that he could start going about his daily business again without constantly looking over his shoulder waiting for some terrible retribution to wallop him.

Irad set off home, a tuneless whistle on his breath. There was a nice gourd of wine waiting at home that the Unfallen had given him the other day. Slightly unnerving his Unfallen grandparents might be, with their unceasing goodwill, but Irad had to admit that his grandfather Lord Adam made rather wonderful wine. Yes, it would be good to toast his reprieve with that. Fitting, somehow.

A lone figure in the distance caught his eye. Well, look who went there on one of his futile tête-à-têtes with the LORD. Shemid. Taking a favoured item, no doubt. Didn't he know that the LORD wasn't interested? Waste of time. Waste of wool, or cheese, or whatever-it-was he was taking. Waste of some of the *best* wool...

Perhaps the wine could wait. Irad could do with a bit of light relief after the last few days. Shadowing Shemid and then laughing at him after his pathetic attempts to communicate with the great LORD came to nothing... that sounded just the ticket. Jeering at Shemid was always fun.

Besides, if his suspicions were correct, it was probably Shemid who'd tipped off the Unfallen that they were coming the other evening to nick those fruits. So Shemid deserved all he got for blabbing to that patronising lot. Not that those fruits were probably anything like as wonderful as Dad cracked them up to be. Who needed immortality anyway? He was young and fit and only a hundred and five years old. Old age was a very long way away. He couldn't really see what the fuss was about. But that didn't let Shemid off the hook for blabbing and for being the Unfallen's lapdog. Shemid needed to be put in his place. And now seemed a perfect time for it.

chapter thirty-two

'The Lord your God is with you …
He will take great delight in you;
in his love he … will rejoice over you with singing.'
(The Ethiopian's Call 3:17)

Oblivious to his brother Irad's intentions, Shemid reached his favourite spot. From here he could make out the distant brightness of the Garden, far enough away that it didn't hurt his eyes, but close enough to drink in its restoring luminosity. Sometimes a zephyr carried the sound of distant songs to his ears, a lilt of golden notes, an arpeggio of joy-filled laughter. Shemid was certain that at times his ears had even been blessed with a whisper of angelic harmonies from Eden, a cascade of melody so beautiful it brought a lump to his throat and re-awoke the joyous yearning of his heart. Today, though, only the southerly summer breeze kept him company, with its hint of sea-salt, a friendly rustle of tree leaves and its gentle touch on his face. A cricket hopped off a dry grass stem, leaving the pale stalk bobbing, and took itself off to a shadier corner before striking up its song again.

From here, too, he was sheltered from the sight of his Fallen brethren by a slight dip and a shady curtain of trees behind him. Oh, his family knew, of course, that his heart belonged to Glory. They had always known. But out of sight meant out of mind, he'd discovered. They had (or at least, *had* had, before this current campaign of nastiness) a grudging respect for him when it came to his care and unsurpassed knowledge of the livestock, or when they needed to call upon his exceptionally strong muscles to carry something. But when it came to him putting Majesty first in his life and priorities… that was different. And as for seeking to model his behaviour on that of the Unfallen – mastering his temper, responding to insults with forgiveness rather than retribution, not partaking in gossip or snide jibes behind others' backs… *that*, they seemed to think, was not merely pathetic, but an affront to them. And suspicious, apparently. He'd actually overheard one of them mutter that such apparent transparency *must* be truly devious cover for ulterior motives...

So all in all, he came in for a lot less mockery if they didn't actually *see* him seeking out Abba. To them, Abba was the LORD, the ineffable, the terrible – and the conveniently distant. They did not approve of seeking greater intimacy with He whom they considered to be the author of their punishment.

Admittedly, just at the moment, even a little normal mockery might have come as a relief to the current hostile iciness with which they were surrounding him. But even so, he preferred his time of solitude with Glory to be just that: private.

He gently set down the lamb he'd been carrying. It was the firstborn of a line he'd been trying to get to breed true, with particularly long, silky-soft wool. It was a descendant of the lamb that his brother Irad had coveted so long ago when they had both been little boys. *That* lamb had grown into a beautiful ewe, and when Irad had tired of her (not too long after he'd obtained her, once he'd realised that she didn't look after herself, let alone milk herself), Shemid had got her back and been allowed to keep her as his very own. Since then, he had been trying to breed her, and now, finally, it seemed he had succeeded. This lamb was the third of its line to have been born with the same quality of wool, and the first of its own generation. Shemid had brought it to give to Glory, in thanks.

He'd only ever brought Abba gifts of... *things* before. A pretty feather. A flower. As he'd grown, the gifts had changed slightly – the finest wool, his favourite ash-rolled cheese. But always a sacrifice of things precious to him, always things he thought Glory might like – the firstfruits, the best, the prettiest. Always the best portion of something. Usually he'd left them there, on the little boulder in his private dell, praying that Glory would see them, would delight in them. They were always gone when he returned, but he'd never asked what happened to them. Perhaps, he thought, Abba had taken them – taken them as his mother said. He'd taken Abel's gifts, storing them in His heart, treasuring them. But perhaps, since Shemid was Fallen, his gifts could never be perfect enough: perhaps, he thought with a pang, perhaps Abba just listens to my heart, but the gifts themselves fly away with the wind, are eaten by passing animals, return to the dust from which ultimately they came.

Which was all very well, but this time his offering, his heart-gift, was not an object but a living creature. A happy, healthy, *beautiful* little creature, the most precious firstfruit that Shemid had ever had. The most precious firstfruit he had ever been able to bring to his beloved Glory. He couldn't very well tell it to sit, stay, and wait for the LORD to decide what to do with it. Lambs, though beautiful, were not known for their trainability and understanding of Fallen human speech.

Come to think of it, the lamb and he were rather similar in one way. The lamb wasn't very good at understanding *him*... and Shemid suspected that *he* in turn wasn't very good at hearing or understanding Abba's voice. Oh, why had Mum and Dad thrown away the Great Relationship, forever barred them all from that intimacy with Creator? If only he could hear Him just once, understand Him just once, truly know that Abba was... content with him. If only he could *know* that he was doing right in Glory's eyes, if only he could know that God truly heard him, there in the dell, in the quiet...

He squatted down and met the lamb's trusting gaze. 'I... er... I don't actually know what to do with you,' he acknowledged ruefully. 'You seemed such a good idea at the time, you know. I thought that Glory might delight in you as much as I do. But I... er... don't quite know what to do now. I don't suppose you do, do you?'

The lamb, oblivious to the fact that its opinion had been asked, butted the palm of his hand and nibbled one of Shemid's fingers. Finding that the fingers didn't taste as nice as grass, it skipped over to some rather more appetising food, growing lushly green by the boulder.

Shemid sighed. 'Abba? I don't suppose that just this once...'

He wasn't, of course, expecting an answer. The Almighty had never yet spoken directly to a Fallen person – or at least, if He had, His voice had never been recognised. Once, Shemid had asked Yan-î what Glory's voice was like, and she'd floundered.

'I can't explain it, Sweetheart,' she'd said. 'His voice... just... *is*. Softer than soft, or more majestic than the greatest mountain. So powerful that all Creation listens, so awesome that the sun, the moon, the stars dance at His bidding, or so intimate that only your heart can hear. He calls the tiniest flower, tells the funniest jokes, serves the most humble creature, is Lord of lords... And that's what His voice is like too... You'd recognise His voice if you heard it, you know. Well, I *think* you would. Really. Well, probably. Maybe...' Her voice had tailed off in recollection.

As a description, it had set Shemid's heart leaping, but as a reply it had not really been very useful.

But whatever he could have imagined, it was not like the reality now. A great wind suddenly swept through the hollow, and then, in the silence that followed, Shemid heard Him. The voice... was... *golden*. Golden velvet, if he'd been asked to describe it. It filled the dell, like the light, the soft-yet-dazzling light, a glow that suddenly seemed to flood his little sanctuary. The voice seemed to come from everywhere at once, and from nowhere: he did not even know whether he was hearing it with his ears or simply directly into his mind.

Shemid had never heard that voice before. But every fibre of his being responded to it, knew it, loved it, worshipped and adored its Author.

'Beloved,' the voice said simply, gently, tenderly.

One word. One simple word. One word, that answered all questions, stilled all doubts, banished all fears, melted all the woundings into irrelevance. One word. Love. Acceptance. Pride. Joy. In *him*!

Shemid, grown man, who had stoically endured mockings and jeerings and teasings and disparagement all his life, who had not cried since he was a small child... at that one tender word, dissolved into tears and sobbed his heart out.

The light did not waver, nor disappear.

Eventually, Shemid, feeling washed out, wrung out, and emptied of all the years of bottled bruisings of the soul, took a deep, ragged breath and sat up. Renewal poured into him, fresh strength. And above all, peace that passed all understanding, serenity that filled and overflowed from the depths of his soul.

His nose was dripping. Embarrassed and a little self-conscious after such an outburst, he sniffed and wiped his nose on the arm of his tunic. Somehow, crying his eyes out had never figured on his list of 'how I would react if the LORD ever spoke to me.'

'A... Abba? Daddy?'

'Yes, Beloved.'

There were so many questions he'd wanted to ask, so many issues, so many deep and meaningful conversations he'd longed to have. Somehow, most of them appeared to have washed away in the flood of tears. They'd somehow been replaced by simple quietude.

'Wha... what did you want me to do with the lamb, Abba? Wi... will you take it with you? Do... do you like it?'

The gentlest of hugs seemed to enfold him. 'Dearheart.' (So that's where Mum gets that word from! thought Shemid inconsequentially, in revelatory comprehension.) 'The lamb is beautiful. I delight in him. I delight in you. Thank you.'

(Thank you?! Thank you? Glory, Lord of lords, Creator of Heaven and Earth, thanking *him*?)

'I won't take him with me, Dearheart, for he is Fallen and would not survive the fullness of my presence in Eden. But I accept him with joy, because you have offered him to Me as a sacrifice. He is Mine, consecrated to Me, and since you have given him to Me, he is Mine in his entirety. You shall not shear his wool, or touch his head, or use him to settle a ewe for breeding for your own purposes: he is consecrated to Me, and I shall lead him to green pastures and watch over him as his Shepherd.'

Shemid nodded. It seemed... right.

Glory's light was withdrawing.

'And Shemid?'

'Yes, Abba?'

'Well done, Beloved.'

chapter thirty-three

A heart at peace gives life to the body,
but envy rots the bones.
(An Anthology of Sayings 14:30)

That... creep! That smarmy, scheming, devious creep! It wasn't fair! Two hampers of perfectly good strawberries, rotting over there in the sun, ignored by the LORD, and here was his brother being *favoured*! For what!? For a stupid smelly lamb that wasn't even *doing* anything particularly clever, just gambolling! He should have known that Shemid had an ulterior motive for mimicking the Unfallen. Sucking up to the LORD, that's what it was, and it wasn't fair, because everyone knew that he, Irad, was everyone's favourite. He'd *always* been everyone's favourite. Well, Dad's favourite. But Dad was everyone that counted, and everyone always agreed with Dad and did what Dad told them. Everyone except that creep Shemid, of course, who'd always had that defiantly stubborn streak of passive resistance when Dad had ordered him to stop sneaking off for his little rendezvous with the LORD. Devious little creep. No wonder Shemid had carried on – all this time, he'd been scheming to curry favour with the LORD! It wasn't fair! *His* strawberries had made a much bigger pile than that pathetic little lamb. And just *wait* 'til he got home and told Dad about what Shemid had been up to! Oh, but then Cain might find out that *he'd* been trying to butter up the LORD himself, and that might not be such a good thing.

But it wasn't fair! If the LORD was going to favour one of them, it should have been *him*, Irad. After all, he was the eldest. And the strongest. *And* everyone's favourite. Well, perhaps not Mum's – he had a sneaking suspicion that she had a soft spot for Shemid, for some reason, but then, she was only a female, after all, even if she was his mother, so she didn't count.

But it wasn't *fair*!

And then those put-on tears. Oh yes, Shemid, thought Irad, very clever. Go for the sympathy vote, why don't you? Devious creep! Couldn't the LORD see through that fakeness? God knew that Shemid never cried, so it stood to reason that the tears were put on. Of course, he hadn't actually heard what the LORD had said to Shemid. He'd only seen the effulgence, and the ridiculous display of tears, and then the smiles. But that had been quite enough, thank you. Enough to make his stomach turn. The LORD, favouring Shemid! It wasn't *fair*.

'Irad.'

He looked round suspiciously. Someone had said his name. He couldn't place the voice. He felt he should know it, but it didn't sound like one of his brothers. Or like any of the innumerable cousins that he could bring to mind.

'Irad. Why are you so angry? Why is your face downcast?'

Irad whirled. 'Who is that? Who are you? Come out, wherever you are. And mind your own business!'

'Irad.' The voice was quiet, firm.

'I told you, come out, whoever you are.'

'Irad. If you do what's right, will you not be accepted? But if you don't do what's right, sin is crouching at your door.'

'Who *are* you? Shut up or show your face!'

'Irad.'

A glimmer of recognition began belatedly worming its way into Irad's mind.

'Irad. Sin desires to have you, but you must master it.'

'Um. LORD?'

But the voice had disappeared, and Irad's grievance grew. Not only was the LORD favouring Shemid, but He'd used the one time He'd spoken directly to Irad to tell him off! It wasn't *fair*! And what was that about not doing what was right, and all that rubbish about sin crouching at his door? Damn it all, he'd wasted two whole hampers of perfectly good strawberries, and then not only had they been rejected, but he'd been told off and lectured as though he were just a naughty little boy!

It wasn't *fair*. And it was all Shemid's fault. Devious, venomous little creep, currying favour with the LORD, and turning Him against Irad. Poisoning Him against Irad. It wasn't fair. *He* should have been the LORD's favourite. He was *everyone's* favourite. It was only right that he should be favourite. He *would* have been the LORD's favourite if that smarmy little creep hadn't turned Him against him.

It wasn't fair. It was time he taught Shemid a proper lesson.

chapter thirty-four

But the way of the wicked is like deep darkness.
(An Anthology of Sayings 4:19)

'Yes. Feed that anger,' echoed the enemy, malicious putrefaction to its core. 'Unfair, unfair! Revenge... revenge is deserved. Come, come into my darkness, away from light. Do not listen to that ... *One*... Hold on to that anger. Feel that hollow. Choose to step deeper into my nothingness. Come, my delicious morsel. Come. Come. Come!'

chapter thirty-five

Refrain from anger and turn from wrath;
do not fret – it leads only to evil.
(Song 37:8)

He'd had a restorative drink of the wine he'd promised himself earlier. It was every drop as good as he'd expected.

It was so good that he'd had a second cup. And a third.

He unburdened himself to a cousin. 'Lectured me, He did! Flippin' told me off like I was a little boy! Told me that if I didn't do what's right, sin would be crouching at my door and desired to have me but that I must master it. Yahdedahdedah. And it's all that creep Shemid's fault, you know.'

He launched into a description of Shemid's crimes, failings and other misdemeanours, mostly centred round his two convictions – one, that Shemid was a devious, smarmy, poisonous creep; and two, that it wasn't fair. Telling it stoked his feelings of injustice to greater heights.

The cousin listened sympathetically and helped himself to a cup of Irad's precious wine. Irad snarled, but didn't stop him.

When the list of Shemid's faults ground to a pause, the cousin asked helpfully, 'So what are you going to do about it?'

'About what? About the LORD treating me like a brat, or about that creep brother?'

The cousin shrugged. 'Well, both, I suppose. Either. Whatever.'

Irad grunted, and glared at his cup. Its contents had somehow evaporated. He refilled it, and growled. 'Hmmph. Well, I can't exactly do anything 'bout the LORD, can I? But just watch me. I,' he said, standing up decisively, and working himself into a deadly rage, 'am going to teach that creep a lesson he won't forget.'

'D'you want me to come with you?'

Irad snorted with derision. 'What, against that little worm? Think I can't handle him by myself? No. Thanks, but no thanks. I'll deal with him. Oh, yes. I'll deal with him alright.'

He launched himself into the late afternoon sunshine and hunted down his brother.

chapter thirty-six

Anger is cruel and fury overwhelming,
but who can stand before jealousy?
(An Anthology of Sayings 27:4)

He found Shemid where he'd expected, in the sheep pens, kneeling in the dirt to clean the hooves of one of the ewes. Shemid's broad muscles were sheened with sweat, and perspiration slowly dripped off his forehead onto his cheek in the afternoon heat.

'Shemid.'

Shemid looked up, startled. He couldn't remember the last time Irad had deigned to set foot in the animal pens. Irad preferred working the soil, gathering the harvest like their father. And Irad had addressed him! Perhaps these last few days of being snubbed had come to an end. Perhaps Glory had done more than restore his own bruised heart this afternoon. Perhaps He'd changed Irad's too!

'Irad!' he said in surprised welcome.

'There's something I want to show you. Let's go out to the field.'

'What, right now?'

'Well of course right now. What d'you think, I came to this stink-hole with an invitation to tea in a fortnight?'

Shemid's ebony face split into his delighted smile. ('Devious creep,' thought Irad. '*I* know how false you really are, how false your pretended pleasure is at seeing me. Don't think *I* don't see right through you. But oh, just you wait. I'll show you. I'll teach you.')

'I'll just clean up then and be right with you, Irad. The little ladies are very sweet, but they *do* make a mess in their pens, I'm afrai—'

'Oh, shut your trap. Just shut up, Shemid, and let's go. I couldn't give a rat's arse about your smelly business.'

'Oh. Oh, ok. Right then. Here I am.' He wiped his hands on his tunic and wished he had time to go via the well to clean himself up. But such an invitation from Irad was... well, unheard of. He was not going to jeopardise this opportunity for reconciliation with a delay, when Irad was clearly bursting with something.

He followed his brother out to the fields, wondering.

He was not prepared for the blow that knocked him, gasping, onto the ground.

Nor for the kick to his stomach.

Soil filled his nose, his mouth, made him try to cough. But there were more kicks. And more, and blood mixed with the earth, choking him.

Red ragged darkness crowded him, smothered him in a haze of unimagined pain.

The last thing he heard was his brother's rage-suffused voice. 'Think you can fool *me*? I'll teach you. *I'm* the favourite, do you hear?'

And then oblivion overtook bewilderment, and pain, and horror, and blanketed him.

And eventually it dawned on Irad that the bloody lump at his feet would never move again. Or breathe. Or curry favour with its devious, manipulative, poisonous wiles.

He spat on it.

He hadn't quite intended to actually *kill* the creep. Just put him in his place, teach him a lesson or two. But, well, it couldn't be helped. Good riddance to bad rubbish.

He stomped off towards home.

All the same, he hoped no one would think to ask him about Shemid's absence. Who knew – perhaps no one would even notice. It wasn't as though Shemid was the most popular kid on the block.

chapter thirty-seven

'Administer true justice; show mercy and compassion.'
(Remnant's Reminders 7:9)

He was drawing close to home. He could see Yan-î drawing water from the well, and his own wife talking to her. His father Cain was discussing something with one of his other brothers. Children were darting in and out on their errands. A tabby cat was stretched out somnolently by the pens, soaking up the last rays of the day's sunshine. A sheep maaahed. Everything was as normal. Nothing had changed. No one had noticed. Everything could go on as it always had.

And then it came. 'Irad.'

This time he recognised the voice. It rumbled, as ominous and omnipresent as thunder. Others heard it too: he saw Cain's head go up. Clusters of people stopped talking, looked around.

'Irad.'

'I heard you the first time. What do you want?'

'Irad. Where is your brother Shemid?'

'I don't know. How'm I s'posed to know?' he snarled.

'Irad. Your brother Shemid. Where is he, Irad? Where is he?'

(They were all listening now. All of them! And what business was it of theirs, anyhow? It wasn't even as though any of them except Mum had *liked* the little creep!)

'How should *I* know, LORD? Am I my brother's keeper?'

'Oh, Irad. Irad. What have you done? Listen! Your brother's blood cries out to Me from the ground.'

(Faces had blanched. Mouths had dropped open. Horror had crept into their eyes. It wasn't fair. It was all Shemid's fault!)

'Irad.' The voice brooked no argument, no excuses. It was implacable, inexorable, terrifying, final. 'You have placed a curse upon yourself. You are driven from the ground, which opened up its mouth to receive your brother's blood from your hand. When you work the ground, it will no longer yield its crops for you. You will be a restless wanderer on the Earth.'

What? Leave here? Leave home? Be cast out? No longer be his father's heir, the favourite son working the soil? Exiled?

Irad's knees buckled. His mouth worked in a wordless cry for a few moments before he flung himself on the ground, begging. 'No! Please! Not that! Please, LORD! I can't bear it. Please. Not that. Anything but that. Anything, LORD. You're... You're driving me from the land, from my home, from everything! I'll be hidden from Your presence. You'll forget about me. And... and... when the others find out... they'll... they'll kill me! They'll kill me, LORD, like an animal, 'cos they'll see You've kicked me out like some beast, and they'll think it sport, LORD, to hunt me down and kill me, 'cos You've turned away from me!'

He was sobbing now, in terror.

It seemed to the listeners that the voice took on an additional timbre, resonating out to the furthest-flung household, the most distant relative. 'Not so. I say this: if anyone kills Irad, he will suffer vengeance seven times over.' And so saying, He put a mark on Irad so that no one who found him would kill him.

No one would meet his eyes as he slowly picked himself up off the ground, covered in dust and ignominy. No one rushed up to him to console him, to offer sympathy or righteous indignation on his behalf at the injustice of such a harsh punishment. It wasn't fair. He... *he* had always been the favourite! Everyone had always agreed that Shemid was a... a wimp, different from everyone else, someone who needed to be put in his place. Someone who was too good to be genuine, who was therefore clearly devious and false. So why were they suddenly acting all shocked and horrified? Why were they acting as though suddenly *he* was the untouchable one? Why weren't they coming up to him to slap him on the back and to tell him never mind, it would all blow over, that they'd be there for him if he needed them? Hadn't he always been the most popular man?

Instead, they parted before him, like shoals of fish before a swimmer, re-forming behind him, never touching him.

Even his wife, whom he'd trained to have proper respect for him, held back in silence and watched as he packed a few things. There wasn't that much he could take. His tilling and sowing materials were of no use to him any longer, now that the LORD had pronounced such punishment on him. The gourd of wine was almost empty – no point in taking that.

He was ready sooner than he might have thought. Only as he was standing there, hesitant before that final, irrevocable move out of his home, out of the only world he'd ever known, towards banishment, did there come a movement towards him.

A single woman.

His mother.

Leading a nanny-and-billy pair of Shemid's prize goats.

'For you. You'll need the milk on your journey. They... don't need much. I think... I think Shemid would have wanted you to have them. He always did forgive you, you know, when you bullied him. He always set his eyes and heart on Glory and Chose to forgive you, however much it cost him. Here. Take them.'

She could hardly bear to look him in the eyes, this son that was no longer any son of hers, this man who had so brutally murdered the gentlest, the purest soul in this Fallen family. But for Shemid's sake, she did, and handed him the goats' harness and leads.

And so Irad went out from the LORD's presence, and went towards the land of Nod, east of Eden.

chapter thirty-eight

You will cry out
from anguish of heart
and wail in brokenness of spirit.
(The Book of the Far-Seer 65:14)

They followed him with their eyes, until the last hair of his head had disappeared over the skyline, and the last dust had settled from that passage of no return.

Nobody spoke.

There was nothing to say.

Later, they would talk, commiserate, discuss, comfort each other. But for now, they were still too numb, shocked. They did not even know where the body was. Later, later they would go and search for him, there in the accusing fields, and bring him back and decide what one did when a human died. This first *human* death, before mortal illness overcame the shield of health that still protected all of them. This first murder. This first fratricide. Burn him, perhaps, as they did when they had killed one of the livestock for its skin and fur, and return his ashes to the soil from which the LORD had created mankind. Or bury him. But for now, such a question still felt out of reach, beyond the horizon. For right now there was only numbness, draining them of thought, of reaction, of energy to think or comprehend.

It was their feet that took them to their homes, mechanical habit untouched by conscious thought. It was their hands that somehow, in slow, shaky motion, fed the babies and milked the livestock when the cries became insistent enough to percolate through to automatic response. It was their mute rawness that drifted them one to another in the silence of shock, staring unseeing at the fires, the walls, the empty spaces.

The silence clung, muffled, shielded.

Time became meaningless.

Cain did not know how long he and Yan-î had sat there in their house. He could not even recall how they had arrived there. But the afternoon had turned to night, and the hearth fire had long sputtered its last. Yan-î's face, opposite him, lit by wan moonlight, was a pale shape under its head covering. His hands were clammy. 'He's... he's gone, hasn't he? They. Both.'

Her voice, dull, monotone. 'Yes. Both.'

The silence stretched again.

'I never told him. I never told him. He... he reminded me too much of Abel. I... I never told him. That I loved him. That I was sorry. That it was my fault we're here – Fallen, exiled. That it was *my* fault he'd never be able to see Glory like we once did. I never told him, Yan-î. I was too busy hiding. Hiding from what I did. Covering it up with anger, bitterness, rage. D'you know, I was *proud* that Irad and the others took their cue from me. I thought... I thought that if they could sneer, too, that would make it right. Make *me* right. Mob rule. Let me off everything... Let me off having to face myself. Face what I did. Oh, Yan-î! I never told him. Oh God, Yan-î, what did I *do*? I never told him! I was too ashamed. He reminded me of what I threw away, how... how *I* once was.'

His voice cracked, broke, continued. 'No. I'm doing it again. I... *I* never sought the LORD with all my heart, with all my strength, with all my mind. Abel does. Shemid did. Oh, Yan-î, why? Why didn't I tell him? How... how could I have treated him like that? All these years! All these wasted years. I should have told him, Yan-î. I should have seen! And you... oh, God, Yan-î. What have I done to *you*? What have I *done*?'

He did not, could not, ask her forgiveness. He would not dare. How could he, faced, finally, with the full force of his sin? It was too terrible. Too huge. Too overwhelming. 'Sorry' was too tiny. Could never be enough. Could never make restitution.

A small, chilled, slim hand gently, hesitatingly, touched his.

She did not lie. Would never lie. She did not say it didn't matter, or laugh it off with facile triteness.

She only reached out her hand. Reached out to him, and he held on to it as a drowning man might cling to a lifeline.

chapter thirty-nine

For this is what the high and exalted One says –
he who lives for ever, whose name is holy:
'I live in a high and holy place,
but also with the one who is contrite and lowly in spirit,
to revive the spirit of the lowly
and to revive the heart of the contrite.
I will not accuse them for ever,
nor will I always be angry,
for then they would faint away because of me –
the very people I have created.'
(The Book of the Far-Seer 57:15-16)

In time, the murder dulled to a mere ever-present ache, and hearts no longer caught at momentary resemblances of face or posture or gait or word.

But the memory of the LORD's voice and verdict remained.

Out of Eden they might be. But not out of reach. Not out of sight.

It did not happen overnight, the slow thaw of hearts. Nor equally. Some responded faster; others never responded at all.

Irad's wife and children and children's children, who found that they could not stand the looks and the whispers, the horror and the accusation-by-association in so many faces around them, followed him. Few carried that thaw with them, and their sons and sons' sons grew with bitterness and violence in their hearts, down to the tenth generation. The mark on Irad promising sevenfold vengeance on any who harmed him was held, vaunted, magnified, became a boast. Murder grew trivial.

'I have killed a man for wounding me, a young man for injuring me,' they said.

And Irad built a city for them all, and named it after himself, and watched his children, and his children's children, and their children in turn, continue to grow. But they no longer worked the soil, for the soil would no longer yield its crops for them. Instead they became tradesmen, crafting tools out of bronze and iron. And even though they had a city, still he and they remained restless at heart, as the LORD had pronounced, and by the time his descendant Lamech's sons were grown, some had abandoned the city and become those who live in tents and raise livestock.

In time, they would look west, and wonder. A Tree was there, they said, a Tree to bring immortality. A Garden of great riches... Who knew what booty there might be there, to covet and trade and snatch and hoard?

But Cain and many of the others east of Eden, humbled and devastated, allowed the thaw to touch them, change them, rebuild them.

Still Fallen. But seeking.

Another son was born to Cain and Yan-î in place of Shemid, whom Irad had killed. Seth. A son in Cain's own likeness, in his own image. And, flanked by his beloved Yan-î, whose hair was at last free again in the glorious sun after all these years of exaggerated covering, Cain... with his own hands, Cain gave Adam and Eve and Abel and M'Burechet the newborn Seth to hold, when the Unfallen came to rejoice with them. Tears were shed that day, but they were tears of joy, of penance, of restoration. The Unfallen came more often now, and were welcomed with heart's gladness by Yan-î and Cain, though their meetings were increasingly held outside the settlement.

For the radiance of the Unfallen, even veiled, was too painful for the eyes of many of the younger generations. And, too, the younger generations, though delighted with the gifts that were given each time, were more intent on their own lives than on catching up on news of those beyond the walls of Eden, with whom they felt increasingly little in common. Who cared any more what distant Unfallen cousins were doing? Who cared what Unfallen beasts supposedly said? The Fallen had other things to think about, now... The rest, therefore, seemed irrelevant. Boring.

Even Elder-grandfather himself now seemed... well, boring. Before his heart-thaw, Elder-grandfather's diatribes against the Unfallen were so much more dramatic, so much more entertaining than watching him relaxed and laughing in their company now. What drama could there be in joy?

True, life was easier now, without that constant anger. Relationships within families were healed, confidence grew, joy began to flourish again. But, with time and forgetfulness, even anger took on the gilt of nostalgia, and was missed.

Evil is fun, lied the enemy. Joy is boring in comparison. Anger is drama, spicing up the bland. Come into my emptiness! Forget that I exist. Just trust me when I suggest that goodness is tedious. Come away from Him. Dismiss Him, trivialise, disrespect Him... Come, my livestock. Choose my darkness!

In time, the grandchildren which Shemid had promised to his mother were born instead to Seth. He named his eldest son Enosh.

And by then, hearts had melted sufficiently that men began to call on the name of the LORD.

chapter forty

Senseless people do not know,
fools do not understand.
(Song 92:6)

But even there, east of Eden, others wondered. The LORD had not struck Irad down. Exile was not death. The LORD had even placed a mark on Irad to protect him. What sort of threat was that, which punished murder with mere exile?

Even Elder-grandfather had become soft since then. They missed the fire, the strength of rage. Rumour had it that Elder-grandfather Cain had once led a mission to the Garden itself. The Garden, full of untold riches. And a Tree, they said, a Tree to bring immortality. Like the Unfallen, those beings whose unbearable radiance had to be veiled whenever they emerged from Eden, to protect the eyesight of their Fallen relatives. The Unfallen, who always bore rich gifts for all, when they visited the Elder-grandparents. Rich gifts that surely were mere fractions of the wealth at hand... Imagine! All those fabulous riches, ripe for the picking!

The Garden was guarded, they said, by cherubim and a flaming sword. But, argued the men, they were many now, and surely a way could be found? Perhaps it was only the east side that was guarded. Perhaps...

And the other, the cunning prince of darkness, fed their jealousies and envies and greeds with glee. Fed *on* those twisted thoughts, the warped emotions, the perverted aspirations.

Elder-grandfather was old now, centuries old. And soft, ever since that murder. They could no longer look to him for inspiration. But *they* were young. *They* were bold. Bright. Audacious...

And when, eventually, aged over nine hundred years, Elder-grandfather died, followed shortly by his beloved Yan-î, then...

epilogue: until...

The watchers in the Garden grieved.

'Again, Father? When will they learn, remember?'

'Never, Beloveds. So long as the Garden is here, it will remain a focal point for their envies and greeds.'

'Is there nothing we can do?'

'Not while the Garden is here, Dearhearts.'

'Then...'

'Yes.'

'We won't be able to visit them any more, will we? Bring gifts, bless them?'

Abba embraced them, gently, sadly. 'No, children. That season is ended for them. For us. It is time. You... will be outside Time, with Me. With Us. Until the first Heaven and the first Earth have passed away, and Redeemer has called all who have ears to reign with Us for ever and ever, reunited.'

'Reunited! When, Glory?'

He laughed then, joyously. 'Ah, Dearhearts. I AM the Alpha and the Omega, the Beginning and the End. Outside Time, all "when" is now!

'Come!'

author's note

This book was not written as a theological treatise. It was simply written as a 'What if...?'

What *if* Genesis were absolutely literal? What might the *circumstances* and dynamics have been which led to each action described in our Bible? The Fall, the dysfunctional family life that led to fratricide, the delay in man calling upon God? And then... what *if* Eve had said, 'No'? How might that have impacted our history, when eventually evil prevailed with temptation? And what might that division – between Fallen and Unfallen – have shown us about the heart of God, since Unfallen humanity must surely, almost by definition, have shared that heart towards their Fallen brethren? And how might Fallen man have reacted in turn towards those who had *not* ruptured that perfect Relationship?

Writing this story required me to work out for myself – even where not highlighted in the story – how things *might* possibly have fitted together. The issue of eating meat, for example. In our Genesis, God only grants meat as food *after* the Flood. So how can one account for carnivores, who need the specific amino acids, etc, that are only to be found in flesh? Hence my invention of the 'bassar' tree: *bassar*, I understand, is the Hebrew word for 'meat'. Had there been such a fruit, containing the nutritional equivalent of meat, then for me it would be possible to respect that aspect of Genesis. (One could then presumably argue that such a plant would have perished and become extinct in the Flood.) For other questions, I am indebted to some of the points I found while browsing on various creationist websites, as well as to my mother and the friends who patiently (and good-humouredly!) put up with me while I demanded how/why/where/what in my thinking aloud.

Various individuals have been beacons in my life, allowing me to see what true love and integrity look like. To others (few, but significant), I owe thanks for showing me what love is *not*. To both sets of individuals: thank you. Your respective impacts on my life permitted me to flesh out the Unfallen and the Fallen in this story. A lifelong adoration of C. S. Lewis' Narnia series has also inevitably coloured both my temperament and imagination. It is a debt I can never repay.

Thanks also to my cat, who divided his hours between alternately snoozing while squeezed between the desk and my tummy, and trying to help me write by standing on keys. He claims, however, that any typos are not his fault. I second him on that.

Too often, it seems to me, Heaven is described as a dull place. The *interesting* people and things, I've heard said, are the ones *not* found in Heaven. Yet, *if* God is God: perfect and almighty, *truly* perfect – then it is in Him that is found all *real* joy and laughter and fun and humour and creativity and beauty and love and delight and adventure and adrenalin. And the same then surely goes for Heaven – and thus for a state of Eden *before* our relationship with Him was forever broken, warped, and perverted. If this book succeeds in capturing even a mere glimpse of such a perfect place, and resonating with that God-shaped hole in our hearts, and if it succeeds, too, in sharing the horror – and ease – of throwing it away, then I am content.

So I hope that, far from this story offending you, it might instead permit you to smile, to wince, to ponder, to yearn, and to look forward…

Bless you.

Follow the conversation on Facebook and Twitter

https://www.facebook.com/pages/Eden-Undone/589966777799655
https://twitter.com/Eden_Undone

references

Since this what-if story has a divergent storyline to that within our own Bible, the books within their holy scriptures would clearly have different names. However, for those in *our* reality who wish to look up the quoted verses in their Bibles, here are the references.

All verses are quoted with kind permission of the NIV. All Scripture quotations in this publication are from the HOLY BIBLE, NEW INTERNATIONAL VERSION ®. NIV®. Copyright © 1973, 1978, 1984 by International Bible Society. Used by permission. All rights reserved worldwide.

Part 1

Chapter 1:   Genesis 1:24-27; Genesis 2:8-15
Chapter 2:   Ezekiel 28:13-17
Chapter 3:   Genesis 2:19-20
Chapter 4:   Ezekiel 28:12, 13
Chapter 5:   Genesis 2:9
Chapter 6:   Genesis 1:26-27
Chapter 7:   Genesis 2:18
Chapter 8:   Genesis 2:21-22
Chapter 9:   Job 7:17
Chapter 10:   Psalm 96:11-13
Chapter 11:   Psalm 52:2
Chapter 12:   Psalm 16:11
Chapter 13:   Proverbs 25:23
Chapter 14:   Psalm 33:5, 8-9
Chapter 15:   Jeremiah 9:8
Chapter 16:   Song of Songs 1:17
Chapter 17:   Isaiah 30:15, 18
Chapter 18:   Psalm 66:1
Chapter 19:   John 1:1-4
Chapter 20:   Isaiah 5:20
Chapter 21:   Psalm 139: 14
Chapter 22:   Proverbs 16:29-30 (NB: I have changed the word 'man' to 'being')

Chapter 23:	Proverbs 19:22 (NB: as above)
Chapter 24:	Amos 6:12
Chapter 26:	Luke 24:28
Chapter 27:	Psalm 95:7-8
Chapter 28:	Luke 1:28
Chapter 29:	Psalm 10:2 (NB: have changed 'man' to 'one')
Chapter 30:	Psalm 64:3
Chapter 30:	For Snake's joke about the ducks, I am indebted to a Christmas cracker.
Chapter 31:	Genesis 20:9
Chapter 32:	Zephaniah 1:17
Chapter 33:	Isaiah 59:7
Chapter 34:	Isaiah 3:13
Chapter 35:	Deuteronomy 1:17
Chapter 36:	Proverbs 19:3
Chapter 37:	Ezekiel 23:35
Chapter 37:	For the image of God 'birthing' woman from man, I am indebted to the beautiful insight, which I had never before spotted, contained in chapter 10 of Wm Paul Young's wonderful book *The Shack*.
Chapter 38:	Psalm 5:4-5
Chapter 38:	I was struck by the lovely description in Matthew Henry's commentary a while back. I cannot remember it verbatim, so this is my paraphrase of why God chose to make Woman from Man's side.
Chapter 39:	Romans 6:23
Chapter 40:	1 Peter 5:8

Part 2

Chapter 1:	Acts 3:23
Chapter 2:	Proverbs 17:17
Chapter 3:	2 Corinthians 8:7
Chapter 4:	Isaiah 43:8
Chapter 5:	Isaiah 26:10
Chapter 6:	Psalm 119:66
Chapter 7:	John 15:13
Chapter 8:	Job 36:13
Chapter 9:	Psalm 10:8-9

Chapter 10:   Proverbs 16:24 (NB: I have changed 'gracious words' to 'grace and love')

Chapter 11:   Proverbs 17:17 and 21:4

Chapter 12:   Psalm 109:4

Chapter 13:   Job 20:5-6, 12-13, 20

Chapter 14:   Nehemiah 9:19

Chapter 15:   Psalm 121:2-8 (NB: have changed 'Israel' to 'Creation')

Chapter 16:   Psalm 68:10

Chapter 17:   Isaiah 30:15

Chapter 18:   Psalm 17: 10

Chapter 19:   Jeremiah 31:15

Chapter 20:   Jeremiah 15:18

Chapter 21:   Psalm 140:4 (NB. In our Bibles, Cain's son is called Enoch; Irad is Cain's grandson. However, since his more famous cousin in Genesis is also called Enoch, and since the two have diametrically opposite characters, I have chosen to skip a generation to avoid confusion.)

Chapter 22:   Ecclesiastes 3:1-2

Chapter 23:   Ecclesiastes 8:7-8

Chapter 24:   Jeremiah 13:17

Chapter 25:   Amos 5:7

Chapter 26:   Psalm 64:5-6

Chapter 27:   Proverbs 1:7

Chapter 28:   Proverbs 14:9

Chapter 29:   Psalm 23: 3-4

Chapter 30:   Psalm 14:30

Chapter 31:   Matthew 5:8; Ecclesiastes 7:7

Chapter 32:   Zephaniah 3:17

Chapter 33:   Proverbs 14:30

Chapter 34:   Psalm 119:150

Chapter 35:   Proverbs 4:19

Chapter 36:   Proverbs 27:4

Chapter 37:   Zechariah 7:9

Chapter 38:   Isaiah 65:14

Chapter 39:   Isaiah 57:15-16

Chapter 40:   Psalm 92:6

Instant Apostle is a new way of getting ideas flowing, between followers of Jesus, and between those who would like to know more about His Kingdom.

It's not just about books and it's not about a one-way information flow. It's about building a community where ideas are exchanged. Ideas will be expressed at an appropriate length. Some will take the form of books. But in many cases ideas can be expressed more briefly than in a book. Short books, or pamphlets, will be an important part of what we provide. As with pamphlets of old, these are likely to be opinionated, and produced quickly so that the community can discuss them.

Well-known authors are welcome, but we also welcome new writers. We are looking for prophetic voices, authentic and original ideas, produced at any length; quick and relevant, insightful and opinionated. And as the name implies, these will be released very quickly, either as Kindle books or printed texts or both.

Join the community. Get reading, get writing and get discussing!

instant apostle